That Perfect Someone

By

L.L. Diamond

That Perfect Someone

By L.L. Diamond

Published by L.L. Diamond

Copyright ©2022 L.L. Diamond

Cover and internal design © 2022 L.L. Diamond
Cover design by L.L. Diamond/Diamondback Covers
Cover photos: Young Couple in Love by Pink Panda and Bluebonnets along a Texas Hill Country by xradiophotog courtesy of Shutterstock.

ISBN-13: 978-1-7373356-6-5

Facebook: https://www.facebook.com/LLDiamond
Instagram: @l.l.diamond
Twitter: @LLDiamond2
Blog: http://lldiamondwrites.com/
Austen Variations: http://austenvariations.com/

Other works by L.L. Diamond include:
Rain and Retribution
A Matter of Chance
An Unwavering Trust
The Earl's Conquest
Particular Intentions
Particular Attachments
Unwrapping Mr. Darcy
It's Always Been You
It's Always Been Us
It's Always Been You and Me
Undoing
Confined with Mr. Darcy
He's Always Been the One
Agony and Hope
His Perfect Gift
That Perfect Someone

For my mother,
who was from the Hill Country.
She introduced me to making Easter nests
out of Texas wildflowers.
She also introduced me to Jane Austen.
I miss her every day.

L.L. Diamond

Chapter 1

Henry stared at her with the most mournful eyes while Lizzy tilted her head and scratched behind the Bassett Hound's ears. He licked her hand with his sloppy, wet tongue, leaving behind a trail of slobber. She sighed. Without a boyfriend, fiancé, or husband, this was the best she could get. What a pathetic testimony to her personal life!

After she injected the sedative into the vein of his front leg, she continued to give him love until the medication took effect. Henry had been nothing but a small puppy when she'd first treated him. She'd been fresh out of vet school. They'd started a journey together that day, so the sad-eyed pup was a favorite out of her regular patients. Who couldn't love such an adorable chunk of a dog?

As soon as his head began to droop, Mary pried open his mouth, and Lizzy aimed the tube.

"Lizzy!"

Son of a—! She jumped back from the dog and shot the fiercest glare possible at Lydia. "How many times do I have to tell you not to yell like that? For one thing, you scared the bejeezus out of me while I was trying to intubate Henry here, and second, I'm sure you could be heard all the way in the parking lot." She nodded to Mary, who once again opened the dog's mouth wide, allowing Lizzy to easily slide the tube down the dog's throat. She scratched under his ear one last time when she laid his head on the table. "Good boy."

"Whatever," her youngest sister said, picking at her neon green nail polish. "You've got a dickhead with a horse out back. He asked for you specifically."

Lizzy rolled her eyes. "Do you know who he is?"

"Nah ah." Lydia dropped her hand and leaned against the doorframe. "I mentioned Chase is fully qualified to treat horses, but he insisted upon you. Besides, Chase is busy with Mrs. Goulding's obnoxious little rat terrier. I don't know why he doesn't tell Mrs. Goulding to—"

"Because his job is to treat animals, who don't always understand that we're trying to help them. That's why." She and Mary rolled Henry to his side. "Now, did you leave the front desk unattended again?" With a huff, Lydia twirled away and stomped from the room.

"You need to talk to Dad," said Mary. "You and Chase run the clinic now, and his lectures to Lydia about showing the customers and you respect have only made her behavior worse. She doesn't care and she never will." They kept hoping Lydia would grow up. She continued to disappoint them.

"I know." Lizzy sighed and lifted Henry's upper lip, giving his teeth a quick peek. "You know the drill. Clean them up. If you find anything concerning, come get me."

Mary nodded and wheeled the machine to scale and polish the dog's teeth beside the table. Once Mary had started, Lizzy headed down a hallway to the back of the clinic, grabbing a hoof pick from a hook on the wall.

The metal bar on the exit door pushed open with ease as she stepped outside. The brisk April breeze bathed her face, the verdant scent of spring tickling her nose. After being inside all morning, she paused, closed her eyes, and lifted her head, taking a deep breath before she reopened her eyes. She loved this time of year. The sun shone brightly in a brilliant blue sky littered with puffy, white clouds. Summer was coming, and she wasn't certain she was ready for the seemingly unending months of scorching Texas heat.

At a heavy stomp, she had to smile. She adored all animals, but horses held a special place in her heart, and this one was gorgeous. A bay, with a striking white blaze and four white socks, stood proud and tall, its lead tied off on the stocks and one foot pointed forward. What a beauty! As with any horse she examined, she approached carefully before she placed a hand against the warm, toned muscle of the horse's neck and stroked toward the shoulder. "Hello, gorgeous." She trailed her palm along the back then peeked under his belly. "You're a big boy aren't you."

"Who are you?"

Lizzy spun around to a man who stood just inside the gate. Woah! He would've been drop-dead gorgeous if it wasn't for the intense scowl upon his face and the derisive tone of his deep voice. He strode up to her, his towering six-foot plus frame almost too close to her not so short five-foot eight.

"I don't need a tech examining my horse. I specifically requested Dr. E. Bennet. Where is he?"

She clenched her hands into fists at her side and refused to budge an inch to his form of intimidation. He could scowl, raise his voice, and invade her personal space as much as he liked. She would not be fazed by him. "I see the confusion here. My name is Dr. Elizabeth Bennet. You must be looking for Dr. Eli Bennet, my father. He's retired. My brother, Chase, and I now run the clinic. I'm capable of examining your horse, or if you'd prefer, my brother can do the honors. There's also Hillside Vets thirty minutes from here, just outside Fredericksburg. They also treat horses."

The man's jaw worked overtime while he glared at her. "You look barely twenty. How long have you been a practicing veterinarian?"

Ugh! What an ass! She suppressed the overwhelming urge to roll her eyes and sigh. Was she really going to have to spell out her credentials? "Let's see. I attended Longbourn Elementary, Middle, and High School, where I graduated with honors. I worked in this clinic every afternoon and holiday from the time I could walk and talk and finished my pre-requisite coursework at Texas A&M in two years when I was accepted into their vet school. I graduated four years later, at twenty-four. I've been a licensed veterinarian for seven years. Chase and I are the exact same age, so his experience and credentials are the same as mine, with the exception that he studied exotics for part of his curriculum, and I'm not fond of snakes." The gelding again stomped his foot but returned it to the same pointed position as before.

"I—"

She turned to the horse and slid her hands down his leg. "Has he recently been lame?"

"A month or so ago, I noticed a limp in that leg while riding him. I rested him for a few weeks, and he seemed fine. He'd stopped limping during short walks around the stable, but when I tried riding him this morning, he favored that leg again."

Lizzy pulled the hoof pick from her pocket and dug the dirt and debris from the underside of the hoof. "How long has he been pointing his foot?"

"I beg your pardon?"

He had no rocks or signs of infection, so she placed the hoof back on the ground. "When I came outside, your horse was pointing this leg." She stood, shoved the pick into her back jeans pocket, and brushed her hands on the soft, well-worn denim. The horse shifted and moved that front hoof back out to its previous position. She bent, resituated the leg, and stepped back once more. Now, would he point it again? No sooner had she straightened than the horse stretched his leg forward. "You see this commonly with navicular disease. Is he a show horse?"

"Dressage," said the man with a slight sneer to his voice.

"Sorry, I get a lot of Western Pleasure horses. We have a small English community around Longbourn, but...Well, this is Texas."

He nodded and his brows drew down a bit in the middle. "Are you sure?"

Lizzy clenched the hand resting on the horse's neck where he couldn't see it. "The pointing is a tell-tale sign. We can x-ray the hoof, but navicular disease doesn't always show up on an x-ray. You see, the name is kind of a catch-all that encompasses damage to the navicular bone as well as the soft tissues in that area. If the problem is one of the soft tissues, an MRI will be necessary to verify the diagnosis."

She shifted back and scanned the gelding's straight profile from its curved neck and back along the strong hindquarters. "Dutch Warmblood?" With a couple of steps, she touched her fingers to the animal's shoulders and traced to its rear where she again slid her hands down the length of the leg. He was a lovely specimen. After she examined the hoof, she gave a wide berth of the back end. She'd been kicked before and refused to be kicked again if she could help it. When she reached the opposite side, she checked the last two hooves, paused for a moment to listen to the heart and lungs, then opened his lips to look at his teeth. "He's twelve?"

The man's head hitched back. "No, he's thirteen, but he is a Warmblood.*"

"Darn," she said with a grin. "One year off." That expression of shock when she surprised a skeptical owner was always satisfying. Her fingers found a sweet spot behind the gelding's ear, and he lowered his head, pushing into her fingers for more. "What's his name?"

"I call him Skylla." His expression remained hard, his lips pressed into a fine line while he watched her work. The man needed to relax!

"Do you enjoy pulling Poseidon around, Skylla?" The name suited him. Even though she'd just met him, his owner seemed as full of himself as one of the Greek gods. She straightened and stopped petting the horse. What was this guy's name? Most owners introduced themselves, but he hadn't, and with his surly attitude, she'd forgotten to ask. "I'm sorry. I neglected to ask your name."

He cleared his throat. "Darcy, William Darcy." His name rolled off his tongue, in a dark, rich voice that sent a tremor through her.

After a couple more scratches, she patted Skylla's neck. "Did you want the x-ray to start, Mr. Darcy?"

The gelding pushed on his owner's shoulder, and Mr. Darcy put a hand to his nose. "Could it be anything else?" He rubbed the gelding's head and straightened his forelock. "What's the treatment?"

"I doubt it's anything else. Arthritis in the knee can cause problems and occasionally the pointing to take the pressure off the joint, but it's not swollen nor is it warm. As for treatments..." She bobbed her head back and forth. "We have several options we can discuss once we confirm the problem."

The man's unusual whiskey-colored eyes shifted from her back to his horse. He stroked the full length of the gelding's nose before shaking his head. "I want a second opinion first."

Her eyebrows rose, and she took a few steps back. What had he expected her to do? Either he wanted a simple answer or something she could fix right then and there. Unfortunately, no miracle cure existed and pushing never helped in these instances. He could haul the horse over to Hillside and let them take a look— unless he wanted to pay the fee for the vet to drive out.

"Okay, then. I'll get the invoice ready for today's examination. Once you have him loaded, go see Lydia at the front desk, and she'll help you check out. He's a beautiful horse. I hope you find the answers you're searching for, but if you need us, don't hesitate to call. We'll be glad to help you treat him."

Mr. Darcy nodded his head.

She lifted her hand. "Have a nice day." Once she was inside, she walked straight to the large treatment room and sat down on a stool in front of one of the computers. "Crap," she muttered at the sharp prod to her butt. She stood, yanked the hoof pick from her back pocket, and slapped it onto the counter. Why did she always forget about that thing? After she sat back down, she punched the exam code into the computer and hit save so Lydia could pull up the invoice at the front desk.

"Was he as big a douche as Lydia said?"

Lizzy spun around and leaned against the counter. "Yeah, a massive douche. I suppose he knew Dad, but hadn't realized he'd retired." She glanced over Mary's shoulder into the next room. "How's Henry?"

"I finished right when you came in. He's unhooked from anesthesia and sleeping it off on the floor."

Lizzy lifted her eyebrows. "You lifted him off the table by yourself?" Mary was no weakling, but Henry was a chunky seventy-five pounds of awkwardly long Basset Hound. She should've called for help.

"He wasn't too bad. I promise I engaged my core."

"Why'd you engage your core?" asked Chase as he stepped through the swinging door.

"I lifted Henry from the table after his dental."

Chase peeked into the room where Mary performed the cleanings. "He's gotten too large for you to do that by yourself. We'll have to persuade Mrs. Shaw to put him on a diet." He set a file down beside the computer and gave Lizzy a shove to move. "Deputy Collins brought his service dog to see you." He snickered as he began to type. "You're welcome, by the way, because nothing was wrong with that dog, and Collins was extremely disappointed to be stuck with me."

She cringed and shuddered. "I don't know how many times I have to turn him down before he listens, but Collins makes the client I just had seem easy in comparison."

"The man with the horse? He looked every bit your type—you know, tall, dark hair, striking eyes."

"Major stick up his ass?"

"Ooh." Chase crinkled his nose. "How big? Like a twig or a full-blown sequoia?"

Lizzy joined Mary laughing, then leaned against the wall. "I'll give him some credit and say a sapling. He looked at my initials, saw E. Bennet, and thought I was our father."

Chase sucked in a breath through his teeth. "Let me guess. He then wanted to know if the female vet had the brains to treat his horse." He sat back and shook his head. "Funny part is, he didn't

8

seem old enough for that. Usually, the old chauvinist boy's club are men Dad's age and older."

"He didn't say anything about me being a woman, but he did ask how long I'd been practicing."

Mary shook her head. "I'm going to get the first surgery. I'll be back."

"You were done quicker than I expected. I thought you'd be outside for another half-hour at least. People rarely bring horses to the clinic for wormer or vaccinations. They get you to come out."

After she explained the situation, Chase hit enter on the computer and dropped the chart into the tray to be filed. "What did the owner say? Did he want an x-ray or MRI?"

"He wanted a second opinion," said Elizabeth with a shrug. "I told him we were here if he needed us and wished him a good day."

"I know that had to be hard after him being such a dick."

She couldn't help one side of her lip from creeping upwards. "I didn't say I gave him no snark at all, and I had to show him I know horses, of course."

Chase chuckled and stood. "I can only imagine."

She followed him into the surgical room. "Are you going to the Hill Country Equine Rescue fundraiser next week? Dad's bugging me about it, but I don't want to go by myself."

"Yeah, he mentioned it to me too," said Chase. "I'm thinking about it."

Hill Country Equine Rescue saved horses from slaughterhouses and abusive homes, rehabilitated them, and found them forever homes—an endeavor she supported whole-heartedly. The charity fundraiser was a huge gala in Longbourn each year, a formal event that raised a huge chunk of much needed money for their work. Bennet Veterinary always purchased tickets and made an appearance, though Chase, for personal reasons, had never attended.

"You know I won't force you, but I'd love to have someone to hang out with." Maybe she could bribe Mary into accompanying her if Chase wouldn't go.

"Jane will be there."

"With Charlie, which means she'll be glued to his hip for the entire night." Her older sister had married Charlie Bingley six months ago. The couple was destined to be one of those who would act like newlyweds for the rest of their lives. They always appeared so blissful.

Chase propped himself on a nearby stool and rested his hands on his thighs. "I've spoken to Maria two or three times in the last month."

Lizzy's head popped up. "You never told me."

"I know." He scratched his head and shrugged. "She was only five when I told my biological family I was trans. She wanted me to know she accepted me, even if the rest of the Lucases didn't. It's hard for her, being stuck in the middle like that." Lizzy chewed on her lip. Yes, Maria had been young and couldn't go against her parents, but she'd turned eighteen four years ago. She could've contacted her brother then, if she'd wanted to. Why now?

When Mary entered with a tiny chihuahua, Lizzy started for the door, pausing to face Chase. "Pizza and wine at Antonio's tonight? You can tell me about Maria."

Her brother glanced up from the chart in front of him. "Yes, absolutely."

"You know you're my favorite brother." Mary giggled at the line Lizzy had been saying to Chase since the adoption papers were signed.

"That's because I'm your only brother."

Lizzy laughed and shrugged. "Who's counting?"

Chapter 2

The ballroom at Seven Springs Ranch glittered with fairy lights and greenery that spilled out onto the large stone patio where guests could dance under the giant Texas sky. Waiters clad in their penguin suits browsed through the crowd, their trays laden with hors d'oeuvres and champagne, while guests milled around the room drinking expensive wine, liquor, and fancy cocktails. The scene could be straight out of a romance novel, except Lizzy was with her brother. What a way to kill the perfect setting for a fantasy!

She squeezed Chase's arm. "Relax. The Lucases won't cause a scene." Every year, the committee for the charity gala was headed by Lindsey "Lady" Lucas, local socialite extraordinaire and the woman who gave birth to Chase. She and her husband Edgar, the former mayor of Longbourn, enjoyed their status and the friends their positions had provided them. They were so pretentious. At one time, the Bennets and the Lucases had been as tight as two families could be—until Chase came out. Now, the two families each pretended the other didn't exist.

"No, I know." He laughed when she adjusted the narrow straps of her gown. "I do not miss dresses."

Lizzy gave a slight snort. "You haven't worn a dress since you were eight years old, and Mrs. Lucas forced you."

"Regardless, just knowing I will never have to squeeze myself into one again makes my heart content." He squinted and pointed to the other side of the room. "Lizzy, is that Momma? I didn't think they were coming." The music faded before the next song, allowing the never quiet voice of Gracie Bennet to carry over the crowd.

Her father had said they'd planned on spending the evening at home. What could've changed their mind?

"I didn't think they'd be here."

"I know. He's always despised breaking out the tuxedo for events like this." He tugged her down the entry steps and into the throng, squeezing them between groups of people who chatted among themselves. Their mother's heavily accented drawl could be heard over the music. Her mother possessed one volume—loud. It made Lizzy cringe.

"I've heard he's wealthy. He bought the old Saddler place off Highway 46, just down the creek from the stables, so he must have a healthy bank account if he could afford all that land. It's a couple hundred acres as I recall. Perhaps I can persuade Eli to take Katy or Lydia over there to meet him."

Chase held up an arm. "Momma!"

With a squeal, their mother raised her hands and danced over to them. "There you are! Your father said you were coming, but I was beginning to think he was lying." She peered over her shoulder to their father, who sat in the corner with a crystal tumbler of what could only be bourbon at his lips. Their mother faced them once again, grabbed Lizzy's hands, and lifted her arms wide, gazing up and down at her strappy, fitted emerald gown. "That's a pretty dress. Isn't it the same one you wore last year?"

Lizzy held in a large sigh. Her mother *would* notice. She didn't hate dressing up, but she refused to purchase a new gown every year when it would never be worn more than once. Plus, who was there to impress in Longbourn? It was always the same small town and the same dull men. "Yes, Momma, I wore it last year."

"Well, I suppose it doesn't matter," said her mother. "But you!" She cradled Chase's cheeks in her palms. "You look so handsome in your tux! Did you get a haircut?" She primped a few spots of Chase's hair. As she took him by the shoulders, Lizzy bit her lips to keep from laughing. "Such a handsome boy! Come with me to talk to Henrietta Smith. I was just telling her the other day how she should have you examine her guinea pig. She keeps complaining that he's losing hair or some such nonsense. I told her you'd know exactly what was wrong with him."

Chase turned to Lizzy with wide eyes as their mother began to haul him off. "Save me!" he mouthed. Lizzy couldn't help herself. She smiled and gave a tiny wave, thankful that Chase was her mother's preferred victim.

She sat in the chair next to her father, making sure her posture was perfect and crossing her legs. Chase was right. Dresses could be a pain! "I thought you weren't coming."

He grimaced and stared into his drink. "I thought I'd managed to avoid tonight. I purchased two tickets and gave them to you and Chase, but it seems your mother refuses to take no for an answer. You know 'Lady' Lucas can't outdo her. She placed one very well-timed phone call, and the next thing I knew, she had two brand spanking new tickets. She also had my tuxedo cleaned and pressed. I swear, Lizzy, I'm going to break out the horse tranquilizer next year. I know it's a good cause, but I absolutely refuse to get all trussed up like a Thanksgiving turkey. Heck, I'd rather volunteer full-time treating their rescues than deal with this bullshit.

"Look at her." Her father jerked his chin in his wife's direction. Momma's mouth moved a mile a minute while she continued to primp and preen on Chase, who ducked and weaved to avoid her. "Do you think she'll ever stop treating him like a little boy?"

Good grief, she hoped not! It was too much fun to watch. "You know how much she wanted a son. If adopting Chase makes her act as if she won the lottery, I say leave her alone. He's known Momma since forever, and he was also the one who brought you the adoption paperwork on his eighteenth birthday. He joined this family with his eyes and ears wide open. It was his choice."

Her father gave a one-shouldered shrug. "I suppose you're right."

She scanned the room and leaned a bit closer to her father. "Dad, why don't you go talk to some friends? Isn't that Mr. Herff over by the fountain?"

Her father patted her hand and took a sip of his drink. "I will eventually. Let an old man sulk and fume for a while first, will ya?" He gave her a nudge to the shoulder. "Now you go have some fun. You don't want to be stuck with an old curmudgeon like me for the entire night." He pointed his knobby finger to a copse of oak trees along one corner of the patio. "Jane and Charlie are holed up over there. You ought to go say 'hi.'"

She nodded and started to rise, then stopped. "We need to talk about Lydia at some point." He had to see reason sooner or later. Lydia needed to find a different job.

"Mary told me she's become impossible. Put an ad in the paper for a new front desk clerk. If you want Lydia to continue until you've hired someone, I'll make sure she goes to work every day."

Wow! That'd been so much easier than she'd expected. "We have Chelsea full-time, and Katy for some afternoons and Saturdays. I think we can manage until we find someone to fill Lydia's spot—if we even decide we want someone else."

He tipped his glass in her direction. "I'll let her know in the morning. I doubt she'll be too torn up about it, at least until I tell her she has to start searching for another job."

Lizzy patted his hand, rose, and tapped Chase on the shoulder as she passed him on her way to the patio. Poor guy! Her mother would parade him around to every single girl in the room if he let her.

When she stepped onto the patio, the cool night air caressed her bare shoulders as she moved closer to a cluster of young live oaks bedecked in twinkling fairy lights. The night was clear and the stars shone in the black sky. It was magical. She could sit out here all evening.

Charlie and Jane stood to one side, and as she drew closer, the man standing with them came into better focus. She narrowed her eyes. He was tall, had dark hair, and when he turned and their gazes met, she gasped and fought the urge to do an immediate one-eighty and run right back inside. How could she forget those whiskey eyes?

Jane looked over her shoulder and smiled. "Lizzy, you're finally here!" She waved Lizzy closer. "Come meet Charlie's friend from Harvard."

Great! Mr. Arsy Darcy was friends with Charlie—her brother-in-law Charlie. Had he been at the wedding? If he had, how had she not noticed or even remembered? The wedding had only been six months ago. There was no way she'd have forgotten that handsome face. When she reached Jane's side, Charlie leaned in to give her a peck on the cheek.

"William Darcy, this is my younger sister, Lizzy," said Jane. "Lizzy's a veterinarian with my brother, Chase, at the family clinic. William and Charlie went to law school together."

Charlie straightened and put his arm back around Jane. "Only William returned to the family business, and I returned to Texas. I hadn't heard hide nor hair of him until he called to say he was interested in moving to the area and asked if I knew any good ranches for sale." Charlie made big bucks in property law. After Chase, Jane was Momma's favorite. She'd earned Gracie Bennet's undying admiration for marrying a man with money. Mary was the forgotten child, Katy was fighting for recognition, Lydia was the baby, and then there was Lizzy. Well, she could never do anything right.

"Dr. Bennet," said Mr. Darcy. "How are you?"

"I'm fine, thank you." She worked to keep her tone as pleasant as she could. "How's Skylla?"

"You've met?" Charlie glanced back and forth between them.

"Yes, Mr. Darcy brought his horse into the clinic."

"Awesome!" The grin on Charlie's face could've lit Houston, it was so bright. "A party is always better when people know each other." He clasped his hands together. "I believe I'm ready for a drink. Lizzy, do you want something?"

"A glass of cabernet, please." She'd need it standing next to Mr. Darcy!

"Darce?"

His eyebrows dipped a bit in the middle. "I'd like a Scotch if you don't mind."

"I know it's been a while, but Aberlour?" asked Charlie.

Mr. Darcy let a small smile cross his lips. "Good memory."

Charlie stepped in front of Jane and kissed her on the cheek. "Don't worry, hon, I've got you covered." They were so adorable together. The two of them were both cheerful and kind, and the love between them was obvious in their little shared looks and the way they spoke to each other. She wished for the same thing one day. If only she could find the right man.

"He's about the same."

She started and stared at Mr. Darcy. Had he spoken? "I'm sorry. Did you say something?"

He shoved his hands into his pants pockets, his shoulders hunching forward. Why did the man always appear so awkward? "Skylla. He's about the same. I thought I'd bring him by this week for those tests."

Lizzy nodded and tamped down that part of her that wanted to evil laugh and cry victory. Had he taken his horse to Hillside or simply come to his senses? "I'll be happy to treat him. If you call first thing Monday morning, Chelsea can make an appointment."

Her sister watched them, her silky blonde hair waving back and forth as she followed the conversation. "I hope it's nothing serious."

"No, nothing serious," said Lizzy. Mr. Darcy's stern eyes rested on her and never seemed to move. Had she said something wrong, or was he judging her? She itched to shift on her feet, more so than when she examined his horse.

His gaze flitted to Jane for a moment but returned to her. "Actually, the stables on my property are a mess. Until I have them renovated, I'm boarding the horses I brought with me at that stable near your office."

"Up the hill?"

"Yes, that's the one."

Jane gave a surprised inhale. "That stable belongs to my father. Lizzy lives in the large two-story house between the clinic and the barn. We grew up there—"

"Until Momma decided she wanted to live closer to town and not where she complained about smelling horse manure every day."

"Thanks for saving me from Momma." Lizzy bit her cheek and smiled at Chase, who approached with his favorite Guinness in one hand and her wine in the other. "I'm pretty sure Harriet is bringing her guinea pig into the clinic on Monday."

"Is there something wrong with him?"

After a quick kiss to Jane's cheek, Chase shrugged and held out a hand. "Chase Bennet."

Mr. Darcy shook her brother's hand. "William Darcy."

Her brother's eyes gave a slight flare before they narrowed somewhat. "William Darcy?" He peeked over at Lizzy then almost let a smile slip before he smothered it. Crap! What was he up to? "Did you bring a horse into the clinic a week ago? Sixteen and a half hand bay gelding?"

His eyes shifted to her for a moment. "Yes, he's been limping."

Lizzy took a gulp from her wine. If Chase started, she'd have to dig her heel into his foot! "I didn't know you saw Mr. Darcy's horse?" she said to the mischievous imp.

"I caught a glimpse of them when I called Deputy Collins back with his dog. Have you seen him yet this evening? I believe he's talking to Christina Murphy at the bar." He pointed inside with a grin.

That was it! She faked an innocent expression and took a sip of wine while the pointy heel of her silver, strappy stiletto pressed into the top of Chase's black dress shoe. At his light laugh, she rolled her eyes and caught the steady gaze of Mr. Darcy, staring her down once again. Ugh! Seriously? Was a boob hanging out or had she spilled something on her dress? She peered down, but nothing was abnormally exposed. Didn't the man have something better to do than watch her as if he were at a movie with a bowl of popcorn in his lap?

Without warning, Chase's foot slipped from beneath hers, and she lost her balance.

"Lizzy!" said Jane.

"I'm fine!" A hand under her arm had saved her from making an idiot of herself, but when she straightened, her brother's wasn't the hand that saved the day. Instead, the penetrating eyes of Mr. Darcy were right in front of her. "Thank you." She glanced down at her dress. Her wine hadn't seemed to have stained the silky fabric, despite the liquid sloshing over the rim and soaking her fingers.

"Here." Mr. Darcy offered a scrap of white cloth. Was that a handkerchief? Did men under sixty still use those?

Charlie laughed as he joined them. "You don't still carry those, do you?"

"You never know when you may need one."

With a shake of her wrist, Lizzy kept the damp hand away from her dress. "Thank you, but the wine will stain it. I'm sure there are napkins on one of the tables."

He wrapped the fabric around her hand. "I'm not concerned if it's ruined. By the time you go hunting around for something else, the wine could stain your gown."

"Thank you." How many times had she thanked him? Was that all she could say tonight? He took her glass while she wiped the wine from her fingers. Where had Chase gone? When she glanced around the patio, she frowned at the sight of her brother, who stood near the doors with Maria Lucas. Lizzy bit her cheek.

"Ex-girlfriend?"

Lizzy whirled back around and shook her head. "No, his biological sister. It's a long story. I just don't want to see him hurt." Chase had been through enough.

Mr. Darcy nodded as he returned her wine, and she took a sizeable drink. If she was going to be forced to socialize with Mr. Darcy, she was going to need it!

Chapter 3

"Mr. Darcy!"

William worked to keep from grimacing at the gushing greeting of Mrs. Lucas. He'd only met her earlier in the evening, right after he'd first arrived, but her voice and exaggerated expressions pointed to a false sincerity he despised. She was one of those women who could make him grit his teeth in sixty seconds flat. "Congratulations, Mrs. Lucas. This evening's event seems to be a great success."

The woman waved away the praise. "Oh, thank you, but I can't take all the credit. We do have a committee, you know."

"Of course," said William while Mrs. Lucas did this odd thing with her eyelashes. Was she batting them at him?

"We are so thankful for your support by attending tonight's gala. I don't suppose I could persuade you to make a further donation to our cause. We have the silent auction, but we're always desperate for funds. The more money we raise, the more horses we can help. Did you hear that we saved eighty horses last year, and we're hoping to increase that number this year?"

William frowned and cleared his throat. "I've bid on several of the auctions, but I'd be pleased to donate five hundred dollars as well. Could I add it to the total if I win an auction? I only brought one check with me tonight."

"Oh, of course! How splendid! We do appreciate the support!" Mrs. Lucas perked up and glanced around him, giving a pretentious wiggle of her fingers. "Yoohoo, Clara! I didn't see you there!" She turned back to him. "You'll simply have to excuse me. I must go speak to Clara Goulding. So far, she's managed to avoid me, but I'll get a donation out of her by the end of the night if it kills me."

"I understand. Have a good evening, Mrs. Lucas."

"You too, Mr. Darcy, you too."

As soon as she walked away, the pain in his neck from how stiff he'd held his shoulders lessened but didn't completely disappear. Charlie had convinced him to come tonight instead of sitting at home with a book and a glass of scotch, but home sounded better and better as the night wore on. Why couldn't he have written a check and been done with it? He stepped forward to continue through the crowd but caught a glimpse of Caroline, Charlie's snobbish sister, heading in his direction and pivoted to avoid her. Right as he slipped between two groups, someone ran headlong into his chest with an "umph." The klutz was female, and by the mass of auburn curls piled atop her head, he would wager Elizabeth Bennet.

She quickly pushed from her vertical faceplant into his tuxedo and looked up at him with wide eyes. "I'm so sorry, Mr. Darcy."

"I'm not hurt. If you'll excuse me?" He pressed his lips together while he stared down at her hand that was still pressed against his chest. The sensation of her palm pressed against him was unnerving.

She flinched and drew her hand away as though he'd scalded her, her complexion turning an impressive shade of scarlet. "Sorry."

He took a breath in the hopes the lingering sensation of her fingers would fade, and fade soon, as he shifted to the side to pass while Elizabeth darted in the opposite direction. He kept an eye out while he made his way to the bar, trying to stay as far from

Caroline as possible. "Aberlour neat, please," he said to the bartender when he reached the far corner.

"William! There you are." Charlie slapped him on the shoulder. "I thought you would've lightened up by now. You always look as though you're in physical pain at a party. I suppose some things never change."

William took a sip of his scotch and swallowed. "I've heard a number of people mention the 'Saddler place' as I've passed, and Mrs. Lucas just hit me up for more money. You know I'm uncomfortable when people start seeing me as a bank account instead of a human being."

"No offence, but everyone in town thought the Saddler Ranch would be sold to a developer and subdivided. When a private party purchased such a huge property and moved in, everyone's interest was piqued. Longbourn is a small hill country town and news travels like wildfire around here. If you wanted anonymity, you picked the wrong place, my friend."

William's jaw clenched and released as his eyes landed on Elizabeth Bennet, who stood about six feet away, speaking to her brother while she gestured in large motions before her.

"For what it's worth, Lizzy could care less how much money you have—if you're interested that is." Charlie wore a sly grin as he looked in the same direction William had a moment ago. When had he given that impression?

"Interested?" William turned back to Dr. Bennet and stared. "She seems to be a competent vet. I'll give her that, but what would I want with a woman who spends her days knee-deep in horse shit and fleas?"

Dr. Bennet's gaze met his, her cheeks reddened, but she didn't rush over to yell at him or start to cry. Instead, she burst out laughing before tugging her brother by the sleeve towards the patio.

He cringed as Charlie whistled. "You really put your foot in your mouth there and based on her expression when she first saw you outside, I'd say she already didn't like you. When you bring your horse in, expect her to kiss his ass before she kisses yours." Charlie walked away, chortling as he went.

"Damn!" he said under his breath. What was it about Elizabeth Bennet that made him react this way? The initial sight of her examining his horse had caught him off-guard, and he'd been abrupt. He'd never handled surprises particularly well, and the reviews online had seemed to have been for her father. His retirement must've been recent.

The bronze glints of her auburn hair captured him from across the room. When she wasn't running into him, she was graceful and intriguing. Her eyes glittered with intelligence but in a way that made him suspect she was laughing at him, even when she'd examined Skylla. What had he done that she found humorous?

Something became like a weight in the pit of his stomach. He shouldn't have said what he had to Charlie. He shoved himself away from the bar and followed the sound of her effervescent laughter to the patio. She spoke to a woman who appeared to be a bit younger by a wizened oak tree off to one side. When the girl left, he took his chance and stepped forward.

"Dr. Bennet," he said softly since she'd turned to stare up at the fairy lights in the tree.

"Yes, Mr. Darcy?" She turned and crossed her arms over her chest, her vivid green eyes burning into his.

"I wanted to apologize."

"Apologize?" Her eyebrows crept up onto her forehead. "For saying you don't want to be around a woman who's up to her knees in shit all day?"

He groaned and shook his head. "I shouldn't have said that. I can't stand events like this, but when Charlie learned I'd moved into town, he insisted I come. The woman who organized this...What's her name?"

"Mrs. Lucas?"

"Yes, her. You see, she'd cornered me right before you ran into me, requesting a donation besides the cost of the ticket and the silent auction bids. I've heard a couple of people talking about me. That didn't help."

Her eyes narrowed. "If you're worried I won't do my best to treat your horse because of what you said, I can assure you, I'd never do that."

"No!" He shook his head and held his palm out. "I know you wouldn't. You were incredibly gentle and good with him when I was such an ass the other day." He could be a dick in certain situations, but he would never imply that.

A laugh bubbled up from her throat. "He's a gorgeous horse. One of my favorite parts of the job is getting to pet and take care of other people's horses—particularly when they're well-mannered, like yours."

"Thank you."

They stood silent for a moment before he had the urge to squirm in place. What should he say? He'd drawn a blank when she was examining his horse too. Why was he so horrible at speaking to her?

"Crap!" she muttered under her breath.

"What is it?"

She moved a bit closer and to the side. "It's Deputy Collins. He's been asking me out since I graduated from vet school. I've turned him down more than once, but he won't take 'no' for a final answer. He keeps insisting I'll change my mind. I've managed to avoid him so far, but he just stepped onto the patio behind you."

He didn't look over his shoulder. If he had, it would've been a dead giveaway to where she was hiding. Instead, he took her by the elbow, tugging her toward him. "Perhaps if you're close to me, I can conceal you better."

She stepped forward until she was almost pressed against him, and every cell in his body shot to attention. He'd never reacted so to anyone before. He'd assumed when she ran into him, that jolt was the shock of the encounter, but the same thing was happening now.

The footsteps behind him drew nearer, and the muscles of her arms stiffened under his palms. Was that a reaction to him or was that the dread of Collins finding her? Her deep green eyes looked up to him, and pulled at him. His breathing became shallow, and his heartbeat thundered in his ears. She flinched at the first contact of their lips, but after a few seconds, she softened in his arms. He teased her lips apart and caressed her tongue with his, the cabernet she'd been drinking sweet on her breath.

His fingers found their way to the back of her head, and he held her to him while they kissed, his mind emptying of everything around them—everything but the woman in his arms: her warm exhales as they fanned against his cheek, the way she gripped the lapels of his tuxedo jacket, and the warm flesh of her back against his palm.

"Oh, William!"

He wrenched himself away and ran his fingers through his hair while Elizabeth stumbled back and pressed her hand to her stomach. Damn, Caroline! Why did that woman always turn up at the worst possible moments?

"There you are!" Charlie's obnoxious sister rushed forward and grabbed his arm, giving him a noisy peck on each cheek. Some things hadn't changed since Harvard. "Oh, and you too," said Caroline while she peered down her nose at Elizabeth.

She propped a hand on her hip. "Yes, me. You do know my name, Caroline. Charlie's told you on more than one occasion."

Caroline responded with nothing more than a titter before she gazed up at him with that cloying smile he'd been trying to forget since college. If only someone would invent a way to laser that from his brain! When he and Charlie shared an apartment and Caroline visited, he'd always been terrified of waking to that same smile beside him in bed. A shudder wracked his spine.

"I'm sorry, but my mother is waving me inside," said Elizabeth with a lighter voice than usual. "Caroline, it was nice to see you again. I'll see you and Skylla sometime this week, Mr. Darcy. Have a good night."

As she was speaking, he narrowed his eyes at her and tried to give an imperceptible shake of his head. He'd helped her with Deputy Collins. She could darned well stay and help him with the female version!

Charlie's sister clutched his arm closer to her breast, and he yanked himself away. "Dr. Bennet, I thought I was going to buy you a drink." He pulled on his ear while he struggled not to speak through his teeth. She couldn't leave him there.

She glanced from Caroline to him and gasped with a hand to her chest. "I'd almost forgotten." She chuckled as though she was always so absent-minded. "How featherbrained of me." Her smile widened. "Caroline, would you care to join us?"

What? No! What was she doing?

Caroline pursed her lips, gazed down her nose at Elizabeth, then looked him up and down like he was an ice cream cone she wanted to drag her tongue across. "Of course, I would. Thank you."

He gestured for the ladies to walk ahead of him, but instead of following Elizabeth, Caroline latched back onto his arm. Was the woman related to a lamprey? Or maybe a vulture with the way her talons were digging into his bicep. Why couldn't she leave him alone?

His eyes drifted down to the luscious curve of Elizabeth's hip, and for one blessed moment, he managed to put Caroline out of his mind—that is until a fingernailed hand grabbed his own ass and squeezed.

He gritted his teeth, and, guiding Caroline by the elbow, pushed her ahead of him. As soon as he had the first opportunity, he'd be speaking to Charlie. His friend needed to do something about his sister. Perhaps he could get Caroline to finally leave him alone once and for all!

Chapter 4

Lizzy squinted and scanned the bleachers until she spotted her father, seated at about the mid-point of the covered arena. He always went to the local horse shows to hang out with his friends, chat about horses, and re-visit the glory days. Why he needed her or Chase to join him was a mystery. Almost every Friday night, he would call her or Chase and rope one or both of them into coming out for the day. "May as well enjoy the show and make a few dollars at the same time," he'd always say. He could treat a horse as well as either of them.

As she drew closer, however, her father wasn't sitting with his friends or Lamonte. Instead, he was with Charlie, Caroline, and... She narrowed her eyes until the other man came into focus. She groaned and sagged a bit. Why did it have to be William Darcy? Charlie was a cheery and good-natured guy, and Mr. Darcy had been pleasant enough when he'd brought Skylla in earlier in the week for the x-rays and the MRI, but would he revert back to the Mr. Darcy she'd first met? The one from the gala still confused her, so she would pretend that one didn't exist. How many men would insult a woman in one breath then kiss her as if he were starved for her in the next? Stop, Lizzy! She had to stop thinking about that. Yes, she wanted to avoid Mr. Darcy, but the person she dreaded dealing with most was Caroline. That harpy always put Lizzy down like she was so much better than her. What crap!

Mr. Darcy's ploy to keep from being alone with Caroline at the fundraiser had been obvious, and if Lizzy were honest, funny as heck. But after that kiss he'd laid on her, she refused to be on her own with him. Sure, they'd been at a large event, crowded with people, but that kiss had nearly buckled her knees and reduced her to a puddle of mush. He was dangerous, and she couldn't and wouldn't sacrifice her heart to someone whose personality seemed to change like Dr. Jekyll and Mr. Hyde.

She clenched her hands into fists and started for the stands. She could do this! She wouldn't let Mr. Darcy know how much he'd affected her, and she wouldn't let Caroline piss her off with her snotty remarks and stuck up comments. "Hey, Dad," she said as she stepped up the metal bleachers. "Did I miss anything exciting?"

"Nah." His voice held that same grumble it always did with that response. "Same old, same old. You missed the halter events and the kids' western pleasure."

She sat beside him and scanned the horses and riders in the arena. "Is this the last of the pleasure events?"

"Yup, but at least you didn't miss Jane. She's signed up for western riding and trail."

"Who's she riding?" she asked Charlie.

"She brought Blue and Jessie, but she brought Jessie more for Blue to have as company. You know how she's been coughing some lately."

Her dad frowned and sat up. "You didn't say Jessie was coughing. I'm gonna go take a look."

"Dad, I told you Jessie started having trouble with allergies last year. I'm sure something is blooming, or she had a dusty bit of hay that stirred all that up." What did he expect? Jessie wasn't a spring chicken anymore, but a twenty-year-old bay mare who every Bennet child had ridden at one time or another. When Lydia had decided to stop riding in favor of chasing boys, Jane started working with the older horse again; however, with the cough that had flared, she had become more of a traveling companion to the horses Jane showed rather than a working horse.

Her father grabbed Lizzy's supply bag and waved Charlie to follow. "Come on, Son."

"Dad, she's fine," she said once more, but he didn't hear her. He'd slung the backpack onto his shoulder and was picking his way down the stands. Why wouldn't he listen?

"Do you ride?"

Her head whipped around, and her eyes met the unusual amber ones of Mr. Darcy, making her stomach complete a triple somersault. "Sometimes I trail ride around the stables, but I don't show anymore. Keeping a horse trained and in shape takes time I don't have."

"How cute!" said Caroline in an overly effusive tone. "Were you like those little girls on the ponies, bouncing out of your saddle when the horse ran?"

Lizzy pinched her leg to keep from rolling her eyes. "No, I had a quarter horse we took in from the rescue. He passed away a few years ago, but he was the perfect horse for a child to learn on. Other than my time in the clinic, I must've spent my entire childhood with him, riding through the woods and practicing for the next show."

"What of your *brother*?"

Lizzy's chin hitched back. What was that supposed to mean? "Sorry?"

"Caroline," said Mr. Darcy with an edge to his voice. "Is that your sister and her husband by the concession stand?"

Caroline screwed up her pointy face, squinting. Charlie had once said she refused to wear her glasses because of how they looked. She was not only rude but vain and one of the most ridiculous people Lizzy had ever met. How Charlie came from the same family—the same uterus for that matter—was a mystery! "What are they doing here?" She huffed and stood before making her way down the stands.

"Maybe she won't come back." When she turned to Mr. Darcy, he was rolling his eyes.

Before she could stop it, she chuckled. "If it were just me, she'd probably stay away, but with you here, I'm sure she'll return before long. I have to admit that I've never seen her chase a man before. When did she start treating you like prey?"

He leaned against the seat behind him with a groan. "When Charlie and I were roommates at Harvard, but she's probably a lot like your Deputy Collins. I've told her *and* Charlie I'm not interested, but she won't take 'no' for an answer." He glanced over his shoulder to where Caroline approached her sister Louisa. "Is she always so nasty to you?"

"She's never pleasant, but I'm assuming she saw us kissing at the fundraiser. She's never been quite this antagonistic—like she's trying to start an argument—and she's never made a crack about Chase before. I want to know whether she's referring to him being adopted or being trans—not that I let anyone give him crap about either."

Mr. Darcy's warm hand covered hers on the bleacher, and her heart stuttered in her chest. "Hey, I get it. I have a sister, and I feel the same way about her. Don't let Caroline bother you. She's not worth the time or the gray hairs."

Lizzy stared at their hands before she couldn't take the contact anymore. She pulled her hand free and swallowed. "Look, Mr. Darcy—" She rubbed her palms up and down her denim-clad thighs. "I'm treating your horse."

"And I'm only five years older than you. Do you address all of your patients' owners so formally?"

Her back stiffened. "How do you know how old I am?"

A sexy as hell chuckle rumbled through his chest. "You more or less told me when you gave me your academic history. You know, you graduated vet school at twenty-four and had been practicing for the past seven years."

Her face heated, and she cleared her throat. "Seven years in May," she said softly. "I turn thirty-one next month."

"So I was fairly close." Their eyes held for a few minutes before she couldn't take the connection and searched the trailers strewn around the parking lot for a glimpse of her father. She needed to get away from Mr. Darcy or join the others so they'd have a buffer.

"I don't know why Dad insists we come to these things if he's going to take the bag and treat the horses himself. He's kept up his license. He doesn't need us."

"Perhaps he likes having you here for company."

She barked out a laugh. "Do you know how many people he's friends with at these things? He's been going to horse shows all over the Hill Country since he was a boy. He knows almost every person here and wouldn't be lonely without me. Besides, he sees me every day after the clinic closes when I stop at the stables to check in on him before I go home."

"Don't you want to see your sister ride?" Like the rest of the family, Jane had grown up around horses, but she'd become a trainer instead of a veterinarian. She and Charlie spent their weekends hauling horses to the different shows around the area.

"I enjoy watching her compete, but I don't attend every event. I work every other Saturday, and I'm sometimes on call. I'd rather stay home where I'm closer to the office." She had other priorities. "You mentioned you have a sister. Does she ride too?" Maybe she could distract him from asking her questions.

"She's an eventer. She may move down here with her horses once I have the stable renovated, but she didn't want to interrupt her training schedule so she stayed behind at Pemberley."

"Pemberley?"

"Where we grew up in Maine. My father still runs a successful stable and breeding program there. I wanted a fresh start, so I moved here." He didn't look her in the eye. Was there something more to him leaving home—moving across country than he let on?

"The Saddler place had been vacant for some time. I would imagine the stables were in pretty bad shape."

"I've had to more or less level them and start over. They'd put concrete in the stalls, and if there were rubber mats, they weren't left behind." She cringed. Concrete was easier to clean but unforgiving for a horse to stand on for long periods of time without some cushion. "I'm living in the house, but it needed work too. Once that's completed, I need to find a decorator but I don't know who to ask." He glanced to where Caroline now sat with her sister and brother-in-law. "I can't ask Charlie because he'll recommend Caroline, and I don't want her in my house. Once she gets one toe through the door, I may never get her to leave." He shuddered.

Lizzy bit her lip while she tried not to grin. She couldn't blame him. "You could do what the rest of us do."

"What's that?"

"Go to the home improvement store, buy a few cans of paint, and do it yourself."

He chuckled and shook his head. "No, I'm no painter. I failed finger painting in kindergarten."

With a smile, she blinked. Mr. Grumpy had a sense of humor. Who knew? A movement in the corner of her eye captured her attention. "Um, Caroline is heading this way. Perhaps we should go see if my father needs help with Jessie."

A wide smile overtook his face. "That sounds like a brilliant idea. Let's go."

Faster than she would've expected, he stood and grabbed her hand, pulling her towards the trucks and trailers in the dustbowl of a parking lot. Before she could get too comfortable with her hand cradled in his, she casually shoved it in her pocket. His touch was too much. He was the most handsome man she'd seen in years—outside of Ryan Reynolds, that is—but she needed to keep her head on straight around him. No matter what, she couldn't let herself develop feelings for him. The last thing she needed was to resemble a schoolgirl with a crush.

"Evie?" Lizzy pulled her keys from the lock and closed the front door behind her. A moment later, a chirp of sorts came from upstairs and a small grey cat barreled down to the foyer. "There you are."

The cat chirruped and trotted behind her into the kitchen where Lizzy dropped her keys and phone onto the bar. "Are you hungry?" The cat moved her mouth in a silent meow, and Lizzy grinned. Evie was the cutest little thing.

After Lizzy measured out a small amount of food and dumped it into the bowl, the young feline pushed her hand away and began eating as fast as she could. "You know if you want food, you have to let me pour it," said Lizzy with a laugh. Evie needed to learn some patience.

Lizzy stroked the cat's silky fur. What was the deal with Mr. Darcy? Today, he'd been a surprise, resembling Dr. Jekyll and managing to be decent company. She couldn't deny she enjoyed looking at him. At a sharp nip to her finger, she startled. "Okay, I stopped. I won't think of him again." Leave it to Evie to know she was thinking something she shouldn't be. "I need a shower. Are you coming?"

As she walked up the stairs, Evie darted past her and toward the master bedroom. The small feline had always been moody and unpredictable, but she had a softer side too.

When she entered the bathroom, Evie was already sprawled, her entire body pressed as flush as she could manage to the bath mat. She adored rolling and rubbing all over the soft cotton. Lizzy chuckled at the kittenish antics and turned on the hot water, letting it warm while she removed her dusty clothes. She dropped her jeans in the hamper but paused, staring at her hand. Was it possible to feel someone's touch hours after it happened? She could swear the sensation of Mr. Darcy's hand still lingered on hers, even now. He was a puzzle and for some reason, she thought of him a lot more than she should. As much as she'd tried to stop, the problem only seemed to get worse. She had a sneaking suspicion he could do a lot of damage to her naïve heart, and she simply couldn't risk it. She couldn't afford to take a chance. So why couldn't she get him out of her head?

Chapter 5

"Morning, Mr. Darcy," said Lamonte as he closed the stall door. "Your horses settling in okay?"

William smiled and nodded. "I think so. They're used to being in a large stable, so they settled in quickly."

The older Black man scratched the gray scruff along his cheek. "Doc Bennet said you have more you intend to bring down. Old Mrs. Vogt sold two of her horses so a couple spots have opened up—if you need them that is." Lamonte chewed on the toothpick sticking out of the corner of his mouth, making it bob up and down. He seemed to be a Jack of all trades. Not only was he a farrier but he also helped Dr. Bennet keep up around the stables. He was often found training a horse in the paddock on most days.

"I appreciate it. I'll contact my sister and see if I can arrange for their transport. I'll let you know as soon as I find out something."

"Sounds good." Lamonte spoke with a lazy sort of drawl. "That gelding of yours seems to be getting around better. I saw you out riding him yesterday. Lizzy's always been good with horses—probably better than her father, but don't tell him I said that. He'd not take that too kindly." A slight smile accompanied the last. From what Lamonte had said while shoeing Skylla, he'd been best friends with Dr. Bennet since elementary school.

"I understand." William cleared his throat and gave a quick glance around. "She mentioned Saturday that she used to ride. I'm curious. Was she any good?"

The man's smile widened, and he laughed. "Yeah, she was good. Mind you, Jane had a natural knack for teaching a horse what to do. She took to training like a duck takes to water. Little Lizzy, well, she was always good at taking care of them. Don't get me wrong. She won her fair share of ribbons. I think there were even a few trophies and a belt buckle one time, but she was one of those little ones who'd bring home a stray kitten or injured bird. Near broke her heart when her father couldn't fix one of them."

Something inside William warmed. He wasn't sure what it was about Elizabeth Bennet, but his gaze always seemed to be drawn to her. Saturday she'd been in nothing but simple dark blue jeans, a clinic polo, and cowboy boots, her auburn curls swinging to and fro in a ponytail as she walked around the horse show, and he'd been mesmerized. What he wouldn't give to see that fine ass clad in breeches and English riding boots! He bet she'd be even hotter. She wasn't a beauty in the classic sense, but those eyes possessed an allure that drew him in like a moth to a flame. What was he doing? He shook himself internally. Lamonte now watched him with an odd curve to his lips.

"Yes, Skylla seems to have improved a lot, but I'm not pushing him. I'd rather keep him as a pet than have him come up permanently lame."

"That's good. Lizzy'd like that." A nearby horse stuck his nose through the top half of the stall door and nudged Lamonte's shoulder. The older man began scratching under his chin. "Too many people are concerned with their horse's worth and what they can do rather than what's good for the animal. Lizzy, Chase, and ole Doc Bennet can tell you some stories that'll make you madder than a wet hornet."

William furrowed his brow. "I've never heard that expression."

"Madder than a wet hornet?" said Lamonte. He shrugged with a chuckle. "I don't know. It's something my father used to say." He glanced at his watch. "Would you look at the time? I got to get over to the Fabra place. They have a couple of horses that need shoeing. This morning, I checked those corrective shoes I put on your horse. Don't want one to come loose and fall off without us knowing."

"I appreciate that. I'll let you get going."

"You have a good day, Mr. Darcy."

"You too." William walked around the corner to Skylla's stall, receiving a nicker when the horse first saw him. "Hey there. I thought you might need a good brushing." He took a small bag out of his pocket and offered the gelding a carrot that the horse grabbed and munched the moment he saw it. With long strokes, William started rubbing the horse down with the scraper. Skylla had always shed more than any horse he'd ever owned. This spring was bound to be worse since they were transitioning to a Texas summer compared to those of Maine. He'd never experienced a summer down south, but how could they not be more severe?

At the clomping of boots from the passage, William glanced out as an unruly auburn ponytail bounced past. Was it her? He paused, stepped up to the door, and leaned forward to get a better look. Dr. Bennet stopped at a stall a couple of horses down, unlatched it, and stepped inside. Was she here as a veterinarian or to ride? Low murmurings filtered down the row but not specifically what she was saying. She was, no doubt, speaking to that horse like she had his. It was one of the things he'd liked about her treating Skylla: she put him at ease more than any vet he'd used in the past.

He shook his head and went back to brushing Skylla. He needed to forget about her and that kiss! But good Lord, how could he? Those soft lips moving under his stoked that current that had raced through him to a crazy high pitch he'd never experienced before. The problem was he'd dated a veterinarian before, and it'd been a disaster. The last thing he wanted was for another relationship to end the way his last had ended with Anne—not only had he caught his fiancé cheating on him, but he'd also lost a good veterinarian when their relationship hit the fan.

After clearing his throat, he shook off the unpleasant memories and continued grooming his horse until those same footsteps followed by a horse's hoofbeats passed them. He looked up, this time to a horse's tail whipping around as though attempting to shoo away flies. Once he'd finished removing most of Skylla's dead hair, he put away the brushes and followed the familiar cadence of a horse's trot. What was he doing?

The brightness of the sun blinded him for a few seconds when he stepped outside, and he blinked while his eyes adjusted, focusing directly on Elizabeth Bennet riding the same large grey mare that had walked by earlier. Her posture was good yet relaxed while the horse moved around the paddock, but wasn't that correct when someone rode Western? How was he supposed to know? He'd never ridden anything but English.

"Good morning, Mr. Darcy."

He peered over his shoulder as Chase Bennet approached from behind. "Dr. Bennet. How are you?"

"I'm good, but please, call me Chase. If you continue to call me, my sister, and my father Dr. Bennet, things are going to be confusing, to say the least."

William smiled. He had a point. "I hadn't considered that, but you're right, of course."

Chase's head barely tilted and his eyes gave a quick dart to his sister before settling back upon William. "Lizzy and I plan to ride the trail by the creek today. Would you like to join us? The path is clear and wide and some of the views are nice. I think your horse can handle it if you want to come."

His body jumped, and he scratched the back of his neck. "Oh, I hadn't planned...That is, I think it's best if I don't. Thank you for the invitation, though." The way Chase watched him for a moment after he responded made the muscles of his back tighten. What was he noticing? "I was grooming Skylla and heard your sister take out the horse. She'd mentioned that she rode when we were at the show. I admit I was curious."

"We all ride," said Chase. "Our father insisted we know-how. Lydia could care less these days, but the rest of us still have our own horses. Mary's is the dun gelding next to yours, Katy's is the sorrel mare just inside the door, and I have the palomino next to hers. He and Momma would cart us all to the horse shows growing up. They didn't ride anymore, but they helped us get our horses ready and watched from the stands. Jane is the only one who still competes, but then it's part of her job. Fortunately, Charlie loves watching her so he doesn't mind."

"Hey!" They both turned. Elizabeth had stopped riding and was watching them. "You going to chat the day away or ride? If you two boys are going to stay here and talk, I'm going on my own."

"Hold your horses!" called Chase. "I better saddle Blondie. You sure you don't want to come?"

He tamped down that part of him that screamed to say yes. "I better finish with Skylla." William followed Chase inside. "I haven't brushed his mane or tail yet."

The younger man opened a stall door and slipped a halter over the horse's head. "If you change your mind, the start of the trail is by that big pecan tree near Lizzy's house. You can't miss it."

"I'll keep that in mind, thanks," said William as he started to walk towards Skylla.

"Mr. Darcy!"

William spun back around. "Please, you can call me William or some people call me Darcy."

Chase frowned and glanced down at the lead rope in his hands then back up to catch William's eye. "About Lizzy. Be careful with her. She doesn't have much experience with men."

His insides flinched, and he clenched and released his hands. "I don't know what you mean."

After a tight chuckle, Chase tied his horse off. "I haven't said anything to Lizzy, but I saw that kiss at the fundraiser. I've also noticed how much you glance her way when she doesn't know you're looking. Before she was my sister, she was my best friend, so I know Lizzy better than most people. She's never taken shit from anyone, and most boys were interested in more than she was willing to give for a few measly dates. After a while, she set her sights on college and vet school and ignored the rest. That's become a sort of ingrained habit—except now she concentrates on work and protecting me."

"Do you need her protection?"

"Nah," said Chase, "but that doesn't mean I don't appreciate it, and that I don't do the same for her." He dipped his chin just enough that his message came through loud and clear. He was being warned not to hurt her.

William exhaled heavily. "Look, my last serious relationship was a nightmare. I'm not searching for anything right now. Your sister's safe from me. Okay?"

The other man's eyes flared ever so slightly and his lips curved to one side. "That's unfortunate. I think you and Lizzy could make a good couple, and despite what she claims, she's lonely. She spends way too much time watching rom-coms and talking to her cat."

"What about Deputy Collins? Perhaps she could give him a shot?" He all but forced the last few words from his mouth. What was he doing? Did he really want Lizzy to date that lumbering idiot with a decidedly unhealthy fixation for his service revolver? He happened to meet the deputy at the coffee shop in Longbourn a few days ago. What an asshole! He admired Lizzy even more after that run-in.

Chase snorted loudly. "Don't ever let Lizzy hear you suggest that. She'd run you over with her horse...or the clinic van, whichever is closest."

"I better let you saddle your horse before your sister abandons you." William raised a hand. "I'm sure I'll see you around."

Chase returned the wave, saying "See ya" before William turned and started toward the far end of the stable. What was it about Elizabeth Bennet? As much as he wanted to deny it, Chase had been correct, his gaze was drawn to her without thought. Saturday at the horseshow had been ridiculous! He'd told her to call him William, then he'd covered her hand with his. He'd decided months ago to avoid women for the time being, so why did his brain conveniently forget the moment Lizzy entered his line of vision?

He seemed to have no control when she was around so he needed to avoid her as much as possible from now on. With their intense attraction—which that kiss confirmed like a slap from a brick wall—what if they ended up in bed together? After Chase's warning, he refused to hurt her with a casual fling. His feelings had been trampled and left for dead, and he would not risk his heart or someone else's until he was certain the relationship would not end in disaster. It was the least he could do. No one deserved that.

Chapter 6

"Lizzy!"

She had started down the hill toward the office but turned as Lamonte and a man she didn't recognize approached. "Everything okay?"

"Oh, yeah," said Lamonte. "Your father wanted to hire someone since the stable has been so full up these days, so I wanted to introduce you to Greg Wilson. He's worked at a place in Maine since he was a boy, seems to know about horses, and certainly has a way with them from what I've seen." He nudged the new guy with his elbow. "This is Dr. Elizabeth Bennet, one of Doc's daughters. She and her brother Chase are the vets at the clinic. If there's an emergency, they're who you call. I'll get you a card with their work phone number when we get back to the office." Wilson nodded with a huge grin. Damn, he was good looking. She'd never seen teeth so white and so straight. That smile must've cost a small fortune because there was no way it was natural.

"I'll make sure to program them into my phone. I don't want to lose them." He turned and nodded to Lizzy. "Nice to meet you, Dr. Bennet."

"Please, call me Lizzy. Everyone does." She clenched a fist, resisting the urge to fiddle with her hair.

His eyes met hers, and he bent a hair closer. "Okay, Lizzy. I must say I've never known such a gorgeous vet before. Maybe we could have coffee sometime? You could teach me more about the horses here."

Her cheeks heated, but she stepped back from him. What the heck! Talk about invading her personal space and coming on too strong. They'd just met. "This isn't a hospital, so there's not much you need to know from my perspective. Lamonte is the best person to teach you what you should learn. I couldn't even begin to tell you which horses are fed by their owners or by us or which horses spend time in each pasture from day to day."

"That's too bad." Wilson flashed a crooked grin, his eyes traveling from her feet to her eyes. "I'm sure I'd pay much better attention with you training me." She swallowed whatever it was that had risen to the back of her throat. Did crap like that actually work with some women?

Lamonte cleared his throat while he glanced back and forth between them. "Yes, well, speaking of what you should know, I think we should get to it. I'm sure Lizzy has patients waiting for her at the clinic. I just thought you should meet either her or Chase."

"I'll let Chase know that we have a new stable hand." She looked to Wilson. "I'm sure the two of you will run into each other at some point." She held up her supersized travel mug of coffee and began walking backwards. "Good to meet you too. Sorry to rush off, but I'm sure I'll see you around." Hopefully not, but she didn't want to be rude, even if his behavior made her skin crawl.

"I'll look forward to it," said Wilson with a wink.

Lizzy pivoted on her heel and began her brisk walk down the hill. Ugh! What was it about a man who gave a slick wink? That single gesture killed the effect of his defined cheekbones and smoldering eyes. She didn't even need to check to know he probably had a fine butt, but she'd never even look now. What a waste of a gorgeous face and top dollar orthodontics.

"Morning, Lizzy," said Katy, who sat at the desk.

"Hey, there. We don't usually have you here on Thursday mornings."

"Chelsea had a dentist's appointment, so you get me instead." Katy shrugged but didn't lose her smile. She was a year older than Lydia, but thankfully, grew out of the self-absorbed teenage years Lydia still inhabited despite turning twenty-two. "Was something going on up at the stables?"

Lizzy set her forearm on the counter and frowned. "No, why do you ask?"

"Oh, no reason I suppose. When I parked my car, I noticed you talking to Lamonte and someone else at the top of the hill."

"Lamonte wanted me to meet a new guy who'll be working up at the stable."

Chase stepped out of his examination room and walked up to the counter. "Dad hired someone?"

"Yeah, but I'm not too sure about him."

They both crinkled their foreheads. "Why's that?" asked Katy.

"You know when a guy is hot, but something about him is too polished?"

"Ew! Did he give you the wink?" At Katy's outburst, Chase started laughing.

Lizzy shot straight up and pointed at her sister. "Yes! He did, actually. I'd been trying not to act like a school girl crushing on the captain of the football team before he started talking and acted all creepy. Completely killed any attraction he held."

"Now you have two Deputy Collinses to follow you around." Chase bit his lip, attempting to hold in his chuckles.

She shuddered and held up a hand. "Don't curse me. One of those is enough." Katy giggled as Lizzy stepped through the door to the treatment room. She dropped her keys into the usual drawer and turned around, leaning back against the counter. "What's wrong with me?" she asked Chase who had followed. Lizzy loved

Katy, but she could always share things with Chase she couldn't share with her younger sisters. "Why is it every man who shows any sort of an interest in me is a dick or a sleaze?"

"Oh, sweetie, it's not you." Her brother took her in a big hug. "What about William Darcy? He was watching you ride Saturday morning. He seemed to be into the view."

She pulled away and blew out a noisy breath. "I don't know. He seems to blow hot one minute and cold the next. I never told you he kissed me at the fundraiser." And what a kiss it'd been!

"No," said Chase, "but I saw the two of you. Carrie did too and was furious! I've never seen her face so pinched. She almost looked rat-like. I have to say I enjoyed that part more than knowing you were knocked out of your stilettos."

"What makes you think the kiss was that good?"

He smiled while he picked up vial after vial of medication and checked the labels. "Because you had that dreamy expression just like after Matthew Denny kissed you at Homecoming sophomore year."

"That crush didn't last long." Matthew Denny had told everyone at school on Monday morning that they'd had sex. They hadn't, of course, but the damage was done and most of the boys after thought she would give it up to them as well. Bastards! All of them!

"Sorry," said Chase. "Bad example. For what it's worth, William seems pretty tight-lipped. I don't think he'd do that, but to answer your question about him running hot and cold, he did mention that he's not looking for a relationship right now. He may be interested but scared to pursue the attraction."

Lizzy took a sip of her coffee and shook her head. "Honestly, I still hadn't made up my mind whether he was a jerk or not. He's seemed decent the last few times I spoke to him, but he's so stiff—it makes him hard to read."

"Hey, not every guy can be as perfect as me." Chase straightened and showed off his profile with a grin.

She burst out laughing at the goofy expression on his face. "Yes, well, you're my brother, so that would make you an amazing boyfriend for some other girl. I'm still stuck searching for Mr. Right, who apparently doesn't exist." She'd never find that perfect someone with the creeps who circled her like vultures.

"He exists, darlin'. Don't give up yet. He'll show soon. I know it."

"Lizzy." Katy peeked inside the door. "Your first patient of the day is in your exam room."

Lizzy grabbed her stethoscope and draped it over her neck while the door swung shut behind Katy. "I'm thinking it's time to buy my cat lady starter kit. You know, some support knee highs that I can roll down my calves and some ugly and unflattering flowery dresses. Then I can go to the shelter and adopt every available cat they have. At least I won't have to pay exam fees for them."

Her brother would've argued with her if Mary hadn't walked in and thrown her purse into one of the bottom cabinets. "Who's going to knock out my first dental this morning?"

"That'll be Chase." Lizzy used her back to push open the door, plastered a smile onto her face, and entered her exam room. "Good morning, Mrs. Washington. How's Tipsy doing today?"

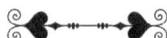

"Hello there, Skylla." Lizzy spoke in soft tones as she approached the large gelding, who nickered in greeting. She set her hand on his nose, and he pressed back into her palm, making her smile. "I know. You're a good boy, aren't you. Can I take you out and see how you're moving?"

She lifted the lunge line from her side and clipped it onto his halter before she opened the stall. Skylla stepped forward, and Lizzy led him in the direction of the paddock. She'd been shocked, to say the least, when William had given her permission to examine Skylla without him. Was this the same man who scowled at her during Skylla's first appointment? By the way he'd behaved that day, she would've pegged him a helicopter parent of sorts. After all, he'd always been a total control freak in the past when it came to this horse. What'd changed? He'd claimed to be busy, inundated all day with contractors rebuilding the stable on his property. Oddly, he'd made a point of breaking away before. What made today so different?

She gave the line some slack when they were in the soft dirt of the paddock, letting Skylla distance himself from her so she could see his gait. The well-trained horse behaved as he surely had so many times before and began walking in a circle around Lizzy. As Lamonte had said, he showed no sign of favoring that foot, so she clucked for the horse to trot. "Good boy," she said when he broke straight into the faster gait. He was an excellent horse—well behaved, responsive to commands, and friendly. Horses like him were her favorite. There was nothing worse than treating a snorting, ill-mannered stallion!

"Woah," she said after watching him canter for several laps. She drew him to her, looping the rope in her hand until he stood beside her. "Good boy." Once she'd patted his neck and kissed his nose, she started back toward the stable.

"I can put him away for you." She turned to where Wilson leaned against the door. Had he been watching the entire time? She hadn't noticed him before, but he was there now, a cigarette dangling from the corner of his mouth and a strange glint lighting his eyes.

"Thanks, but I can do it."

"If I didn't know better, I'd swear he belonged to someone I knew back in Maine. Darcy has a Dutch Warmblood that looks just like him." The cigarette dangled and bounced while he spoke. When he finished, he dropped it on the ground and stubbed it out beneath the toe of his boot.

"Did you say Darcy?"

"Yeah, I was friends with a guy whose father managed the Pemberley Stables. After my friend dropped out of college, he worked for the Darcys until his father died. He had a way with horses. He was good with them, you know. But when his father passed, they fired him instead of promoting him to his father's place. Bullshit, if you ask me."

"Did they give a reason?"

"Nothing reasonable. I assure you. Personally, I've always believed the owner's son was jealous of my friend's natural ability with their horses. It was just as well, though. Too much at Pemberley reminded him of his father, so he moved on. Last I heard, he was in Kentucky working with racehorses." If it was the same Darcy, the characterization didn't seem to fit. Yes, he was overprotective, but she'd never pegged him for the jealous type.

"I'm sorry. I can imagine that must've been difficult. Since he was such a good friend, you must've missed him after he left."

"I did. He was a lot of fun, and we used to hang out a lot."

She led Skylla into his stall. Once she turned him around so he faced the door, she unhooked the line, and when he nudged her, she let him rub his forehead on her arm. She laughed when he almost knocked her over. "Okay, boy. I know you're my last patient for the day, but I'm not going to stay all night so you can scratch to your heart's content."

"He likes you," said Wilson.

Lizzy gave the big horse one last scratch to his cheek. "I like him too." She closed the stall and started toward the tack room. "I hate to rush off, but I'm having dinner with my sister and her husband. If you don't mind, I'd like to shower and change before heading over."

"I could help you with that." Wilson wore a smirk that turned Lizzy's stomach.

"No, and I would appreciate it if you kept your comments professional."

Wilson raised his eyebrows with a bit of a smirk. "Hey, don't get your panties in a twist. I was teasing. I never thought you'd take it so seriously."

She propped her hands on her hips. "Mr. Wilson, we are not romantically involved and do not know each other well enough for that form of teasing, as you put it. For that matter, I never have nor will I ever accept that form of harassment. Perhaps you should find Lamonte. I'm sure he requires your help since it's feeding time."

Wilson's face contorted into a sneer. "As you wish, princess," he said before he walked off. He didn't look back.

As soon as he rounded the corner, Lizzy let loose the almost convulsion she'd been holding back. "Eww! What a sleaze!" The words were not said loud enough for him to hear, not that she would care if he did. What was it about some men? Gah!

Chapter 7

"William!"

He spun around at the high-pitched squeal just in time to catch his younger sister, who barreled into his arms. "You told me next week," he said. He squeezed her tightly then kissed her forehead. It was so good to see her. "I had everything planned."

Ana drew back and spread her arms. "Surprise!"

He couldn't help but laugh. His little sister was smiling and happy and here. He'd missed her. Her company for the next few weeks was just what he needed to distract him from a certain curly-haired veterinarian. "You know I won't complain about this kind of surprise. It's great to finally have you here." He peered over her shoulder at the massive combination motorhome-horse trailer she'd driven down from Maine. "You didn't make that drive by yourself, did you?"

All five-foot-four inches of his baby sister pulled back and crossed her arms over her chest. "Why wouldn't I?"

He ran a hand over his face and sighed. She'd kill him with worry one day. "What if something had happened, Ana? Did anyone know you were on the road by yourself?"

"Mrs. Reynolds knew, of course." Well, that was something. Martha Reynolds had been their mother's best friend and the closest thing to a mom Ana had known since their mother died ten years ago. She would've insisted Ana check in constantly while on the road. "I stayed with her in Pennsylvania, then Aunt Catherine in Tennessee, and I stayed at that place you told me about in Arkansas last night. I was fine, and the horses were given space to exercise and a stall each night along the way. Speaking of horses, where are we putting them? Because that sure as hell isn't ready yet." She pointed over her shoulder to the framework for the new stable. The demolition of the old structure had taken longer than expected, so they were behind schedule.

"I'll call Dr. Bennet about those two stalls. I'm sure we'll be able to run them over right away."

His little sister bit her lip. "What about the other four?"

He abruptly halted and gaped. "Georgiana Elinor Darcy, what've you done? I told you I had access to two stalls. What did you think I was going to do with the others? The fences on this property are in disrepair and made of rusty barbed wire. They're going to take some time to replace."

"I was certain there'd be somewhere we could keep them," she said. "All of my belongings are in the living quarters of the motor coach. I wasn't planning on returning to Maine."

His jaw all but dropped. "What did our father say?" That conversation couldn't have been pretty. George Darcy had been angry when he'd left, but Ana? Their father lived and breathed horses since their mother died, and his sister had earned more of their father's attention than William. With her mad skills at jumping, she could do no wrong.

She shrugged and started walking to the camper door. "What I expected him to say. Swore I'd never get another penny—or another horse from him again. I told him that didn't matter since I had my inheritance from Mom. He tried to claim he could keep me from accessing my trust fund until I informed him the money was mine at twenty-two, and I'd moved every last cent of it to a different bank. Once he dropped the f-bomb and called me an 'ungrateful little bitch,' I walked off. I'd already packed my belongings and put them in the motor coach. I just had to load my horses then drive over to Waterside and load yours before I left."

"When are he and Anne getting married?"

"Two weeks," said Ana. She grabbed his hand and swung it between them. "You need to let that skank go. She's not worth whatever brainpower you give her. Besides, he doesn't treat her like he did Mom. I'm not sure why he's marrying her, but it's not because she's 'the one.'"

"That doesn't surprise me, and I know I need to forget about them both. I was just curious—a glutton for punishment I suppose." He scratched the back of his head and stared at the trailer. "Okay, let me call Dr. Bennet. We'll get two of them settled in with Skylla and the horses I brought with me, then we'll figure out the rest. Either Dr. Bennet or Lamonte may have some idea of where we can keep them."

She cocked her head slightly to one side. "Is this the Dr. Bennet who has been treating Skylla?"

"No, her father. He's retired." This time, he crossed his arms over his chest and gave her a side-long stare. "What?"

"Nothing," said Ana. "You simply mention her a lot in our texts. Do you like her?"

He groaned and tugged at her blonde ponytail. She was way too observant if you asked him. "That's complicated, Squirt, and we have horses that need stalls. We'll talk about it later." With any luck, he could distract Ana from *that* situation for as long as possible. Maybe he'd never have to speak of it at all.

The early arrival of his horses didn't cause any sort of uproar at the stable. When he and Ana had arrived, Lamonte waited for them out front and helped them get the two stallions situated and their feed and supplies put away. No sooner had they finished than his phone rang.

"Hey, Darce," said Charlie as soon as he answered. "Doc Bennet called and said you needed to put up a few horses."

"I do. Ana showed up a week earlier than planned with her two horses as well as the four I'd left in Maine."

"Look, bring them on over. We always have an empty stall or two on hand, and Jane returned a horse to its owner this morning."

"I don't want to get in the way of Jane's business—"

"Nonsense! Besides, all of Jane's time these days is taken up by a young stallion she's training. He's a real piece of work, and the owner is paying her big bucks to get him ready for the NRHA open reining futurity. She'd only accepted the other horse because he was already trained. The owner was having surgery and didn't want him sitting around for six weeks until he was cleared to ride."

"You're sure?" He hated imposing.

"I'm positive."

A click came through followed by some static. "William, this is Jane. You aren't causing me any difficulty. I promise. Bring those horses over. They can't stay in a trailer until that stable of yours is built."

When Charlie's voice had changed to Jane's, William had almost pulled the phone away to look at it but managed to stop himself. "Yes, ma'am. We'll be over in about ten minutes."

"We'll be waiting for you."

"Jane," he said then paused.

"Yes?"

"Thank you."

"We're happy to do it. I'll see you soon."

Ana lifted her eyebrows. "Well?"

"Do you remember Charlie Bingley?"

"Your roommate from Harvard? Yes, of course."

"His wife trains horses, and they have a small stable at their house. They've offered for the rest of our horses to stay there." He couldn't thank Charlie or Jane enough for their generosity. He would've been cold calling stables all over the area if they hadn't contacted him.

"That's amazing. Should we get them loaded up again?" Fortunately, the paddock and the one-acre pasture near the entrance to Lizzy's driveway had been open. Lamonte had insisted they release the horses to exercise while they set up the stalls and made arrangements for the remaining horses.

"I'll bring in the two that are staying here later," said Lamonte. "They've been on the road for a long time. Let them stretch their legs for a little while longer. I can feed them, if you tell me how much."

Once they gave Lamonte the particulars, they drove five minutes down the highway to the Bingleys'. The horses weren't thrilled to be back in the trailer after four days of travel and stomped until they pulled up to the stable and killed the engine. Jane and Charlie came out to the trailer as William and Ana were getting out of the vehicle. The couple wore jeans and boots as though they'd been working in the stalls. When had Charlie started wearing cowboy boots?

Charlie stepped up to Ana and hugged her as if he were another brother. "Ana, I'm glad you could come down. You need to get your brother out of that house of his. He hides away too much for his own good."

"I went to the rescue gala," said William with a frown.

"We've invited you to dinner three times, and you've made some ridiculous excuse on every single occasion." Charlie held up three fingers as though they didn't know what three meant. William wasn't going to explain why he'd avoided those dinners. That would open a can of worms he'd already managed to successfully escape.

"Hi, Ana. I'm Jane." Charlie's wife leaned forward and extended her hand, which his sister took with a grin.

"I'm glad to meet you."

"Lizzy is inside finishing the shavings in the last stall. Why don't we get these guys unloaded? I'm sure they're sick to death of being in that trailer."

"They stomped the entire drive over," said Ana.

Charlie chuckled. "I don't blame them. I'd be fit to be tied after four days cooped up traveling. I get claustrophobic during any plane ride over four hours."

While they chatted and opened up the back of the trailer, William remained quiet. Lizzy was there? He'd managed to avoid her for the past week and a half, which was saying something considering she lived next to the stables, and they both boarded horses there. With his sister joining them, he needed to be careful. Few knew him as well as Ana. If he let even the slightest hint of his attraction show, she'd notice. Heck, she'd noticed his mention of Elizabeth in his texts. Ana handed him the lead rope attached to his mare, and he followed Jane to the closest pasture.

"Can they be let out together?" She opened the gate. "We have another smaller pasture on the other side of the barn if we need it."

"No, they all get along." One at a time, they released the horses, who galloped to where they had plenty of room to buck and kick and get some of their energy out. "If you show us where we can put their food and hay, we can get that unloaded."

Charlie laughed as he heaved the first bag of food near the door onto his shoulder. "When we were in law school, you always helped everyone else. I'm certain if we saw more of you, you'd prove to be just the same. Let someone help you for a change." William and Ana each grabbed a bag of feed, and Jane led them to the storeroom.

"Jane?"

William stiffened in an effort not to react to Lizzy appearing before him. He'd known she was there. Why had it come as such a shock when he came face to face with her?

"Where are some spare water buckets?" Lizzy glanced around, and her cheeks pinked. "I'm sorry. I hadn't realized you'd arrived, or I'd have come out to help." She nodded at him. "Hi, William."

"Dr. Elizabeth Bennet, I would like you to meet my sister Ana Darcy."

"Oh!" Lizzy stepped forward and extended her hand. "Your brother has mentioned you. It's nice to meet you."

"I've heard a lot about you as well." Ana peeked at him out of the corner of her eye. Little imp! "I'm overjoyed to finally meet the legend behind Skylla's improvement."

Lizzy's cheeks turned even redder. "I wouldn't say legend. I'm just glad Skylla's feeling better. His gait had improved when I examined him a few days ago. That's reward enough for me."

"The limp is gone," said William. "I haven't started trotting him yet, but I've been riding some of the trails on the property to try to build him back up slowly. The last thing I want is to cause him pain."

"That's perfect. Rushing a horse back can injure them worse than the original problem. It's always wise to take things at a gradual pace, no matter how conditioned the horse was before the injury."

"Hey, do you have plans for dinner?" Charlie's wide grin was a dead giveaway for what was coming next. "We're gonna grill some steaks. Why don't the two of you join us?"

"Charlie," said William. "You're already putting up our horses. We can't impose last minute on your dinner plans."

His friend waved away his objection. "You aren't imposing. Lizzy is staying, and Chase will be here soon. What's two more? We have plenty of food, and if you drink too much, it's not as if you don't have your own place to stay. I've seen those camper trailers online. You wouldn't be roughing it."

"I'd love to stay for dinner. William?" His sister grinned at him. He should've known she'd play matchmaker if given the opportunity.

He did his best to disguise his sigh. "It looks like we're staying, then. Thank you for the invitation."

"So, Dr. Bennet," said Ana, "while we have you here, you'll have to leave me your card. Jazzy is due for vaccinations and needs to be wormed."

"You know, I keep some supplies in my trunk. I don't have any vaccinations since they need to be refrigerated, but I'm sure I have a tube of wormer in there somewhere. I'm coming out to vaccinate one of Jane's horses tomorrow. I can bring the injections for your horse then."

"Perfect!" Ana clasped her hands in front of her. "I'll give you my email and phone number before we leave so you can bill me."

"Sounds great," said Lizzy. "I'll go run out to my car and check my supplies."

Ana waggled her eyebrows at him, and he swallowed a groan. His sister was usually rather reserved around strangers, but she was behaving downright chatty toward Lizzy. He didn't know who this girl was. She was not the sister he watched grow up.

"This all worked out better than expected." Charlie rubbed his hands together. "Tell you what. I'll go start prepping dinner, so as soon as y'all get the horses fed, we can fire up the grill."

"Please," said Jane, "I'm starving. In the meantime, we'll get the horses inside. They should've gotten most of their energy out by now. I'll make sure they get out again first thing in the morning and spend the entire day in the pasture. I'm sure they'll be overjoyed with the freedom."

Ana pressed her palms together in front of her in a stance William knew well. "Would you mind if I came over and rode? I don't want Jazzy to get too lazy. He's a bear to ride down after a break."

"Of course not." Jane waved her hand for them to follow her back outside. "Some horses are like that. I've ridden plenty who become hyper when they aren't worked regularly. You're always welcome. You don't even need to call. Just follow the drive around the house like you did today."

His sister took a couple of quick steps to catch up with Jane. The pair then chatted about horses while William remained behind them.

Dinner with the Bingleys, Chase Bennet, and Lizzy Bennet? What was he going to do? He'd need to avoid Lizzy as much as he could, but how to do so without being rude? Tonight was going to be difficult, to say the least.

Chapter 8

"All righty! Chase just showed up. I've got the steaks ready for the grill, the salad is made, and the potatoes are in the oven. We've got beer, wine—" Charlie glanced at William— "scotch, or sodas. What does everyone want?"

Jane and Charlie never stood on ceremony, so Lizzy marched up to the counter-height bar and selected a bottle of merlot. "I'll have wine, thanks."

Her brother-in-law grinned and passed her a glass. "By all means, help yourself. You know where everything is. Make yourself at home. Chase, how about a Guinness?"

"I always knew you were my favorite brother-in-law," said Chase, grinning while he took the bottle from Charlie.

Charlie chuckled. "I'll ignore the fact that I'm your only brother-in-law."

"May I have one of those, please?"

When Lizzy turned, Ana stood beside her. What had made her shy all of a sudden? "Yes, of course. I'm assuming you're old enough?"

Ana rolled her eyes. "Yes." She spoke in a low, drudging voice. "William sometimes behaves as though I'm still a teenager, but I was old enough five years ago."

"Overprotective?" After treating his horse, she could only imagine.

"Very," she said with a slight smile. "But he's amazing, so I can't complain much. I wouldn't trade him for anything."

After Lizzy handed her a glass, she sat on the barstool. "Your brother mentioned you live in Maine. Did you drive the entire trip with six horses by yourself?"

"Why is that such a big deal? I've driven myself to competitions all over New England. On this trip, I had friends and family along the way where I could stop and where the horses could get out of the trailer. When he realized—the way William looked at me—you'd have thought I walked through a men's high-security prison naked."

Lizzy hurried to swallow her wine so she could laugh without choking. "Warn me the next time you're going to say something like that." She pressed a hand to her chest and coughed until she could talk in a normal voice again. Thank goodness she'd managed to get the wine down! "As for that trip not being a big deal, I've been riding and traveling around Texas with horses since I was a little girl, but I wouldn't have attempted a four-day drive with six horses on my own. I'm not scolding you, believe me, I'm not. That tone in my voice is awe."

Ana's shoulders slumped a bit. "I'm sorry, but Mrs. Reynolds, my aunt, and now William have all either lectured or had that expression of terror at what could've happened. I mean, I had a bathroom in the camper so other than filling up at the gas station and stopping for the night, I never had to get out. I even stocked the cupboards with snacks and water so I didn't need to go inside the convenience stores."

"You obviously planned well, but since it's a sore subject, let's talk about something else."

"How about my brother?" Ana's lips curved to one side as she tipped her glass for a sip of wine.

"Um, what about him?" Had her necklace suddenly become tighter? Her cheeks were burning. She glanced around. Where was Jane or Chase when you needed them?

"Do you like him?" Ana's voice was higher and had a sing-song quality that set off alarm bells. Was this the same girl who was shy just a moment ago?

"He's a client. I treat his horse. I don't know what you want me to say." She buried her face into the wide mouth of her wine glass. Hopefully, the color of her cheeks and her expression wasn't betraying her, or she could at least hide them. They'd never gone on a date, but that kiss William had laid on her at the fundraiser—Oh, holy heck! Her legs had nearly given out, and her toes had curled in her stilettos. The man could kiss! Not that she wanted Ana to learn any part of that.

"Hey, Sis." Chase's arm came around her shoulders. "You have fun riding with Jane today?"

"Chase Bennet, have you met Ana Darcy?" Her brother had impeccable timing!

"No, sorry." He extended his hand to Ana. "I should've introduced myself before butting into your conversation."

"No worries." Ana smiled, and her clear, pale cheeks turned a faint shade of pink. That was interesting!

Lizzy grinned. "Chase is my brother. He's a veterinarian too, *and* he treats horses."

"I think William mentioned your father was a veterinarian also."

"For the most part, he's retired," said Chase, "I suppose the occupation runs in the family like a disease." Chase had been making that joke for years, but you'd never know by Ana, who laughed and seemed to have a hard time looking directly at him. He used the arm around Lizzy's shoulders to shake her. "And I do treat horses but not as much as you."

Lizzy rolled her eyes. "If you'll both excuse me, I'm going to see if Charlie needs anything."

After a covert pinch to Chase's arm, Lizzy walked outside and checked the thermostat on the grill. "How's it going?"

Charlie took a long draw of his favorite craft beer and grinned. "Almost hot enough." He peered over his shoulder at the house. "Is William's sister doing okay?"

"Yeah, why do you ask?"

"I remember her being kind of shy. William said at the gala that she hasn't changed much, so I wanted to make sure she wasn't overwhelmed in a group of strangers. She was more animated in the stable, but she always was around horses."

"That explains why she seemed a bit timid a moment ago. She'll be okay, though. I left her with Chase. You know he'll make sure she's comfortable."

Charlie nodded. "He can be hesitant in certain situations himself."

"True, but not here when he's in a room full of people he knows and loves."

"I'm going to grab the steaks. Are you going to stay outside?"

"I think I'll pet Jessie." Lizzy pointed to the old bay mare. "I see her watching us from over the fence."

"That's your sister's fault. You know she feeds her apples and carrots almost every day."

Lizzy laughed and shrugged. "Jessie should be able to enjoy her retirement. We've always given her treats, and she's never become mean." Not like that pony of Maria's who bit Lizzy when she was eight years old; but the Lucases had given her peppermints, which Jane would never do.

"No, I don't think she's capable." Charlie pointed toward the house with a huge grin before heading in that direction.

Lizzy walked from the patio through the grass to the pasture fence. They'd had more rain than usual for spring in the Hill Country so Jane's lawn was a verdant green. There was even some grass in Jessie's enclosure. The horses were hopefully enjoying it while they could. It would all be brown by fall. "Hey, girl," she said as she drew closer. "Are you enjoying the sun and breeze today?"

The mare nuzzled the hand before Lizzy slid it up to the horse's cheek to offer a scratch. Jessie leaned her head into Lizzy's palm. She'd always been an affectionate horse. After a few minutes, the old mare lifted her nose and attempted to sniff the glass of wine. "Oh, no you don't. Carrots and apples are one thing, but you don't need my merlot."

She stepped back and started toward the patio at the same time Charlie opened the door, gabbing away to William as they moved outside. "I can't thank you enough for letting the horses stay. I panicked when Ana said she'd brought them all."

"Do you know what happened to make her do this?"

"Who knows? I think our father said or did more than she's saying, but we haven't had a chance to discuss all of it yet. She may have simply been fed up. You should remember how he is."

"I do," said Charlie, "and we're glad to help. When her father called, Jane wouldn't hear of those animals going anywhere else. I swear, that woman would open her own zoo if she could. Did you see that chicken coop behind the stable? Those were removed from their former home by animal control, and when Lizzy heard of it, she called Jane. We have three cats: one has three legs, one is missing an eye, and she adopted the third when it was twelve—and can you believe she's friends with everyone at the Longbourn animal shelter. I'm sure next time a cat or a dog isn't adopted, they'll call to see if she'll take it. That woman's an angel." William was laughing while Charlie went on and on about Jane's pet hoarding tendencies. At least she was an exceptional pet mom, and she had access to vet care for cost—especially for rescues.

"Regardless, we appreciate the help."

Charlie slapped him on the back. "I'm glad you agreed to stay for dinner. We haven't really had a chance to talk since you became engaged." Lizzy's stomach plummeted to her feet. He was engaged? She spun back around, flattened her hand, and held it under the old mare's lips to let her nibble. Maybe if Jessie was busy, she wouldn't make any noise.

"Yeah, well, not all relationships are meant to be," said William.

"Well, there are a lot of pretty ladies around Longbourn. I'm sure you'll find someone to keep you company after a while." Lizzy glanced to the stable doors. This conversation should be private. She shouldn't be listening, but how to get inside without someone noticing. Had Charlie completely forgotten she was out here?

"No, not for me. I'm done with women—at least for now."

"Spoken like someone who was burned."

"No offence, Charlie, but I just want to forget the entire drama and move on. Now that my stallions are here, I can advertise them for stud. I'll want to have Dr. Bennet examine the mares since I bred them before I left Maine. I need to know if they took before I try again."

"So you're serious about starting your own operation." Charlie snickered. "Your father will be furious."

"He will, but he took advantage and bred his mares to Eddie, thinking I wouldn't find out. Instead, he told me he'd bred them to

some other stud and sold the offspring without giving me my part."
Lizzy's eyes bulged. What kind of father would do that?

Charlie whistled. "What was his excuse?"

"At first, he claimed that he didn't think I'd mind, that he'd
referred several people who'd purchased stud services so I owed
him. He always has some excuse."

"Then why lie?"

"I said the same thing when I confronted him," said William.
"Honestly, I haven't trusted him since I caught him screwing my
fiancée, so I don't know why this shocked me so much."

Lizzy clapped her hand over her mouth before she spit red
wine all over Jessie, and began tiptoeing toward the stable. She
peeked back, but thank heavens, William had his back to her. She
continued to creep along the fence line. Don't step on a stick! As
long as she made it to the doors, she could get inside without
William knowing she'd heard. She'd have to double around
through the paddock and return to the house through the front
doors, but that would be a hell of a lot less awkward than coming
face to face with William right now.

When she made it inside, she let out a long exhale, and her
shoulders relaxed. No wonder the man was so hot and cold!
Anyone who'd been cheated on would be gun shy, but his own
father had been the other man. What kind of childhood had he and
Ana had? Her heart clenched for the two of them. No wonder
they'd moved across the country and far away from him.

She let herself through the paddock gate, then climbed the
fence on the other side, setting her wine glass on the post so she
wouldn't spill. Before long, she'd made it around to the front door,
pulled her phone from her back pocket, and texted Jane to let her

in. A moment later, her sister opened the door and stuck her head through. "How'd you get out here?"

"Sort of a long story. Can I come in?"

Jane laughed and opened the door the rest of the way. "Yes, of course. Sorry!"

"No worries."

"There you are!" Chase held up his beer with a grin. "We were wondering where you'd disappeared to."

"I decided to walk around for a bit. You know to enjoy the fresh, spring air."

Chase's head hitched to one side. "And Monday morning, you'll be downing antihistamines like they're Tic Tacs." Ana grinned and took a sip of her wine, watching them like they were the newest episode of her favorite sitcom.

"Ha ha, Chase," said Lizzy. "I'm sure I'll be fine." She put an arm around Ana's and led her to the sofa. "So, how long will you be staying in Longbourn?"

Ana sat beside Lizzy and shifted so she faced her. "I'd planned on staying for as long as my brother will have me—indefinitely if he doesn't mind. If I get in his way, he mentioned a guest house somewhere on the property. I'm sure he'll let me live there."

"I'd forgotten about that old place," said Jane. "I think it's back by the creek."

With a nod, Ana wagged a finger at Jane. "He did mention a creek."

Chase frowned while he swallowed a sip of his beer. "If it's the cabin I'm thinking of, it'll need a lot of work. We pass it on the other side during trail rides."

"That's okay. I don't mind," she said. "William and I have always been close. I'm just glad I can be nearby."

"That's sweet," said Jane in a gushy voice.

Lizzy could only take a sip of her wine and nod. At least William had someone who cared about him. He needed someone.

Chapter 9

"Lizzy!"

She turned around from unlocking her door as Lamonte ran, as much as his long, thin legs could, in her direction. Not only was Lamonte running an unusual occurrence, but his forehead was also furrowed. "What's wrong?"

"It's that gelding of Mr. Darcy's. He's salivating like nobody's business and biting at his stomach. He isn't rolling yet, but I suspect it won't be long."

She stepped inside, set her coffee cup and keys on the table in the entry. "Okay, let's go. We should call Mr. Darcy, though. I'm sure he'll be fine with me treating Skylla, but I'd rather have his permission first."

Lamonte glanced over his shoulder as they walked toward the stables. "You do that. I'm gonna go ahead and start walking him before he rolls." The older man started his awkward lope towards the entrance while Lizzy pulled her cell phone from her pocket. Why did he seem to think she had William's phone number? She selected the clinic from her contacts and pressed call. Maybe Chelsea hadn't left for home yet.

"Bennet Veterinary Hospital, this is Chelsea, how may I help you?"

Lizzy exhaled in a whoosh. "Chelsea! I need Mr. Darcy's phone number. It's an emergency."

"On it!" After a few audible keystrokes, Chelsea read off the number.

"Thanks!" Lizzy hit end and rushed to punch in the number before it escaped her.

"Hello?" answered William in a hesitant voice.

"William? This is Lizzy Bennet. Lamonte just tracked me down to check your horse. He believes Skylla has colic, so I wanted to make sure it's okay before I examined him myself or started any treatment."

"Yes, of course. Do whatever he needs. I'll be there as soon as I can." His speech had quickened, and his tone had become urgent. "This is so odd. He's probably had colic no more than once or twice in his life."

"Something unusual may have triggered it." Lizzy bit her bottom lip. They would need to check everything: his food, his hay, and the possibility someone fed him a treat not on his diet. "We'll go over his stall and be on the lookout for anything out of the ordinary."

"Thanks. I'll be there as soon as I can."

"I promise to take excellent care of him."

"I know you will. Thank you," he said before the line clicked, and he was gone. A sharp pang went through her chest. Since their first meeting, he'd come to trust her. He was relying on her to save his horse. This was no different than any of her other client's owners, so why did his approval cause such a reaction?

As soon as Lizzy reached the far doors, she headed straight for Skylla. "How's he doing?"

"He's sweating and keeps stopping to paw at the dirt. I'd say he's hurting pretty bad."

She lifted his lip and smelled his breath. "Doesn't smell off, but we'll need to see if his teeth need floating." A long line of saliva dribbled and dripped from his mouth onto the dirt of the paddock. Something wasn't right. Colic didn't cause drooling. If a horse needed his teeth floated, that could cause drooling as well as colic, but if Lizzy had learned anything about William in the past month, it was that the man was meticulous about caring for his horses. After checking his hooves for warmth, she ran her hands over his stomach and rump. "I'm going to go search his stall."

"You think this is something besides colic?"

"No, I think he has colic. The salivating is weird, though. You get that when a horse's teeth aren't floated and the need of that can cause colic, but Mr. Darcy—"

"Isn't the type to let that go. You should see him talk to this horse. If you couldn't see that it's a horse, you'd think he was talking to a girlfriend." Lamonte chortled. "He doesn't talk to his other horses that way. Those stallions of his would surely bite his nose if he tried. They're well-behaved for stallions, but I caught them trying to nip at me when I shoed them."

"Yeah, even the most placid stallion is unpredictable." Of course, Lamonte didn't need her telling him that fact. He knew it quite well. "Look, you keep walking him. I'm going to get some Banamine and check his stall."

She rushed back into the stable and unlocked the medical cabinet. Her father had always insisted some supplies be kept in the storeroom in the case of emergencies. She grabbed a syringe, the vial of medicine, a thermometer, and a stethoscope. After she'd given Skylla more of an examination followed by the injection, she hurried back to his stall.

At first glance, everything seemed normal. The water bucket was clean and full, the wood shavings were new, and none of the wood on the door or walls had been chewed. She picked up a handful of his feed, smelling it and letting it flow through her fingers back into the bucket. When she turned, a flake of hay was in the opposite corner. Why was it there? She peered up. The hole to the loft was above her. When she stepped over, she didn't have to pick it up or smell it to know that had to be the problem. The hay was darker than normal with a white fuzz. "Moldy hay."

"Is he okay?" She turned to a pale and frazzled William.

"Lamonte is walking him in the paddock. I gave him an injection to see if we can't help his discomfort, but somehow, he's gotten moldy hay."

William stepped into the stall and picked up the flake. "This isn't the hay I purchased. I opened that bale myself yesterday and checked it thoroughly."

"I'm sure you did. I'm not looking to blame anyone. He was drooling, which is unusual for colic, so I came to see if I could find anything that could be the cause. Now that I know, I'd like to tube him and give him some oil and medication to help it all pass and give him some relief. We can also give him some water in case the salivating is dehydrating him."

"Yes, sure," he said. "The vet in Maine did that when he had colic before."

"Why don't you go see him while I get everything together."

"Are you sure I can't help?"

Lizzy nodded and waved him to follow. He had to be worried sick, so if helping made him feel better, she'd let him. "Yes, of course, I never turn down a free vet tech." One side of his lip twitched. That was a relief. She'd hoped to lighten the mood some.

He trailed behind her to the supply closet where she grabbed everything she needed. Lamonte brought the horse into the corridor, and she performed the procedure while William stroked the horse's neck and whispered sweet nothings near his ear. Lamonte was right. He spoke to that horse as though he was the most important thing in the man's life. How did any woman in her right mind cheat on someone who could be so sweet?

When she was finished, she coiled the tubing and returned it to the steel bucket. "Now we walk him and wait."

"I'll do it." William took the lead rope from Lamonte and continued talking to the horse as they headed back to the paddock.

"You think he'll be okay?"

She looked at Lamonte. "I hope so. We'll need to get that hay out of his stall and make sure there's nothing left for him to inadvertently ingest if he likes to nibble on his shavings."

"Yeah, I'll get it done. I just wish I knew where that bale came from. I've fed him from the supply Miss Darcy brought and it's good hay. Our latest batch is nice and dry too. You know I always check it before I feed."

"I know you do. I'm not sure where it could've come from either. The last time we had something like this, it was that eleven-year-old who came in with his aunt and thought it would be fun to feed a horse a Twinkie."

"I remember that," said Lamonte. "But this isn't a kid with junk food."

"No. We'll need to call Dad so he can email everyone with a horse. They'll need to check their hay. I don't think anyone here would do it, but if someone has a bad bale and they had a visitor with them, they may have fed it to Skylla by accident."

"Gotcha!" Lamonte took out his phone. "I'll call Doc, then do a walk around to see if I can find anything. You keep an eye on Mr. Darcy's horse."

"Thanks," she said. "I appreciate it, and I know Mr. Darcy does too."

"I don't like that someone hurt a horse in my stable—even if it wasn't intentional—and I want to know how it happened." That was why Lamonte and her father had been friends since they were young. They both had an intense love for horses that went all the way down to their bones. Lamonte wanted to take care of them, and her father wanted to heal them. Together, they made a great team.

As the older man ambled off, she walked out to the paddock. The sun was beginning to set and the sky was awash with a brilliant array of reds and oranges. The shadow of William and Skylla made for an impressive silhouette against the colorful backdrop. They walked at a brisk pace, which was steady enough to keep the horse standing and not rolling.

The two of them approached. "If you need to go home, I can message you if we need you. I don't want to keep you from anything important."

She shook her head and smiled. "I'm happy to wait it out with you."

"You have no plans?" he said in a slightly higher tone. Why had that surprised him?

"I have no life." She shrugged then stroked down the horse's nose. She lifted her stethoscope, putting the earpieces in her ears while she moved to the horse's side. His heartbeat was still a bit rapid, and after a moment of being still, he pawed the dirt. "We should keep him moving. I could use some water. How about you? I can run to the house and grab a couple of bottles for us."

"Water would be great."

"It'll be dark soon, so I'll turn the lights on. You can also take him up and down the drive if you want a change of scenery."

"I hadn't considered using the road. In that case, we'll walk you to your door." They fell into step beside her.

"Where's Ana tonight?"

"She's at Charlie and Jane's. Every morning, she heads over and spends the day with the horses, riding. I know she's set up a dressage course. That's always been her weakest event, and she wants to give her horses time to settle so she figures it's a suitable way to work out any anxiety from the move."

"Sounds like an excellent plan to me." She glanced beside her, happening to meet his eyes. The jolt that went through her made her jerk her gaze back to the path in front of them.

When they reached her house, she pointed with her thumb toward the door. "I'll find you in a bit."

"Hey," he said quickly as she turned.

"Yeah?"

"I'm sorry, but can I use your bathroom?"

She startled and stepped forward to take the lead. "Yes, by all means. Please. We could be here all night and the one at the stable isn't always the cleanest. Pass the staircase, and it's the first door on the right."

"Thanks."

Once he disappeared inside, she waited with Skylla in front of the house. "Are you feeling better? I hope so. I know William wants you better. He's really worried, if you couldn't tell."

The horse nickered and nudged her arm.

"Well, that's promising. Tonight, you haven't been as touchy as you usually are. I guess we'll just keep you moving for a little while. I'll give you some advice: the sooner you poop, the sooner you can go back to your stall and the sooner I'll stop poking and prodding." She said the last at a whisper in case William came outside.

"You're a handsome boy." Just like his owner, which sucked. All of the guys who were decent were either unavailable or gay.

The door closed, and she pivoted around quick. "Okay, thanks," said William.

"You're welcome. The road has lights down to the highway if you want to walk all of the way."

He gave a hint of a smile. "The things you learn when you come after dark."

She pointed toward the house. "I'll find you in a few minutes." After she went inside, she closed the door behind her and leaned against it, letting out a long exhale. She needed to stop reacting to him this way or she'd be in big trouble. She'd managed to avoid heartbreak this long, but how could she prevent that from happening with William? The problem was she never consciously started liking him, so she had no idea how to stop. Some mischievous force was setting her up for a fall and she didn't like it—she didn't like it at one bit.

Chapter 10

William took a sip of water as he watched Lizzy examine his horse. She pressed a hand to Skylla's neck while she listened to his heart and his breathing, she petted him softly and spoke to him, and she scratched behind his ears, right in Skylla's favorite spot. Was it ridiculous to be envious of a horse? Because at that moment, he was.

He clenched and released his hand and took another drink from the bottle of water she'd brought him. She rubbed along the bottom of Skylla's belly and listened to his stomach. "There's a lot of noise in there. Let's hope that means we'll see something soon."

"He seems to feel better. He's stopped pawing and biting at his stomach."

"I agree, but I gave him Banamine to help with the pain that causes those behaviors." She took Skylla's halter and began leading him down the long hallway while William leaned against the stall. The night had become humid and the mosquitos had come out, making the paddock a miserable place to remain, so they'd hurried inside the stables and shut the doors in an attempt to keep the biting pests from finding their next meal.

As she strode away, William's gaze immediately went to her butt before he averted his eyes. He wouldn't be a creep. "Get it together," he said in a mumble. He rubbed his forehead and resisted the urge to turn around and watch her some more. A loud "Whoop!" made him whip back around. "What is it?" He really had no need to ask since it was impossible to miss Skylla's tail in the air, and Lizzy's wide grin.

"Thank God." He wiped his hand over his face. Of all the horses he owned, the big bay gelding was special—a gift that couldn't be replaced. He couldn't lose him.

Lizzy approached and handed him the horse. "I think we can put him up. He should be good now, but I'll sit with him for a while longer to make sure."

"You don't have to do that," he said as he led him into the stall. "He's my horse."

"And I live closer. It's easier for me to go home. I don't have to drive."

"Then I guess we're both staying." He grabbed a pitchfork and started down the corridor. "We can argue about it some more after I clean up Skylla's mess."

She took off her stethoscope and wrapped it around her neck. "Would you like a beer? I'm running home for some snacks. I have Guinness in the fridge. I know it's not what you normally drink—"

"Guinness will work. I think this is definitely worth a celebration. Don't you?"

"Good enough reason for me," she said with a laugh.

As soon as Lizzy rounded the corner, he made his way back to Skylla's stall and scratched his chin. "What do you think about a sleepover? You'll have to act as chaperone though. I like Lizzy, but it's more important that she stay your vet. I'm not willing to screw that up." A part of him also didn't want to be hurt again. The entire relationship with Anne had been a nightmare. Thank goodness, he'd managed to get out before they'd actually married. A cheating fiancé was one thing, but a cheating wife compounded with a messy divorce was an entirely different beast.

After one last scratch to Skylla's chin, William rummaged through the bins in the storeroom until he found the quilts he kept for those cold mornings when Ana rode cross-country. He grabbed three of them and threw one down on the shavings before setting the other two on top. The added cushion would be nice if they were going to sit there for any length of time.

Skylla came over and gave him a thorough sniff before nickering and stepping back to the other side of the stall. His mother had purchased Skylla for his college graduation present. She'd known his preferences in a mount so well, she'd picked the perfect horse. He'd never found another he enjoyed riding as much the large gelding. Since then, he'd ridden a good number of horses before even discussing their purchase. The mares and the stallions he now owned were bought for bloodlines and as breeding stock. Ana had jumped a few of them at different events to help give them some recognition and accolades to increase their value. He'd also ridden a few of them at several dressage and jumping events for the same purpose.

He leaned his head back against the wall and closed his eyes for a second, but the click of the door unlocking made him lift his head and turn. "Hey," he said softly.

"Are you sure you want a beer? You look about to fall asleep."

"No, I do. Between the contractors at my place and this, it's been a long day. I'm beat. A beer sounds amazing."

She sat down beside him and handed him the bottle. "Why don't you take off? I don't mind staying. Really. If you're dead set on being nearby, you can sleep at the house. I don't have any clothes for you or a spare bed at the moment, but you'll at least have a comfortable sofa to sleep on."

He took a draw from the beer. "Thanks, I appreciate it. I do. I just prefer to stay here with him. When you came in, I was remembering when my mother gave him to me. He was a two-year-old then. She died six months later."

"I'm so sorry," she said with her brow crinkled.

"I suppose he's become my keepsake of her, which is completely impractical since he can't live forever. I don't know what I'm going to do when he's gone."

The warmth of her hand on his was a shock. "Hey, don't think about that. If you go by average lifespan, he's got another ten or fifteen years. You don't have to say goodbye yet or even anytime soon."

His head still rested against the wall when he turned to look at her. Her eyes held his until he cleared his throat and redirected his gaze to their joined hands. "I know, and I thank you for that. You did exactly what he needed."

"I did no more than any other vet would do."

"Not every vet puts an animal first. Some are motivated by money—"

Lizzy raised a finger. "I prefer to believe they started because of a love of animals. They've simply lost their way and started loving the money more. Dad had a classmate who became like that. It's sad. I couldn't ever think of an animal as a bottom line. I mean they ask you about situations in the vet school interview—how would you counsel an elderly couple whose pet will take thousands they don't have—but I've never been in the situation where I had to tell a client in no uncertain terms that they had to put their pet down for financial considerations. Chase and I keep a savings account to help out with those cases, my father did as well and still contributes to it. None of us wants to put down an animal we can save. I know I may be forced to do it one day, but I thank the Lord it hasn't been necessary so far."

"Have you ever had anyone want to put an animal down because they don't want it anymore?"

Her lips pressed into a flat line, and she began to pick at the bottom of the plastic beer label. "I had a man bring in three cats once to be euthanized. His son had been diagnosed with asthma, and he couldn't keep them. I offered to take them instead, and he agreed. He simply didn't want the hassle of persuading a rescue to take them. I made sure their vaccinations were up to date and fostered them until they were adopted. One of the local rescues listed them on their webpage for me, and we posted them on the clinic's social media accounts. They found a good home." Anne had mentioned similar situations in her practice, which seemed to be one of the unfortunate aspects of the job. He wouldn't want to make that choice.

"Do you foster pets often?"

"We occasionally get pets dumped at the clinic, so Dad, Chase, and I take turns. If the kittens are feral and don't tame at all, they sometimes live here as barn cats. We also know a few other stables or companies that will adopt them. One of the waterparks will take feral cats too. Just like with the case I mentioned, one of the local rescues helps us out by listing the ones we can domesticate, and we put them on our social media pages. The pet is spayed or neutered as part of the adoption and we've usually wormed them and given them all the initial vet treatment. It's a good deal for those searching for a pet. Fortunately, it's not something we handle often. We always share rescue listings on our social media pages and the adoptions are through the different agencies so we don't become known as the 'it' place to abandon animals."

"You'd go broke if that happened."

"No shit," she said shaking her head.

He took a sip of his beer and watched Skylla while he nuzzled the shavings. He had to admire their set-up. Lizzy was an idealist when it came to her job, but she'd been fortunate enough to live up to her high standards. "When my stables are done, I'll need a few cats to help with the mice."

She turned with a smile. "If we don't have any, I can help you find a couple who might be in rescue or one of the shelters. There are always cats who need their perfect home." The genuinely content expression on her face pulled at something inside him. Her lips were pink and full and looked oh, so soft, and he wanted more than anything to know how soft they were. A moment later he blinked and jerked back. When had he begun bending in to kiss her? Where was his self-control?

He cleared his throat and shook himself. "Forgive me."

"I understand." When he looked back at her, she shrugged. "I actually owe you an apology. The evening you brought your horses to Charlie and Jane's, I'd been outside talking to Charlie while he warmed up the grill. When he stepped inside for the steaks, I went to pet Jessie for a moment. I was going to keep chatting with Charlie, but you came outside with him. I overheard you mention what happened with your fiancé."

He winced, averting his gaze to his beer bottle. "Oh!" He combed his fingers through his hair. "I hadn't noticed you there."

"As soon as I knew the discussion was so personal, I headed into the stable and doubled back around to the front of the house. I'm sorry."

"No, please don't beat yourself up. I hadn't planned on telling Charlie that much. One second we were talking, and the next, I suppose it all sort of slipped out."

"How long ago did the two of you break up?"

"Six months ago. The entire situation was...an ordeal to put it mildly. We'd just moved in together and were planning a wedding for this summer. My father owns a stable and a successful breeding program, but I was the one who often met the owners of mares who came to see the studs for themselves. I did a lot of the leg work for that. That evening, I'd met someone who'd been breeding their mares to our stallions since I was a little boy. He offered to take me to dinner, which I accepted. When I arrived back at the stables, I heard a noise in my father's offices. No one should've been there at that time of night, so I went to see what it was. We'd had someone stealing a year or so before, and I wanted to make sure the safe and paperwork were secure. I found Anne on her knees in front of my father."

Lizzy gasped, her expression pinched. "Bitch!"

He laughed but not because anything was funny. How often had he used that same word when referring to Anne? "Looking back, I should've noticed her car parked over by my father's."

"She shouldn't have been there to begin with. Do you still speak to your father?"

"God, no," he said in a growl. "If you heard my conversation with Charlie, you know he did more than just screw my fiancé. Ana remained for a while, but after her own disagreements with him, what he did with Anne was the final nail in the coffin. She was to wait for me to get settled, then get some help to travel down with the rest of the horses."

"Instead, she came on her own and brought them before you were ready."

"Pretty much." He dropped his head back against the wall again. "I can't blame her. She'd moved from her studio our father was paying for into her own place and was shelling out a lot to board her horses. She has a trust fund from my mother that allowed her to go out on her own, but our father kept calling and harassing her to come back home. She just wanted to leave the drama behind."

"She's an adult though."

"She's twenty-seven. Pemberley is a large property with a main house and several cottages. Ana liked being close to the stables, so she lived in a studio over the offices next door. I think he and my mother thought we'd each eventually move into one of the cottages. I was expected to inherit the entire operation, but I told him I wanted no part of it when I left. I haven't asked Ana how she left things with him. That's her business. I'm always there to listen if she wants to talk, but I don't pry."

"That's good," said Lizzy. "My mother sticks her nose into everyone's lives. I think she expects Chase to tell her about every date he goes on—not that he goes out often. She'd probably pass out cold if I ever went out." She peered up at him. "She wants me to date Deputy Collins."

He tried not to show his disgust at that option, which made her chuckle. Even though he couldn't go out with her, his gut rebelled at the idea of her dating anyone else. He needed to keep that ball of trouble inside and squash it like a bug. He had no right to dictate what she could and couldn't do. As much as he hated it, he had no claim to Elizabeth Bennet, none at all. So, why did that make his chest hurt?

Chapter 11

Lizzy stretched her legs before she blinked two or three times. Where was she? The scent of wood shavings, dust, and horse lingered in the air, and when her eyes finally opened, Skylla's nose puffed several blasts of warm air into her face.

Oh crap! How could she forget what happened yesterday? Skylla's colic; she and William walking him and staying with him until late into the night. They spent the remainder of time talking about anything and everything until...Well, she didn't know what happened. She must've dozed off.

The hard pillow under her head lifted just a bit, and she looked down to where her hand rested on someone's chest—William's chest. She pressed her lips together to keep in the groan welling in her throat, and in slow motion, lifted herself carefully from his shoulder.

A quilt fell around her waist, and she touched the soft cotton. She hadn't been covered while they were talking, so he must've draped the blanket over her after she fell asleep. Her heart tightened and twisted. What was she going to do? She liked William, she liked him a lot, but he wasn't looking for a relationship or wasn't interested in one, for all intents and purposes the same thing in her opinion. The problem was she was beginning to resemble herself in high school when she crushed on the same guy who had no interest in her for months or a year at a time, only William did have some interest in her. He had to or he wouldn't have leaned in to kiss her last night. But a relationship wasn't possible, not on his end anyway, and she had to respect his feelings.

She rose to her feet, picked up the two empty bottles of Guinness, and took them to the recycling. After, she grabbed her stethoscope and did a quick examination of Skylla, who seemed to be on the mend.

"Good morning," came a gravelly voice after she'd listened to the gelding's belly sounds.

"Good morning."

"It's been a long time since I slept in a stall." He gave a crooked smile that melted something deep inside of her. "I suppose you still do this from time to time."

"Not too often." She wasn't going to tell him that usually when a horse improved as Skylla had, she gave the owners specific instructions and let them take it from there. The last thing she wanted was for him to ask why she'd stayed last night. She couldn't even answer that question for herself.

William shoved his hands in his jeans pockets and rolled on the balls of his feet. "It's Sunday and the clinic is closed. Do you want to get coffee with me?" No, no, no! The Lizzy of high school would smile and say, "yes," and go without further thought, but the adult Lizzy knew that path would never lead to happiness, only that mad crush that went nowhere.

"Thanks, but I have plans with Chase." She didn't really, but Chase was good at covering on the fly. He'd never tell. At that moment, she needed to get away from William, needed to put some space between them to save herself.

"Oh, sure. No worries." He nodded while he spoke then pointed over his shoulder. "I'll get him some fresh hay. Once I've showered and changed, I'll come back and see how he's doing. Do you think it would be okay to try a bit of feed then?"

"I'd stick with grass hay for today," she said. "If he's still fine by tomorrow, go ahead and start slowly with his usual feed. Let Lamonte know too. He'll help keep an eye on him during the day.

Anyway, I better go shower so I can meet Chase, otherwise, I'll be late. I'll see you around." She did that little hop thing she always did when things were awkward. Ugh! Why couldn't she just shut up and leave? "If he has any more problems, you have my number." Be quiet, Lizzy! Go, just go!

"I'll definitely call."

"Sounds good." With that, she finally stepped out of the stall and closed it behind her. Lord, why couldn't she speak, get out no more than what was necessary, and leave?

As soon as she entered the house, Evie chirruped and ran over from the chair in the corner, making her squeaky little chirps and trills, obviously disgruntled at being left on her own for the night but also excited not to have been forgotten. "I know, and I'm sorry. You act as though I do this all of the time." Lizzy treated her to an entire can of food before she rushed through a shower and threw on her most comfortable pair of jean cutoffs with a vintage Journey t-shirt. The top was one of her favorites that she'd rummaged out of some boxes of old clothes her mother had left in the attic. After she threw on a pair of black and white checkerboard Vans, she locked the door and took off in her small hybrid SUV.

Ten minutes later, she pulled up to Chase's townhouse, which was close to the old main street of Longbourn, and jumped out, striding right up to the door and knocking hard. Yes, Chase liked to sleep in on Sunday mornings, but he was going to have to get over it. She needed to talk to someone, and he was the best person for the job. They'd been best friends before they were siblings. He was used to it.

Lizzy tapped her foot for a bit, then checked her watch. Even when sleeping in on a weekend, he never took this long to answer. Lizzy rapped again and unlocked her phone so she could text him.

It was eight o'clock. He should've been getting up about now anyway.

The door began to open and a female voice called, "Don't worry! I got it!"

When the girl became visible, Lizzy about fell over onto the ground in a dead faint. "Ana?" Her entire upper body burned. Was it too late to crawl back into her car and disappear?

"Lizzy!" Ana ran her hand over her fine blonde hair and glanced behind her. "Was Chase expecting you this morning?" Her fingers fiddled with the buttons on the pale blue oxford. Was she wearing one of Chase's shirts? Lizzy's eyes widened. Were those Chase's boxers?

"Um, no, he wasn't. I'm so sorry. I should've called. I didn't know." Lizzy pointed over her shoulder. "I'll go. Just forget I was here." This was horrifying! First William, then his sister. Was she going to get any kind of a break this morning?

Ana tilted her head then reached forward to grab Lizzy's arm. "You don't have to go. You caught me by surprise is all. The coffee shop down the road delivers, and Chase ordered us drinks and some scones for breakfast. I suppose when I think about it, he called in the order five minutes ago. They'd never have gotten here so quickly." She perked up. "Do you want something? I can call and add it to the order."

"Thank you, but I'm interrupting." Lizzy tried to back from the door, but Ana tugged her inside instead.

"You wouldn't have come this early on a Sunday morning if you and Chase didn't have plans or if you didn't need something. At least that would be me if I showed up at William's door at eight in the morning."

"But I can talk to him about it later."

Ana didn't listen, and instead, pushed her onto a barstool. "What do you want? Latte, cappuccino, Americano?"

"Extra-large amaretto latte with whip," said Chase from the stairs, "and a chocolate croissant. Although, if she's here this early on a Sunday, you should make it two."

Lizzy began biting her thumbnail as if it were on the menu while Chase jogged down the stairs. "It's not that big of a deal. I can talk to you about it tomorrow." She really didn't want to discuss Ana's brother with Ana in the room.

He laughed and lifted his eyebrows at Ana, who giggled. "Oh my God! Is this about my brother?"

Lizzy's face burned, and she groaned, pulling the neck of her t-shirt over her face.

"Okay, I'm going to call the coffee shop and add to the order," said Ana. "Then I'm going to take a shower. By the time I get out, if you're still uncomfortable talking about him with me in the room, I'll take my coffee and head over to the stables."

"No!" Lizzy dropped her shirt. Chase had been on his own for so long. If he'd found someone who accepted him for who he was and liked him, the last thing she wanted was to horn in on their time together.

Ana stepped over to Chase, who grabbed her hand and pulled her over for a kiss before she pranced up the stairs. As soon as she was out of sight, Lizzy lifted her eyebrows. "That seems fast."

"It's not what you think."

Lizzy lifted her eyebrows higher.

"Okay, so it is, but we didn't have sex. We just slept together."

She held up both hands, palms out. "You don't have to tell me anything you don't want to. I was shocked when she opened the door, but as long as you're happy, you know I'll never stand in your way."

"I know," he said, sitting beside her. "We've been hanging out a lot since she arrived two weeks ago. We've spent every evening together talking about our histories and what we like and dislike. Last night, we were drinking and talking, and I didn't want her to drive home so late, so she stayed over." He gave a one-shouldered shrug with a lop-sided smile. "I really like her."

"I'm thrilled for you." She gave him a nudge on the shoulder.

"So, why are you here this early on a Sunday?"

Lizzy bit her lip. "I suppose you could say I slept with William in the way you slept with his sister."

"Okaaay," said Chase. "I'm trying to figure out how that happened because while both of you are crushing on the other, neither of you have seemed inclined to act on it."

"He confused the hell out of me at first. He kissed me at the fundraiser—"

"Yeah, I saw that, remember."

She covered her face with her hands and shook her head before dropping them to her lap. "Then he went all weird and very formal. I overheard why at Charlie and Jane's—his story—and I get it. Then Skylla had colic yesterday."

"What?" Chase frowned. "Is he okay?"

"Yeah, he's fine. Lamonte is now on a one-man mission to figure out where the moldy hay in his stall came from, but Skylla pulled through. William and I walked him and kept him occupied until things resolved. I was going to stay for a while to make sure he was good, but William insisted on remaining with me."

"And?"

"I suppose it was a lot like you and Ana. We talked about why he's not interested in a relationship, his father—"

"That man's a real piece of work, isn't he?"

"Tell me about it. And I thought Momma was a mess."

Chase chuckled. "Then what?"

"I woke up this morning, my head on his shoulder, and a quilt over me. He'd brought out a couple of blankets before we sat down. I suppose he covered me after I fell asleep." It was so sweet. Crap! She was in trouble—heaps of trouble.

"You like him."

"I do." She set her elbow on the bar and covered her face with that hand. "I feel like such an idiot. I mean, if he'd stayed an asshole like that first day when we met, I'd be fine, but I can see who he really is around Ana and his horse. I'm so confused."

"You're not the one who's confused," said Ana coming down the stairs. "Sorry, but there's a call for Chase." She held up Chase's cell. "I believe you're on call this weekend?" Her brother sprang from his seat and took the phone out of the room. "I hadn't intended on eavesdropping."

"It happens. That's how I know about Anne."

Ana sneered. "That bitch? I wish he'd stop letting what happened with her dictate his life. I get why he wanted to move away from Maine and totally support him, don't get me wrong. I needed to leave too for that matter. But you'd be good for him. The problem is he's being a first-class, Grade-A chicken shit."

Lizzy spluttered out a laugh. "I can understand why, though, can't you? That wasn't just a betrayal by her, but also your father. It was huge."

"It was, but I never felt that William loved her as much as he should. Our aunt pushed him to ask Anne out, and one day, he gave in. I think he became comfortable in the relationship. They got along. I don't think they ever argued, and since Anne was a vet—like you—she was content to ride or go to my three-day competitions. The problem was I don't think there was a spark—no chemistry at all. William has never said that, but nothing was natural between them. When William told me he proposed, I was so disappointed. I never told him that, of course, but she wasn't what I expected him to marry. They were just so vanilla, you know? I'm thankful he got our mother's ring back from her after their engagement imploded."

Wow! What a description! Vanilla? So they were dull? Boring? "But I'm not going to push him," said Lizzy. "That wouldn't be fair. He needs to work out whatever is going on in that brain of his without my interference."

Ana bobbed her head back and forth. "True, but don't feel that you're an idiot or be confused. Chase has been pretty observant, and I've noticed his interest too. At Charlie and Jane's, he watched you whenever you weren't looking at him. He's into you—bad. He just has to get over himself, but I can't see that taking too long, not with how he looks at you." She laughed and rolled her eyes.

"I don't know, Ana. I feel like I should try to move on." As if she had all of these other options to move on with!

"I get it. I do," said Ana, "but he'll eventually come around. Don't let it shock you too much when he does. I think he's going to have to let things burst before he'll let you in."

Burst? What did Ana mean by that? Whatever it was, it didn't sound good. Well, that settled it. She would go on about her life. If another man came along, other than Deputy Collins that is, she'd go for it. She wouldn't wait around for William Darcy to get over his past. So what if her heart whispered he was worth the wait. What did her heart know anyway?

Chapter 12

William stepped up to the hostess's stand and glanced around the room. "Ana Darcy?"

The girl in the tailored black suit skimmed over her reservation book. When she lifted her head, she smiled and picked up a menu. "This way, please." She then led the way to the back of the dining room where Ana's blonde hair stood out in the dim lighting and candlelight.

"Will," said Ana with a grin as the man she sat with rose to his feet. Chase Bennet? She was here with Chase Bennet. "You know Chase, don't you?"

"I do." He shook hands with Lizzy's brother. "How are you?"

"I'm good, thanks. You?"

"Couldn't be better." When Chase sat, his arm draped across the back of Ana's chair. Ana had been back three weeks, and she was seeing someone? He knew she'd been at Charlie and Jane's every day. She had messaged him twice and said she wouldn't be home. He'd assumed she'd slept in Charlie and Jane's guest room.

When the waitress came over, he ordered a local craft beer from the menu and relaxed back into his chair. "How long have the two of you been dating?"

Ana looked over to Chase with a smile. "We ended up talking for a while that first night at Jane and Charlie's house. I took a chance and invited him to come watch me ride sometime. He showed up the next day after work. We've gone trail riding a couple of times up at the Longbourn Stables, and since my horses were coming due, he ran their Coggins tests too. He invited me for coffee at first, then we went out to dinner a few times." She shrugged and smiled again at Chase.

"Sorry, I'm late!" When William turned, Lizzy stopped in her tracks, but only for a second before she stepped forward and took the last remaining seat at the table. "I hope y'all weren't waiting long."

"Not at all," said Ana as Chase took her hand. Lizzy grinned and picked up her menu. Obviously, she'd known about this little development. Why had Ana left him out?

The waitress set his beer in front of him and looked at Lizzy. "What would you like to drink?"

"Oh!" She checked the menu and requested a glass of merlot. "I can order my food now if everyone else is ready. I don't want anyone to starve because of me."

They ordered their meals and, after handing their menus to the waitress, settled in. "I thought you were walking out right after me," said Chase.

"You know how Mondays are. Mr. Pfeiffer showed up at closing with Stewie."

Her brother groaned. "What's he eaten now?"

"Their new carpet. I took x-rays, and he's fine. After a bit of medicine to help out with the situation, I sent him home with instructions. Mr. Pfeiffer knows the drill. He'll call the after-hours number if there's a problem. Since Dad's on call tonight, I let him know."

"I thought your father was retired," said William.

"Mostly." She bobbed her head back and forth. "He still takes two on-call days a week, will come in if one of us is sick, takes a Saturday here and there, and of course, will work at a horse show."

Ana grinned widely. "So, this dog you mentioned. He's eaten things before?"

Chase chuckled and nodded. "All of the time. We probably see him every month or two. He's become the cornerstone of our practice."

"What's he eaten?" Ana propped her chin on her hand and raised her eyebrows.

After blowing out a breath, Lizzy looked up at the ceiling and pointed to her index finger. "Let's see, there've been those rectangular elementary school erasers." She folded that finger down and moved to the next. "He also chewed and swallowed their grandchild's stuffed animal, I believe there were a few pens, some money—they wanted that back in a useable condition if possible—a couple of hair bands, and more sticks than I can count."

"You had to surgically remove the erasers," said Chase. "And from what the owner has said, Lizzy's count doesn't include the Legos and things they discover he's eaten after the fact."

Ana laughed and shook her head. "He's as bad as a goat. Do you remember those goats our father rented to clean that back field?" She rolled her eyes at William. "He thought they'd just take out the bushes."

"They wiped it clean," said William, "and I mean clean. He was furious since he wanted the grass for the horses, but it was his own fault. He should've asked or done some research." He turned to Lizzy. "You don't look like you came straight from the clinic." Her hair appeared damp, and she wore a slinky, black top with a lacy trim that dipped into the "v" between her breasts. His eyes darted back to her face before they ventured too low. He didn't want her to think he was a letch.

She glanced at each of them before her eyes rested back on him. "Um, I did go home to shower and change. I don't like going out to dinner covered in pet hair and all other manner of nastiness from the clinic."

"I only meant that you look nice." He scratched the back of his head. Had Ana snorted? Good Lord, kill him now and bury the remains under his chair.

"Thank you," she said a bit slowly. "Ana, I do love that dress. Where'd you get it?"

"This?" Ana pinched part of the fabric between her fingers. "I believe it was a birthday gift from Mrs. Reynolds two or three years ago."

"She was my mother's best friend," said William.

Ana tipped her glass in Lizzy's direction. "Thank you, by the way. I'm afraid I wear breeches with some t-shirt and riding boots so often, I tend to hold on to clothes forever. They just don't get worn."

"So what's Maine like?" Lizzy took a sip of the merlot the waitress delivered a moment before. "I've heard it's beautiful, but I've never been."

"You should definitely go!" Ana's face lit up like the sky on the Fourth of July. She loved Maine. Her willingness to move to Texas surprised him in a way. If it hadn't been for wanting distance from their father, he couldn't imagine her leaving. "You know who would make an excellent tour guide?" Ana bit her lip and gestured toward him. Wait! What was she doing? "Will!"

"Ana," he said in a low voice.

Lizzy fidgeted with her hair. "Tell me about *your* favorite part, Ana." And with that, Ana began describing the coast and the lighthouses she adored. Not long after, their food arrived, and their conversation turned to what was happening in Longbourn and the surrounding areas of the Hill Country in the next few weeks.

After arguing with Chase over who was going to pay, William pocketed his credit card while they walked out to the parking lot.

Lizzy scrunched up her nose. "The nights have gotten hot. Summer came way too fast."

"Do you need a ride home?" he asked Ana.

"No, thanks. I left my car at Chase's." She peered over her shoulder at him. "I'm staying there tonight."

He nodded. Her private life could remain private, but he was thankful he wouldn't spend all night waiting and worrying when she didn't come home. "Good night, then." After kissing her cheek, he shook Chase's hand. "Night," he said to Lizzy, who lifted her hand in response.

As he walked to his car, an odd clicking made him turn around. Lizzy was sitting in her car, but it wasn't starting so he strode back and knocked on the window. "Are you having trouble?"

She opened the door and shook her head. "I just took it in for servicing. I don't know what could be wrong."

He glanced around the parking lot. Chase's truck was stopped at the exit on the far end of the parking lot about to pull onto the highway. "I'd offer you a jump, but it's not a great idea with an electric car. Why don't you lock it up, and I'll drive you home? Since we can't tell what's wrong in the dark, we'll have to come back in the morning or have it towed."

Her shoulders slumped, and she dropped back into the seat. "I hate to bother you. I can call my father. He'll come get me."

"It's not a problem." William opened the door wider. "I have to pass where you live to get home anyway."

"That's true," she said, grabbing her purse. "Thank you."

"I'm happy to do it."

Before she followed him, she took another bag out of the back. "Chase and Ana must've been in a huge hurry to leave." She laughed as she gazed over to where her brother's taillights disappeared into the darkness. "It's nice. I'm pleased for them."

"When did you find out?" He opened the passenger's side door for her, then walked to the other side to get in. "I only ask because you weren't the slightest bit fazed when you sat down." She lifted her eyebrows. "Don't get me wrong. I'm not upset. Your brother seems like a good guy. I suppose I was a bit surprised. Ana never mentioned anything."

"Chase didn't say a word either. I found out when I went over there, and Ana answered the door..." She scraped her teeth along her bottom lip.

"She answered the door?"

"She was wearing one of Chase's shirts and his boxers. That's all. Chase said they'd stayed up all night talking, and he didn't want her to drive home so late by herself."

"I wouldn't want her doing that either. I'm glad he kept her where she was." He gave a chuckle. "I thought she was sleeping at Charlie and Jane's so she wouldn't need to get up at the crack of dawn to drive over." Lizzy laughed, a sound that made his heart lighten and float in his chest.

She sat quietly for a moment. "You know, I don't know why, but I had you pegged for a guy who drove the biggest SUV he could find. A sporty electric model was the last thing I expected."

"Oh, I have one of those too, but it's strictly for when I have business meetings where I have too many people to fit in here, or if I'm pulling the smaller trailer, which I did to move down here. I wanted to leave Ana the big camper-trailer."

"I can understand why. The drive down was much safer for her because of that."

"And she had more horses than I travelled with."

"She thought of everything, though. You have to give her that." Lizzy shifted in her seat. Was she uncomfortable or just uneasy with him?

"I do give her credit. She managed brilliantly."

"I wouldn't have done it. I suppose I'm somewhat of a chicken."

"I wouldn't say that." He gripped the steering wheel a little tighter. He itched to take her hand in his and entwine their fingers. Stop! He had to stop this. "I can tell you now that Ana would never do half the things you do as a vet—anything that requires a long glove for example."

Lizzy burst out laughing. "Do you know how often I get that? No veterinarian loves that part of the job."

He adored her laugh, but what didn't he like? She had a certain bravado that came out at opportune moments, such as when they'd first met and she'd listed her academic history. That had put him in his place when he was being a complete ass. She loved animals, which he did as well, and she accepted everyone. What wasn't there to like?

"I don't know how often you drive out here in the dark, but the turn is just around the corner. It sneaks up on you if you're not careful."

"Thanks," he said, letting off the accelerator. "I've noticed that during the day."

When he reached the top of the hill and pulled into the driveway, he frowned at the lights on and the front door wide open. That didn't seem right.

Lizzy gasped. "Evie!" As soon as the car stopped, she threw open the door and started toward the house, but William grabbed her by the waist.

"I'm guessing you didn't leave it like this."

"No!" She wiggled in his grasp. "Let me go. I have to find my cat. She's small and there's a barred owl that lives on the property."

"And what if whoever did this is still in the house?"

"Fuck," she muttered.

He took out his cell, searched out the sheriff's phone number, and dialed. "All I'm asking is for you to wait until the sheriff's deputies make sure no one is in there. Then we'll find your cat. I promise." He cleared his throat and tried to keep his brain occupied with what he was going to say rather than the feel of her stomach under her slinky top. Otherwise, he'd sound like a complete idiot when someone answered.

Distance! What happened to his vow to keep his distance from her? At some point during dinner, that had been long forgotten. He couldn't leave her now, not when she needed him, but once he made this one call, they would wait for the sheriff, and find her cat. After that, she was on her own.

Chapter 13

The moment the baby-faced deputy told her the house was clear, Lizzy tore through the door and up the stairs. If Evie was in the house, she was tucked away in one of her preferred hiding spots. She'd never been one to venture outside, so once William convinced Lizzy to wait, they'd watched the door like hawks in the event the petite feline tried to escape between the time they called the sheriff and when the first cruiser arrived. One of Evie's favorite past-times was stalking the birds from the window, but she'd never shown any inclination to do more than watch. That didn't mean she wouldn't try when an empty door was beckoning her to explore what fun hunting adventures were waiting for her in the great wide open.

Lizzy pushed through the door to her childhood bedroom and opened the closet doors. She hadn't lived in this room since her parents moved out, before Evie, but for some reason, Evie seemed to like it. Maybe the room still smelled like her? Only Evie could say, and she wasn't talking—not anything Lizzy could understand anyway. Lizzy slowly opened the closet doors. They were never fully closed since Evie would hide and nap in there, but no sign of her tonight.

"Where does she go when she's frightened?"

Lizzy startled and turned around, bumping right into William. "She has a couple of hiding spots. I thought if someone had come into the house, she'd come in here or my closet, but she could also be in the laundry room. She'll hunker down behind the washing machine if she's in there."

"Where's the laundry room?"

"Downstairs off the kitchen." She hurried down the hall to the master bedroom and rushed straight to the closet, but it was a mess. Clothes were strewn across the floor and bags had been taken off shelves, opened, and dropped at the intruder's feet. Evie would never ever stay with someone who was not only a stranger but also ransacking the place. Her soft travel carrier sat empty in the corner, but no little grey ball of attitude.

Her eyes began to burn, and she swiped a hot tear that trailed down her cheek. "Evie! Come here Ickle Bit! It's okay. I'm home."

"Lizzy!" She brushed away another tear, grabbed the carrier, and followed William's yell to the laundry room. "Is this who you're looking for?"

She shifted the dryer, slid between it and the washer, and stifled a sob when the small grey cat came into view. "Evie, come here, baby. It's okay."

Evie hissed when she was picked up but buried her face into Lizzy's elbow. "Shh, I'm sorry. I know you must've been scared."

"She hissed and growled at me," he said.

"I've never seen her warm up to anyone else, and she'll growl if anyone but me picks her up. She doesn't even like me to hold her for long periods of time. Usually, she'll give me a slight growl to let me know she's had enough." Lizzy scratched the top of Evie's head. "She does love to cuddle when I'm sitting on the sofa, and she'll snuggle up to me in bed. I've woken up with her curled up against my back under the covers."

"She likes to spoon you?"

Lizzy choked out a chuckle. "I suppose as much as she's capable."

"Miss Bennet?" came the voice of the deputy through the partially open door. Evie began to squirm in a frantic attempt to flee back behind the washing machine.

"Give me a second." She pointed to the carrier she'd dropped, and William set it on the dryer so they could slip the small cat inside. "I think she'll do better in here until everyone's gone." They zipped it up and left her on the floor in the laundry room, closing the door to give her some quiet.

The baby-faced deputy stood just outside. "Miss Bennet," he repeated.

"It's Dr. Bennet," said William.

"Oh, sorry. I'm new." The deputy held a small notebook and a pen. "Have you noticed if anything is missing?"

She shook her head and swallowed. "No, not yet. I was too worried about my cat. If you'll give me a minute, I'll look around and let you know."

"Yes, ma'am." He walked to the older deputy, who stood in the living room.

A warm hand to her back returned her attention to William. "Where do you keep your valuables?"

"I don't have much that's worth anything." They strode into the living room. The television and internet equipment were still there. He followed her upstairs where she opened her jewelry box. "My ruby earrings and necklace are gone. Those were from my parents when I was accepted to vet school. I wore the diamonds they gave me when I graduated tonight, so thankfully, I still have those as well as my Aggie ring." She held up her hand where the ring was proudly displayed on her finger.

"Nothing else is missing?" He turned in a circle.

"I don't see anything. I mean, both TVs are here." She frowned and tossed her sheets and quilt back on the bed. "My laptop is gone."

"Do you own anything else that can be carried easily?"

"No, not that I can think of."

At a knock on the doorframe, they both jumped to face the deputy who stood in the entrance. "Did you find anything?" He noted what was missing then looked at her with his eyebrows drawn toward the middle. "You said you're a doctor. Do you ever keep drugs here?"

An odd sort of giggle burst from her throat. "I'm a veterinarian. I've heard of people drug-seeking Tramadol through their pets, but I've never known anyone to do it. Chase has never had someone try it either."

"But what if they were hunting for drugs and settled for your jewelry?" said William. "You have to admit this place is pretty torn up for no more than a necklace, a pair of earrings, and a laptop. Maybe we should check the clinic."

"We keep some Tramadol in the lockbox in the stables too." They both stared at her strangely. "New research shows it's effective for laminitis." When their expression didn't change, she sighed. "Most people call it foundering."

William nodded. "We should check both places. Can you call Lamonte? He may want to make sure the horses are okay."

"I think a horse would be fairly difficult to sell," said the deputy.

"I agree, but my horse had colic a couple of weeks ago caused by moldy hay."

Lizzy's eyes flared for a second. "And no one knows where it came from. Do you think they set that up to see where I store my medical supplies?"

"It's possible."

They walked as fast as they could to the stable while Lizzy called Lamonte. They were probably overreacting but better safe than sorry since most of the horses they boarded didn't belong to them. When they reached the office, the door had been kicked open and the room ransacked.

She groaned and stepped into the storeroom next door. The medical cabinet was wide open. "Son of a—"

"Don't touch anything," said the deputy when she went to lift a vial.

"But you want me to tell you what's missing." She held up a finger. "Wait!" After retrieving and putting on a sterile set of gloves, she lifted her hands and wiggled her fingers. "Now am I good?"

He nodded, and she began sorting through the different bottles and vials that remained. Crap! They'd even managed to get into the smaller locked cabinet in the back—only Chase, her father, and Elizabeth had those keys, but it didn't take an expert to see that the lock had been cut. "Tramadol, ketamine, and diazepam are missing."

"I'm sorry. I don't know what those are," said the deputy.

"Tramadol is a pain reliever, ketamine is an anesthetic—excellent for short procedures outside of a hospital setting and requiring anesthesia—and diazepam is also known as Valium." She shifted the controlled substances log so the deputy could see it. "As you can see here, we keep a log of every horse, owner, and dose administered by date and time. The supply cabinet is kept locked, and the controlled substances are also kept in another cabinet inside with a separate lock. Only my father, my brother, and I have those keys since we're licensed veterinarians. Whoever did this knew where the outer door key was kept and used bolt cutters to cut the lock on the interior cabinet." Two other deputies entered, and the baby-faced officer excused himself to talk to them.

"Do you think you should call Chase?"

Lizzy shook her head. "I've known Lamonte my entire life. I'm willing to bet you everything I own, he'll show up with my father. We need to check the clinic, but I think the alarm system would've gone off if someone had tried to break in. We keep very little in the way of controlled substances here. Whoever this was stole what we had left, which wasn't much. I think I had one more dose left in the ketamine and three or four in the diazepam. In fact, we only bring medications up that have already been opened for this very reason, so if there's a break-in, the thief doesn't get their hands on a full bottle. My father always insisted upon the precautions even though we'd never needed them before. I'd made a note to myself to bring more ketamine the next time I had a procedure up here. It's just easier to leave the medications in the cabinet for the next time we need them. We keep a large room of sorts at the end clear for treating horses who need anesthesia. It's not a full-blown surgery like at a vet school, but it works for simple procedures."

William grabbed her hands and gazed directly into her eyes. "Hey, I'm not attacking you."

Ugh! Her head was beginning to pound. What she wouldn't give for a drink! "I'm sorry." She dropped her hand to her side. "I'm angry as hell at whoever did this, and all I want is to get back to Evie and make sure she settles."

"Lizzy?"

She gave a dry chuckle at the sound of her father's voice. "What'd I tell you," she said as Lamonte hurried in with her father hot on his heels.

"Are you okay, darlin'? They said someone broke into the house." Her father swooped her into a huge hug.

"I'm fine. I was out at dinner with Chase, Ana, and William. The thief stole my ruby necklace and earrings and my laptop and scared the bejeezus out of Evie, but we're okay." Her eyes started to burn again when she pulled away. "It's been one thing after another since we left the restaurant. First, my car wouldn't start then this."

Lamonte embraced her after her father. "Where's your car?"

"At Cibolo Falls Grille," said William. "Since it wouldn't turn over, I'm guessing it's a battery issue, but I own an electric car, so I couldn't give her a jump.

"He gave me a ride."

Her father frowned and scratched his stubble. He rarely shaved since he retired, instead keeping it clipped close to his face. "Where was Chase?"

"He was at the far exit when I realized the engine wouldn't start. I wasn't going to call him back. Besides, it was dark and trying to figure out what was wrong without light would've been a pain."

"Lamonte and I will give it a once over on our way home," said her father. She suppressed the urge to roll her eyes. Her father had selective hearing and could be downright overprotective in some situations. "If we can't get it going, I'll call Goulding's. With as many times as his wife's rat terrier has bitten one of us, he owes us." He gestured to the cabinet. "Anything missing?" After she summed up the situation, her father's jaw clenched and released and clenched and released. No doubt about it. He was furious and that anger was simmering just below the surface. "Who could've known what was kept in here?"

"The new guy," said Lamonte. "Wilson followed me in here when I was getting some Bute for Mr. Vogt's grey mare. Mr. Vogt had been keeping it in his storeroom, but I offered to keep it under lock and key instead. Thought it would be safer that way." Lamonte shook his head with a furrowed brow. "Greg seems like a good enough guy. I hate to think he did this."

William held up a hand. "I'm sorry, but did you say Greg Wilson?"

"Yeah." Lamonte tilted his head, and his forehead crinkled. "He did mention being from Maine. Do you know him?"

"What does he look like?" William glanced from one to the other while he shoved his hands in his pockets.

Lizzy crossed her arms over her chest. "Dark hair, brown, cut short with brown eyes and a killer smile I'm sure probably charms the panties off most ladies, but gave me the creeps."

His mouth flattened into a thin line, he pulled out his phone, and fiddled for a moment before holding it out. There, as plain as day, was a photo of a younger William standing beside a younger Greg Wilson. "Is this him?"

"Sure is," said her father.

"Son of a—" William gave a dark laugh and rolled his shoulders back. "You know, I wondered when that moldy hay turned up in Skylla's stall. I should've known."

"What do you mean?" asked Lizzy.

"I'm sure you can see by the picture that I know your Greg Wilson, only his name isn't Greg Wilson. It's Greg Wickham."

The deputy, who'd been standing back from them, stepped forward and pointed to the phone. "Do you have reason to believe it's him?"

"Yes, I do. He stole from my father's stable in Maine, mostly cash my father had left in the office, and he gave Skylla moldy hay, causing him to colic. We had security camera footage that proved it was him, but it wasn't until my father caught him trying to do it for a second time that he fired him."

The young officer handed William a card. "Could you please send that photo to this email address? Do you know if he has a criminal record?"

"Yes, he's actually wanted in Maine on charges of unlawful sexual conduct."

"Oh, God." Lizzy clutched her stomach. Thank goodness she hadn't been swayed by that too slick smile and had agreed to a date. When the deputy moved away to call in the information, Lizzy shifted closer to William. "I'm almost afraid to ask but based on something Chase said…"

In that moment, William's eyes tore at her soul. "Yes, it was Ana."

Chapter 14

"So, you went to Harvard Law, but you don't actually practice law?"

William turned to face Lizzy and propped his elbow on the back of the sofa, resting his head against his fist. "You ask a complicated question."

"Do I? How?" One of her eyebrows arched in a way that fascinated him. Had he ever known anyone else with that talent? If he had, he couldn't remember who.

"Because there are a number of reasons I went to law school, but practicing as an actual attorney was never one of them. I suppose I could stand up in a court of law and make an argument. I took part in a mock trial in law school but hated every moment of it. Everyone's attention focused on me alone was nerve-wracking."

She took a sip of her Scotch, and he stared at a droplet clinging to her lush bottom lip. Her tongue peeked out, not letting the precious liquor go to waste, and made him take a deep breath. This was it! He was going to die a painful death right here in Lizzy Bennet's living room. Why had he volunteered to stay at her house to make sure Wickham didn't return? She had family for the job. Hell, even Deputy Collins had made an appearance as everything was wrapping up and offered to sit in his patrol car in front of her house. But no! He had to be the good guy in every situation. Now he was paying the price. Her head tilted, and her hair fell to her back, revealing the elegant line of her neck. "That's a lot of money for a degree you weren't going to use."

His gaze shifted back to her face. "Who says I don't use it?"

"Well, you said you never planned to practice."

"But I write contracts for stud fees and sale contracts when we sell a horse. In Maine, I purchased properties for investment purposes which I sell when the time is right. Since I'm an attorney, I handle all of the paperwork myself."

Her hand swirled the Scotch in the glass almost absent-mindedly. "How well has that worked?"

"Which part? Taking care of my own legal documents or investing in property?"

A soft curve graced her lips. How he wanted to kiss them and...and...He cleared his throat. "I've doubled my initial investment on most of the properties. I have yet to lose money, and I didn't have to pay an attorney, so I've done well."

Her head hitched back a bit. "Impressive. I think I'd be too cautious for that."

"Every venture can be risky and takes a lot of research prior to purchase." His eyes darted down to his drink. She was too tempting. "My mother's family also owns a conglomerate, which includes several magazines, a newspaper, and a publishing company. Ana and I inherited our mother's shares. As her heirs, we took her place on the board with a few other family members, like my uncle and aunt. Most of our meetings are conducted online these days, so no one has to travel."

"That explains a lot." She rested her head on the back of the sofa. Was she tired? The evening had been stressful, so fatigue would be understandable.

"What's that?"

"Well, you don't seem to really work, but you had enough money to afford the Saddler Ranch. You don't seem like the type to do anything illegal, so..."

He chuckled and rested his drink on his thigh. "So, you were curious if I was a spoiled trust fund child?"

With a laugh, she lifted her head. "Funny, I considered family money but never lumped you in with Paris Hilton or one of the Hearsts."

He clenched his glass, resisting the urge to brush back that curl that'd fallen across her cheek. "I appreciate that. I admit that I'm not a fan of the limelight." A change of subject would be ideal. He never liked talking about himself, but how to swap the topic back to her? "How long have you lived here by yourself?"

She stared at the mess around her and winced. "My father purchased a house in a subdivision closer to town when he started taking steps to retire. Our mother had been after him for years, but he liked living close to the office. The location is easy if a late-night emergency comes into the clinic."

"You don't have to wake up early and no drive to work."

"See, you understand perfectly," she said with a grin.

The situation was easy to imagine, and he couldn't blame Mr. Bennet for holding out for as long as he had. "You said something earlier about fixing the place up?"

"When they started searching for a house, Dad asked me and Chase if we wanted to buy the house before he put it on the market. He offered it to us for less than he would've listed it, but Chase had recently purchased a townhouse down where the creek enters the park. I'd been living at home, so I'd saved enough for a down payment and didn't want to move so I bought it. The one drawback is Momma's decorating. It makes me cringe. When the house became mine, I started remodeling and updating as soon as they moved out. If Ana and Chase keep seeing each other, I'm sure you'll be invited to the Bennet home for a Sunday dinner. You'll see what I mean."

"What've you done so far?"

"Oh, I painted in here and changed out the flooring and the ceiling fan—I'm not a fan of carpet, so Chase and my father helped with the hardwood floors, and we updated the molding. Last spring, I renovated the master bedroom and bathroom, and this winter, we overhauled the kitchen with new cabinets, countertops, and appliances. A lot of the painting and the little stuff my father, Chase, and I can do is done when we can between the big projects, allowing me to save up."

"It's comfortable. I like how it's turned out." He meant it. Her home suited her. The colors were inviting and the furniture was just what he'd pick, cozy and attractive.

She settled into the cushions a little more. "How far along are the renovations at your house?"

He blew out a noisy breath. "I've found a decorator who's going to submit a proposal. We'll see how it goes. I'm still concentrating on the stables, which are coming along well. It'll be nice when we can move the horses in. I don't want to take advantage of Charlie's generosity any longer than necessary."

"I doubt he minds. He's always struck me as the type who would give you the shirt off his back."

William smiled and propped his head back on his hand. "He is." He suspected the Bennet family was as well, especially considering the way Jane insisted on keeping the horses for him.

One thing he hadn't expected when he'd accompanied Lizzy back after the sheriff's deputies left was this comfortable domestic scene. When she'd offered him a drink, he'd accepted, but at the gala, at Charlie and Jane's, and at the restaurant, she'd never ordered anything but wine. The moment two tumblers hit the granite countertop, and she began pouring Aberfeldy, he was even more in lust than when he first saw her gorgeous ass clad in denim. Who didn't love a woman who could drink fine Scotch?

She grabbed the bottle from the coffee table and uncorked it. "Do you want some more?"

He nodded and held out his glass. "Yes, thank you."

"We're going to have to call you a cab to get home," she said as she poured a generous two fingers.

He stiffened. "I wasn't kidding when I said I would sleep on your sofa until Wickham was caught."

She huffed and rolled her eyes. "I know you weren't, but I can manage on my own. I'm a big girl."

"Don't forget your father feels the same as I do. Neither of us wants to see you hurt. If I hadn't shown up that night, Ana would have a completely different story to tell. Even though Wickham didn't rape her, she was still traumatized and needed therapy. You can't underestimate him."

"Why does he dislike you so much?"

He scratched the back of his neck and blinked. Why? How many times had he asked the same question? "I wish I knew. When we were young, I think he was jealous. He wanted to ride. I remember him begging his father to be allowed to ride one of my mother's eventers, but his father refused and he was punished for talking back when he argued. I'm not sure when he started using drugs, but his life went downhill after. He's never taken responsibility for his actions, so I'm sure he blames everyone but himself for the things he's done. Ana's experience alone is why I don't want you on your own with him. I wouldn't put anything past him."

With a groan, she rubbed her eyes. "Okay, I understand." She took a sip of her drink, then looked at him, her emerald eyes soft. "Do you ever wonder if that's why he went after Skylla?"

After he shook his head, he relaxed. Maybe she wouldn't fight him on this. "Wickham had given Skylla moldy hay before that. He didn't attempt harming Ana until after he was fired. That was when he had nothing more to lose."

"Oh," she said all of a sudden. "I apologize. I hadn't considered that he'd worked for your father. I suppose trying to rape your boss's daughter would be a pretty stupid thing to do."

He reached out to take her free hand with his. "Don't worry about it. I don't remember giving you what he's done in any particular order." His thumb caressed that spot just above her thumb. What was he doing? In as normal a movement as possible, he drew his hand away. He didn't want to be abrupt as if she had some contagious illness.

She scanned the room and frowned. "I suppose I should clean some of this up."

"I say let it go for tonight. I'll help you tomorrow."

"No," she said, shaking her head. "I don't want you cleaning my house. It's bad enough that you're staying here. Yes, you offered, but only after my father started pushing me to move home or stay with Chase for the time being. Please don't think me ungrateful, but I don't want you feeling obligated just as I didn't want to butt in on Ana and Chase's time together."

He leaned forward to ensure he caught her eye. "Hey, I get not wanting to give up your independence, and after living alone, I imagine moving back in with your parents and three sisters could—"

"Make me start exhibiting symptoms of insanity?"

He smiled. "Sure, that. But Wickham watched what was going on around the stable. I don't know that he gave Skylla tainted hay to see where you kept the supplies—from what Lamonte said, he could've witnessed him opening the cabinet. The problem is that I'm sure he's stealing at least part of the drugs for himself, and he'll run out sooner or later. If he gets desperate, I'm not sure what he'll do. I don't want you to get caught up in whatever disaster he brings next."

"You don't think that after this he's fled?"

Had Wickham fled? William couldn't know for sure, but he was certain Wickham was low on funds—he'd just sacrificed his job for a few measly hits and trinkets. He would be an idiot to return if he was the thief. "No, I think he probably has little to no money left and is holed up somewhere using the drugs he stole from you."

She sighed. "Hopefully, he's caught before too long, and you can go home."

If he didn't know better, he could easily be offended, thinking she was dying to get rid of him. "We'll see. I'm not holding my breath." Once she downed the last of her Scotch, she rested her head on her hand. "Are you tired?" he asked. "You can go to bed whenever you want. I don't expect you to keep me company."

"Mmm. I'm getting a little sleepy, but I'm okay."

He took her glass and set it on the table so the remnants wouldn't spill on her furniture.

When he sat back, her eyes were closed. "Lizzy?" She frowned and nestled further into the cushions. As soon as he finished his drink, he stood, lifted her into his arms, and carried her up the stairs. He poked his head into the first room, which had some obnoxious pink flamingo wallpaper, the next had a lavender damask wallpaper with a bright floral border. Both were empty. It was easy to see why Lizzy was renovating. Obviously, she'd started with the rooms she used and closed off these.

The master bedroom ended up being the last room. With crisp cream walls, the room had an interesting shiplap section behind her white headboard. He'd never seen anything like it, but when combined with the fluffy white bedding and décor, the room was cozy and welcoming.

When he laid her on the bed, she stirred and gazed up at him with soft eyes. "You aren't really going to sleep on the sofa, are you?"

Where else did she think he'd sleep? "Of course."

She made a sort of grunting "uh ah," and patted the other side. "We'll figure out what to do if you stay again tomorrow night. You'll sleep better here."

Was she serious? How was he supposed to sleep a wink next to her? He laid down on top of the covers but remained stiff as a board—in more ways than one. He took a deep breath and closed his eyes. This was going to be the longest night of his life.

Chapter 15

William blinked and stretched his legs as he became aware of the room around him. A strange ceiling fan above him whirred in swift circles. Where was he? He rubbed his forehead and turned toward the steady breathing next to him where a mass of dark curls spread across the pristine white pillowcase. Lizzy. The events of the night before suddenly flooded back, and he blew out a breath. From on top of her chest, a pair of gold-green eyes stared at him without blinking.

"Hi, Evie," he said in a whisper. He had to laugh quietly at the feline's position, propped up on Lizzy's side so she could stare him down. He'd always been a dog person, but she seemed to have an interesting personality. "I promise I'm not here to hurt her, but I'm glad to see she has such a devoted attack cat." He attempted to scratch behind her ears, but Evie dodged his hand and swiped at him, managing to scratch his fingers with her claws. "Well, that wasn't nice."

"What'd she do?" Lizzy's voice was low and a little rough and sexy as hell. It wasn't helping his resolve to be a perfect gentleman.

"I tried to pet her, and she scratched me."

"She's funny about people she doesn't know. You're lucky she didn't hold your hand in place with those claws." Lizzy turned her head and smiled while she scratched the little grey cat under the chin. "If I touch the wrong place, she'll bite me. Never, ever rub her stomach. She won't tolerate it for a second. The only time I can stroke from her head to her tail is when I'm in the bathroom. Every pet has its quirks, and she has more than most."

"How'd you sleep?"

She sighed. "I know I fell asleep easily but I woke up a good bit. Having my house invaded by that asshole disturbed me more than I realized. Evie never left my side either, which isn't out of the ordinary, but sometimes she'll roam around and play. I've woken up to her stuffed lizard slapping against the floor. With how much I jolted awake last night, I was surprised she was still cuddled up to me."

"Her stuffed lizard?"

"One of my clients saved her after a pack of dogs chased her into some bushes. When she brought Evie into the clinic, she brought a baby blanket and a stuffed lizard with her. I have to admit that I fell in love with her then and there. I'd always wanted a polydactyl cat, and she has the most adorable little mitten paws." Lizzy held up one of the cat's feet for him to see her extra toe, but she had to release it quickly when the petite feline lunged to bite her. "She couldn't keep Evie, and I told her that I'd take her— something I've never done before. The toy is somewhere around here, and the blanket stays on the foot of the bed. She likes to knead it."

He rolled to his side and propped his head on his hand. "You may feel more comfortable at the ranch, you know," said William. They'd been through this yesterday, and she'd refused. What were the odds one off night of sleep would change her mind?

"No." Her expression was hard. "He won't take my security away from me. This is our home, and after being terrified by Wickham, Evie is not being moved. She'll settle in faster in her own home."

"Are you going to work?"

"Yes, I am. I'm not calling in sick on Chase. You'd have to have worked there when it happens to know how hectic things get."

"Your father did offer to go in for you." The sheriff's deputies weren't finished until after midnight, then, of course, they'd been up another two hours drinking Scotch and talking. He was tired. She had to be exhausted.

With a laugh, she sat up with a slow movement, giving Evie time to move. "I'm sure my father will show up whether we want him to or not." She lifted her arms and stretched, providing a glimpse of her toned stomach when her top rode up. "What are your plans for the day?"

"Not much," he said. "I'll go feed the horses. I wish Charlie and Jane had a few more empty stalls. I'm worried about Skylla being here."

"I still can't believe that he tried to harm him the same way he did in Maine."

"I can." Nothing Wickham did surprised him, whether it was feeding Skylla moldy hay for some odd sort of vengeance, or attempting to steal drugs. The reprobate wasn't his father, who'd been an excellent man. The younger Wickham was nothing but a menace.

Lizzy stood and strode into the bathroom, Evie trotting along behind her. While he lay on the bed, Evie's chirps and trills filtered into the bedroom and made him smile. She was a cute little thing, even if she was moody and wouldn't come within a mile of him.

When Lizzy emerged, she was twirling her hair into a clip. "Do you want some coffee?"

"Coffee would be amazing."

"I set a new toothbrush on the counter for you. The toothpaste is on the shelf."

"Thanks." He rose but paused before he passed the doorway to watch Lizzy walk to the top of the stairs. Evie ran ahead, but waited for Lizzy at the top, pawing at her ankles.

Lizzy chuckled. "Okay, I'm coming." As soon as they disappeared, he made his way to the bathroom, brushed his teeth, then splashed some cold water on his face before he followed them downstairs.

"Will you wait a second?" Evie pushed Lizzy's hands out of the way so she could get to her food bowl. "You wouldn't get it all over your face if you'd have some patience."

"Do you always feed her on the counter?"

She nodded and put the spoon in the sink. "When I first adopted her, my parents had moved out a few months before and their dog was still here. Momma wanted the house all set up and their three cats acclimated before she brought over Lucy. If I hadn't fed Evie on the counter, Lucy would've gobbled up all her food the moment I put it in the bowl. She knows she's supposed to stay on the part of the counter where her food bowl and kitty fountain are. She does make attempts to push that boundary, but when she's caught, she'll run back to that part of the counter before I can catch her. I have to admit, she's pretty smart, and she has a very determined mind of her own."

"Not unlike her owner."

Lizzy grinned when she looked up from the coffee maker. "I'll take that as a compliment. Thank you very much."

He laughed and leaned against the counter while he watched her work. When she opened the refrigerator, she leaned back and lifted her eyebrows. "Milk?"

"No, thank you. I prefer my coffee black."

Her hips swayed in her wide-leg pajama pants as she moved around the kitchen. She stopped and bent over to touch her nose to Evie's with a grin before pulling down a sizeable blue travel mug covered in stickers. He couldn't resist and picked it up, scanning the different designs: a rainbow heart with "Love is Love," a cat holding a cup of bubble tea, a teacup that said, "That's the tea, sis," and a pawprint with flowers.

"Do you like my stickers?" Her hand was on her hip and one side of her lips curved in a way that made him want to kiss her senseless.

"I do. Where'd you get the 'Love is Love' sticker. I'm sure Ana would go nuts for one."

"I got that at a Pride march with Chase. I think I've seen it on Etsy, though." After a few swipes at her phone, she held out a page. "Here, I can send you the link. I think they have one with the Pansexual colors too. I noticed Ana has a keychain with the Pan flag on it."

"I bought her the keychain, but she's really not into labels. She adores that quote from *Schitt's Creek*."

"Oh, you mean 'I like the wine and not the label.'"

He nodded. "Yes, that's it."

"Chase likes that one too. You're welcome to hang out until you finish your coffee, but if you need to run errands or go home, I have an extra travel mug. I also have bagels and eggs if you want breakfast. I hope you won't consider me rude, but I do need to get changed for work. Help yourself to whatever you want."

"I know you have to be at the clinic soon. I'll just finish my coffee and maybe toast a bagel, then I'll go feed my horses."

"Sounds like a plan." She poured him a cup of coffee before she fixed her own. "Bagels are on the counter over there. I'm going to go get changed."

He smiled when Evie jumped down from the counter and followed Lizzy out the door. His phone buzzed, and he pulled it from his pocket.

"Is she going to the clinic?"

"Yes, she insisted she had to," he typed back.

"That obstinate, headstrong daughter of mine would feel that way. Are you going to the stable? I'll be there in ten minutes."

"Going to check on my horses. Did you go to the hardware store?"

"Lamonte and I were there when it opened."

William peeked around the corner. Good! Lizzy was still upstairs. He had a feeling she would shit a 24-carat gold brick when she discovered what he and her dad had planned.

William sipped from his glass of merlot while he chopped the last of the garlic, adding it to the bowl of ground sirloin. With his hands, he mixed the combination of meat and seasonings and formed it into patties. The kitchen door opened, and he grinned. "Hi, honey, how was your day?" The words were exaggerated, and he couldn't keep from chuckling after he said them.

Lizzy paused mid-step and stared. "You're still here." She lifted her eyebrows and shifted further inside. "And you're cooking."

"I hope you don't mind. Your father and I did some work around the house today. When we were done, I ran out to the grocery store and purchased what I'd need to make dinner." He stopped and leaned against the counter. "Do you live on box mac and cheese? I swear, you must have a dozen boxes of that stuff in there."

She set down her travel mug and keys on the counter. "You snooped through my cabinets?"

"No, I was searching for a plate for my bagel. After seeing the contents of your cupboards and fridge, I thought I'd cook. I told you I wasn't going to let you be on your own until Wickham was arrested, and I meant it. Wickham was brazen enough to break into your house, so he's stupid enough to try more."

Lizzy happened to catch a glimpse of something in the corner and zeroed in on it, narrowing her eyes.

"Wine?" He poured a glass of merlot and hurried to put it in her hand, but instead of taking the glass, she pointed to the corner near the ceiling.

"What's that?"

"What?" Yes, he was being intentionally dim, but what else was he supposed to do?

She turned around, opened the kitchen door, looked outside, then slammed it shut. "You installed a security system?" Even if he hadn't had a response, the beep of the unit when she'd opened the door answered her question for her. To tell the truth, he'd been shocked she missed it the first time.

He shoved the wine into her hand. "Technically, your father, Lamonte, and I installed a security system. Now, I'm sure the grill out back is good and warm, so I'm going put the burgers on."

After taking a gulp of her wine, she pinched the bridge of her nose. "I should've known my dad would do something like this." She dropped her hand. "But I can't believe you helped him."

"Hey, after what happened with Ana, I agreed with him. Please understand that we just want you safe."

A low rumble came from her as she turned and marched upstairs with her wine clutched in her hand. She had to understand. None of them believed her incapable, they simply didn't want her hurt.

He grabbed the plate of hamburger patties and made his way to the patio in the back. Constructed out of pavers with a huge firepit, the back of the house looked out on the creek below. The view was incomparable. He liked his ranch, but the rock face on the opposite bank topped with mesquite and spindly oak trees was stunning contrasted with the vivid colors of the sunset.

While the meat cooked, he sipped his wine and enjoyed the view. He loved Maine—the coasts and the wooded countryside were beautiful—but Texas had its own scenery, and the Bennets' old house was incredible. There was a certain serenity sitting out here with the crickets chirping and the dark slowly enveloping him. He could understand why Mr. Bennet would have preferred to stay—the man groused about nothing else while they set up Lizzy's new alarm system. The house also wasn't shabby: five bedrooms, four and a half bathrooms, and three-thousand plus square feet, tucked back beside the creek and giving a certain privacy from the comings and goings of the stables. He couldn't understand Mrs. Bennet's desire to move closer to town. She hadn't been living in squalor, that was for sure!

"You brought over a bedroom set?" She stood outside the faux French doors with her arms crossed over her chest. "We're not even dating, and you're conspiring with my father? I need to understand this because I'm coming up with nothing but more questions."

One side of his lips curved. Her father had said she'd be...How'd he put it? "Madder than a hornet in an old Coke can?" "When you refused to stay with your parents as well as at my house, your father cornered me and asked me a half dozen questions about whether we were seeing each other. I told him we're friends—"

Her hand rose. "I'm not meaning to be rude, but that could be stretching things a bit, don't you think? I mean, we avoid each other more than we talk. Friends don't do that."

"I never said we were besties or that we had sleepovers, and who says I avoid you?" Had he been obvious? He hadn't meant to be.

She shook her head and pressed her palm to her forehead. "Forget that part." She sat in the chair beside him. "Are you really cooking dinner?"

"I've got burgers on the grill with all the toppings you could want inside."

She pressed her hand to her stomach. "I love cheeseburgers."

Her father had said as much. The man had known exactly how to soothe Lizzy's ruffled feathers. He stood and flipped the burgers. "I've got potatoes in the air fryer."

"Fries, too? Sweet!" She took a sip of her wine and relaxed. "I'm still mad at you, by the way. I'm just not in the mood to argue. At this point, you're also holding my stomach hostage." She looked over her shoulder at him. "Don't do anything like this again without talking to me—even if my father *is* involved. Got it?"

"Got it," he said. He couldn't see when or why he'd ever need to conspire with her father again, so that was an easy promise to make. Now he just needed to survive the next few days until Wickham was captured.

Chapter 16

When the door opened, the alarm system beeped, making her flinch as she entered the chill of the air conditioning from the stifling late June heat. It'd been five days since they'd installed that stupid alarm. You'd think she'd have become used to it by now. She dropped her keys on the table in the foyer and walked through to the living room, the scent of something amazing making her mouth water.

What was she doing? This was absolute craziness! Who let a man they were attracted to live with them for an unknown amount of time for protection? And what man would do it without a commitment of some sort? While no one could say she and William behaved like an old married couple, they weren't able to avoid each other in the same house. Yes, the former Bennet homestead was large, but they had to share a kitchen and laundry room. Neither had their own private wing.

Her stomach growled, and she looked down. "Traitor." The man cooked every night, and not simple Rachel Ray 30-Minute Meals, but real food: burgers and fries, salmon, spinach pasta. He'd even made a dish with tofu—and she'd loved it.

Food aside, she couldn't continue to live like this. She'd called her father today, who'd laid out the most manipulative guilt trip she'd heard in years, and she'd relented. Moving into her parents' house was out of the question, which was her only option if she booted her easy on the eyes roommate, at least until Wickham was caught. So, she was stuck with the whiskey-colored gaze and drool-worthy body of William Darcy for the duration. She was doomed.

At a chirrup, she looked down to Evie who sat primly in front of her. "I suppose you want your dinner." The petite cat needed no further invitation and trotted toward the kitchen. When they entered, she all but groaned at the sight before her. Who said he could cook without a shirt on? His back was to her, and he was wearing an apron and a pair of cargo shorts that were slung low on his waist. Dear Lord, if he turned around without the apron, would his happy trail be showing? If she could've, she would've slapped herself.

"You're early," he said smiling over his shoulder.

"My last appointment cancelled, and Chase was fine finishing up on his own." Her eyes devoured the muscles of his shoulders and trailed to his defined biceps. She'd never seen him work out, but he had to with his toned physique.

He turned and started when he caught her staring. Crap! "Oh, sorry. I went to the gym this afternoon, and couldn't cool off after my shower." He untied the apron and tossed it over the counter while he reached for his t-shirt. Holy hotness, Batman! The man had a six-pack and a toned body she had only imagined, and sure enough, that trail of hair she'd questioned was right there and disappeared beneath the button of his shorts in an unspoken invitation for her tongue to...to...Was she drooling?

She whipped around and dumped some food in Evie's bowl. "How long until dinner's ready?"

"About fifteen minutes."

"Sounds good. I'm going to take a shower." A hand to her arm made her turn. Damn! He'd put his shirt on.

"Lizzy, are you okay?"

"I'm fine." Where had that high-pitched tone come from? Ugh, she was making a fool of herself. She needed to get his hand off her arm before she jumped him and ruined everything. "I'll be back in a minute." Without any sort of pause, she fled the room, but in a way she hoped and prayed wasn't obvious. What would he think if she ran like a little girl?

Shower! Freezing shower—ice cold shower! She stripped off her clothes into the hamper and stepped under the spray. "Fuck!" Screw it! She'd rather spend the day miserable and turned on than freeze her ass off in that frigid water. For one thing, she needed to shave her legs (she'd shaved them every day since he'd moved in), and she didn't want to shave off goosebumps, and for another, she hated to be cold.

After she was done, she dried off and put on a comfy pair of cotton shorts and a t-shirt, then returned back downstairs and poured a large glass of sparkling water. "Did you do anything exciting today?" She ignored the tension in the room. Was it her or was the air so thick it was difficult to breathe?

"I had an online call with my aunt and uncle. Ana joined us from Chase's. I have to travel to New York in a few weeks for an in-person meeting. Those don't happen too often, which is why they messaged us and requested the conference."

She lifted her eyebrows. "I hope it's nothing serious."

"No, just the usual business, I think. We have some paperwork to sign that has to be witnessed." He held out a plate for her. "Food's ready."

Dinner, as usual, was amazing. When she lifted her head from her plate, he chuckled. "Hungry?"

"Huh?"

"I don't think you looked up once since I set the food down, and you haven't said a word."

Her face burned as she stood to put her plate in the dishwasher. "I suppose so. Sorry. It was good, as always. Where'd you learn to cook, anyway?"

"My mother taught both Ana and me to start. After she passed away, I continued. I think Ana still cooks, but I don't know how often."

She grabbed her glass of water and chugged down what was left. "It was excellent, really. I'm going to have to start running more often, or I'll get fat. I'm not used to eating like this."

His eyes raked from her head to her toes and back. "I doubt that, but if you want, I can plan for some salads and lighter foods."

Now her entire body was hot, as if she'd spiked a fever. "We'll see. I'm sure Wickham will be caught soon, and it won't matter." She laughed, but it came out odd. What the heck was she doing? She rushed out to the living room and wedged herself into the corner of the sofa, turning on the television.

"Lizzy, are you sure nothing's wrong?"

When she looked at him, he stood at the other end of the couch, his arms crossed over his chest. "It's just been a weird day. I'll be fine by tomorrow."

"You're sure?"

"Yes, I'm positive." Don't push! She might just break if he pushed, and that would be horrifying.

"You can say anything to me. I hope you know that."

Okay, you win. I'm horny as hell and want to jump your bones. No, she'd die a million times over if she said that.

"I'm good. I'll do dishes in a bit. For now, I want to sit for a little while."

He shook his head; his eyes had an odd shade over them. "No, don't worry about it. There's not much to clean up." As soon as he disappeared into the kitchen, she pulled out her phone, retrieved her contacts, and pressed Chase's name. She turned on the television for some background noise.

"Lizzy? What's wrong?"

"Can I stay on your sofa tonight?"

"What about Evie...not to mention William?" His voice changed. He was smiling. Jerk!

She turned her face away from the door to the kitchen and lowered her voice. "One of us has got to get out of this house, Chase, or something terrible is going to happen."

"You see, I don't see that as a bad thing. Ana and I both think that both of you need to get laid, and if it's with each other, then it's all good. Two birds with one stone and all that." Ana's giggle filtered through the line, and Lizzy clenched her hand into a fist.

"I can't keep living in this house with him."

"Lizzy, it's Ana. I get it. I really do, but the two of you would be great for each other."

She groaned and buried her face into the quilt she'd pulled over her legs. "I'm going to do something stupid, Ana."

"Why is it stupid? You're lonely and horny, and he's lonely and horny. I fail to see the problem." The line was quiet for a second. "Has he cooked for you?"

"Yes, and if he doesn't stop, I'm going to weigh five hundred pounds."

"Wow! You're wound up tight. Go get a glass of Scotch, then sit in my brother's lap. You'll feel better. I promise."

"I can't believe you just said that about your brother."

Ana laughed. "Don't get me wrong. A part of me is grossed out at the thought, but I want to see him happy. He's smiled more since he moved into your house than I've seen in years. Imagine how he'd look if he's having sex too."

"The two of you are as evil as my father."

"Dad wants you safe," said Chase, who came back on the line. "And I can imagine the guilt trip he used to keep you from kicking William to the curb." He exhaled loudly. "Look, if you really can't take it anymore, come on over and you can stay here."

She straightened and winced. "Will Ana ever be going home?"

"No," he said, laughing. "But I think you knew that."

With a groan, she dropped her head back. "I'm so horny, Chase. I'm not kidding when I say I may just throw him down and do wicked things to him."

"Hey, I say go for it. He wouldn't fight you, you know. You forget that I've seen the way he looks at you. He's harboring some serious lust and feelings. Before you say a word, I know he has a ton of baggage, but who doesn't these days. He needs to put it behind him and move on."

A tell-tale beep of the dishwasher meant he'd turned it on. "I've got to go. He'll be coming in here in a minute."

"Good luck."

"Yeah, yeah," she said before hanging up.

When William entered, she sat stiffly in the same corner, her foot bouncing in a never-ending rhythm. He sat all the way to the far side, turned and opened his mouth, but then seemed to reconsider since he turned back to the TV.

She shook herself in an attempt to stop focusing on him and noticed what show was playing, hurriedly swapping the channel for something else. Netflix had started when she'd powered it up, but when had she hit play? She didn't even know what show it was, but the naked ass and graphic sex scene was the last thing she wanted to watch with William when there was a moratorium on sex.

Her hands fidgeted, and she tossed the remote across to him. "I'm tired. I think I'm going to bed. Thanks for dinner. It was delicious." Evie, who'd spent the past ten minutes playing with her toys on the living room floor trilled and followed Lizzy as she started up the stairs. Meanwhile, she kept her face down so he wouldn't notice that she was blushing, something she'd been doing a lot tonight, but the way she said the last as if it were one long rushed sentence couldn't be any more obvious.

The crisp, clean bedsheets slid along her newly shaven legs in a way that she'd always loved. It wasn't sex, but hey, she had to find some sort of fulfillment, even if it wasn't an orgasm.

He was going to turn her into a babbling mess if he didn't leave. She needed to do something or she'd explode, and it wouldn't be pretty.

No, uh-uh! This was her home, and she wasn't going to suffer under her own roof. Tomorrow, she'd just have to start working on her father and William. One of them would have to come around eventually. They'd have to see that she didn't need someone here twenty-four hours a day, seven days a week. She'd no longer kowtow to her father's guilt trips either. Nope, tomorrow she was a new woman!

The low sounds of the television filtered through the house, and she pulled the covers over her head with a huff. She had to get William Darcy and his fine ass out of her house once and for all.

Chapter 17

Lizzy marched up the hill all but stomping as she went. Enough was enough. It'd been a week—more than a week—and she still didn't have her house to herself. Who had given William Darcy permission to squat there, anyway? Certainly not her! Okay, so she hadn't fought him that hard, but her father was legendary for his guilt trips and this one had been epic. The minute he pulled out the 'darlin',' all bets were off, and this coercion included either William staying in her house or her staying with her parents. Like that was going to happen. She'd sooner move in with Deputy Collins than live with her mother again.

But seriously! Who'd have thought William would still be there after all this time? Wickham had broken in ten days ago—ten days—and now William's constant presence was making her batshit crazy. How were you supposed to live with someone you were attracted to, but wasn't interested in you? Hell, if she knew! She'd been trying to figure that one out since the first night. In the meantime, he cooked her dinner every day, sometimes walked around in nothing but shorts—she'd required a bib on those mornings—and he'd hired a maid. Why did she need a maid? Lizzy kept the house clean. She was the only person who lived there, and she and Evie didn't make much of a mess.

She slammed the door behind her, strode straight into the kitchen, and held out a finger.

"Hi, honey, how was your day?"

Gah! Why did he always say that? Her jaw hit the floor. He was half-naked...again. "Where's your shirt?"

A crease formed between his eyebrows. "I was warm so I took it off. You've never had a problem with me being shirtless before. Is something the matter?"

"Is something the matter? Yes, something's the matter! You're still here!"

His eyes narrowed, and he held a spoon in one hand, which looked a bit odd at the current moment. "In case you haven't noticed, Wickham hasn't been caught."

She slapped her travel coffee cup down on the granite countertop. She couldn't do this anymore. He didn't want a relationship, and all he did was wind her up. How horny could someone get before they finally exploded, or imploded, for that matter? Well, she had no interest in finding out. "He's got to be long gone, so you can go home."

He leaned back on the counter and folded his arms over his chest. "Wickham's never long gone. I'm willing to bet he's lying low and will come back out when his drug supply has run low. What's really going on here?" He stepped closer, and the woodsy scent of his cologne hit her.

"You need to put on a shirt." He looked down to his pecs with a frown. "Gah!" She rushed upstairs. She needed to get away from him. After she took a long shower, she threw on a comfortable dress she liked to wear around the house and padded downstairs barefoot.

When he turned, his eyes raked over her, and her nipples hardened. What in all that was holy? How'd he manage that? He wasn't staying. She had to make him leave, because if she didn't, she just might throw herself at the man, and she refused to humiliate herself that way. She strode over to the open bottle of wine and poured a generous glass.

"What are you wearing?"

This time, she frowned and looked down. "A dress I love because it's comfy and soft. Why?"

"It's short."

She turned to face him. "Okay, so? I've worn shorts this length in front of you without a problem." He paraded around *her house* half-naked but had a problem with a baby doll she was wearing. Dickhead!

He scratched the back of his neck. "And you're not wearing a bra."

"I don't wear a bra with pajamas either, but you've never commented before."

"That's different. Your tank tops kind of press everything down and they're more..." He waved his hand over his chest. "...covered. I can ignore it better when you're wearing those."

She set down her glass and stepped closer. "Are you saying this is sexier?" Could she really be affecting him the way he did her?

"Lizzy," he said in a low growl.

So, she *could* get under his skin just as easily as he burrowed under hers. She bit her fingernail and smiled. "What?"

"You need to stop doing that."

"What am I doing?" Yes, she was intentionally being stupid, but if he wasn't going to leave, then maybe...

"You know what you're doing." He slammed the spoon onto the counter.

"Do I?"

Without warning, he took a deep breath and lunged, his lips crashing against hers in a bruising kiss. Lizzy threaded her fingers through the hair at his nape with one hand and gripped his shirt with the other. Oh, holy heck! Not that she'd lost her memory since the gala, but the man could kiss. Despite the intensity, his lips were soft and moved against hers in a way that made her knees weak and her toes curl. He'd been drinking wine, and she couldn't mistake the bold flavor of the merlot on his tongue as it slipped along hers.

One of his large hands landed upon her breast and squeezed, making her whimper in the back of her throat. More, she needed more. She wanted to touch him and him to touch her—everywhere. How had she become so desperate and needy? Her fingers grazed the bare skin of his stomach and spread out so her palm flattened against his warm flesh. His firm abs shifted under her hand, and she slipped her fingers under the waistband of his shorts. A moan rumbled through him as he cupped her rear.

She'd been tiptoeing around him since she'd heard him talk about his ex-fiancé, but with all of this self-imposed abstinence, her restraint had finally snapped. A better description would, no doubt, be blown to smithereens. It was impossible to live with a man she lusted after day after day, night after night. How many times had she lain awake in bed, unable to sleep because of the sound of his sheets rustling in the next room? The situation was ridiculous, and giving in would probably bite them both in the ass, but at that moment, as he began walking her backwards through the door to the living room, she didn't care. She didn't care one bit. She wanted him more than she'd wanted anyone in her life.

His lips moved to her neck, and his fingers found their way between her legs. She gasped, and when her legs collapsed out from under her, he caught her and lowered her into the armchair. He dropped to his knees, hiked up her dress, and yanked her panties down to her feet. Was he as desperate for her as she was for him?

While his hands stroked up her thighs, his eyes followed their movements with a gleam that made her ache in anticipation. He drew her forward, so she was at the edge of the cushion, and his hands gripped her hips. The moment his mouth touched her, her head dropped against the back of the chair. "God, yes!" Holy shit! A few swipes of his tongue, and she was lost. This beat the hell out of her vibrator. How was she supposed to go back to a cold, hard piece of plastic after having William Darcy's mouth and tongue working her like he was?

Every cell in her body shook. She couldn't breathe, and her mind lacked the ability to concentrate on anything but what he was doing to her. Her fingernails dug into the upholstery as she climbed higher and higher. Just when she would have expected to peak, he changed his tactic. She cried out, but he only glanced up with a wicked smile and started to build her up again. Before, she'd thought she'd die from frustration, but was he trying to kill her instead? He teased her body over and over until she was buzzing from head to toe. When she couldn't take any more, the wave finally pulled her under, a guttural cry echoing through the room while she drowned in pleasure.

When she once again came aware of her surroundings, she was panting. His head rested on her hip, and his shoulders heaved under her hands. This was amazing, but she didn't give in to go halfway. That orgasm had left her with an ache that hadn't been relieved. He lifted as she sat up, and watched while she pulled her dress over her head and shook out her hair. His fingers grazed along her breast, trailing a circle around her nipple before she reached down and tugged at his shorts. After he removed them, he yanked his wallet from one of the pockets and pulled out a condom. He grabbed her wrists and pulled her closer for a deep kiss. "I've wanted you for so long. Did you know that?" he said against her lips.

Was this really happening? How long had she wanted him too?

When he finally buried himself inside of her, he pressed her back into the chair, his face buried into her neck. "Good Lord, how are you this tight?" He started to move, and groaned. "This is better than I imagined it would be."

"I would hope so." Her eyes fluttered with a broken laugh, and she shifted her hips in an attempt to take all of him.

He grasped one of her legs and hiked it over his shoulder, going oh so much deeper than before. She gasped. If this was what being with William was like, she was a goner. No one else would ever do. She'd only had two lovers in her life, and they were both in college. They'd never made any effort to satisfy her, but he'd brought her to one mind-blowing orgasm, and even now, he studied her every reaction. He shifted his hips, bringing an incoherent, high-pitched noise from her throat, and he lifted his eyebrows. "There?" She nodded and grasped his hip to pull him as deep as he could go.

They moved together while he caressed her breasts, her stomach, and her leg. "You've been driving me crazy for months," he said low and gravelly. "That night at the fundraiser, when I kissed you."

She struggled to keep her eyes from rolling back and fluttering closed. "Me too." She wanted to watch him but keeping her eyelids open was next to impossible. Her skin was over-sensitized, and what he was doing seemed to touch every part of her. His movements accelerated and became erratic as his thrusts grew harder. She began that steady climb again, but this time, he didn't stop and start and build her to that fever pitch, instead he brought her straight up to that towering peak and dropped her off the ledge. Her entire body trembled and her back arched off the chair. His voice permeated through the roaring in her head as he called out her name and collapsed on top of her. Her leg slid down his arm until her foot landed on the floor.

They lay there panting until William pulled his face from her neck. "Um, Lizzy?"

"Yeah?"

She pried open her eyes and followed the direction of his pointed finger. Evie sat on the coffee table, staring at them without blinking. "Is your cat a freak?"

With a smile, she shrugged. "Seems so."

Twelve hours later and her body still hummed. Could one night make someone a sex addict? If so, she was a junkie looking for her next hit. She buried her face into the pillow and held in a groan. This was not going to go well. They'd given in to something they shouldn't have, and William would certainly have buyer's remorse.

She peeked from the pillow to find him gone, so she pulled herself out of bed and padded into the bathroom. At the first glimpse of herself in the mirror, she gaped and brushed back her hair. That was going to take some conditioner and a wide-toothed comb to fix. She touched a spot at the base of her neck. How was she going to hide a hickey in July? If she wore a scarf, Chase and Mary would know why in two seconds flat. The snickers and laughs at her expense wouldn't be avoided.

She put on some deodorant, brushed her teeth, then wound her hair into a clip. Hiding that bird's nest was the best option at the moment. After, she found her dress from last night on the foot of the bed. When had it been put there? Last she knew, it'd been discarded on the living room floor. She shrugged and pulled it on before she headed downstairs to face the music.

William smiled when she entered and took a mug out of the cabinet, filling it but leaving enough room for milk. "Coffee?"

"Please." She tried to smile, but how well she pulled it off was something only he could say. She fiddled with the top button on the front of her dress while she fixed her cup. After a deep breath, she opened her mouth, but right when she tried to speak, Evie jumped on the counter and chirped. "Sorry, Ickle Bit, I almost forgot."

While she fed Evie, he loaded a couple of dishes from their late-night forage for food into the dishwasher. She finished feeding the cat and returned to her coffee as his toned arms snaked around her waist. "I think we should talk."

"Hmm?" She turned in his embrace, and his eyes roved over her.

"Sorry," he said with a sexy grin. "It's that dress. I'm a sucker for a gorgeous woman in a skirt, but that short little thing makes me want to hike it up and do dirty things." His hands slid up her thighs, and he groaned. "And you're not wearing panties. Are you trying to kill me?" He buried his head into the crook of her neck, nibbling along her shoulder.

She closed her eyes. "This is not what I expected this morning."

He lifted his head and tucked a curl that had escaped her clip behind her ear. "You thought I'd regret last night?"

"The thought crossed my mind. You've been pretty adamant you weren't interested in a relationship, particularly with me."

"I didn't lie last night—when I said I'd been attracted to you from the beginning. I wanted to kiss that snarky mouth when we first met, and that night at the fundraiser, I wanted to drag you away, peel that tight dress off of you, and make you scream my name." He sighed and pulled her tighter against him. "The more I got to know you, the more the attraction increased and shifted beyond the physical. Despite every barrier I've tried to put up, I've found myself falling for you. When Wickham broke in here, the thought of him hurting you terrified me. You became more and more irritated the longer I stayed, but I thought I was crowding you, robbing you of your independence."

"No," she said, staring at the hollow of his neck instead of his face. "That was frustration, sexual frustration, pure and simple."

His lips claimed hers in a soft kiss, his fingers trailing across her cheek. When he pulled back, his eyes captured hers. "I'm sick to death of fighting myself. I don't want to go back to the way things were when I avoided you out of fear. I'd rather embrace what we've found and see where this goes. Are you okay with that?" he asked, his lips a hairsbreadth away from hers.

"Yes," she said in a whisper. "I'm definitely okay with that."

He kissed her once more before he sighed and put a few inches between them. "Now that we've settled that, it's time for the super sexy conversation."

She laughed and drew back a little. "Super sexy conversation?"

"Yeah, like whether you're on birth control and all that fun stuff."

She bit her bottom lip and shook her head. "No, I've never really needed birth control. My experience is limited and consists of a couple of guy friends from vet school. Those were mostly because I hadn't found someone to have a relationship with and I was curious." Her face burned, and she couldn't look him in the eye.

He smiled and pulled her bottom lip from her teeth. "Don't freak out. I just thought we should talk about it. You know, be responsible adults."

"We'll have to go out and buy more condoms. Chase always insisted I keep a small pack just in case, and well, we've used all but one of them."

"Wait, back up a second. You've only had two lovers or two experiences?"

How her face could get hotter was puzzling, but it did. "Um, I've been with two men, each of them once."

He lifted her chin so she couldn't avoid his eye. "I think we have some time to make up for, but before we go out, I say we use that last condom. We may as well run out before we have to buy more. I'm sure it's burning a hole in your nightstand." He flashed an adorable grin while he waggled his eyebrows.

She laughed and rolled her eyes. "Seriously? Burning a hole?"

"Hey, I didn't say it was a good excuse." His clever fingers slipped between her legs and she shamelessly shifted out a foot, giving him more room. "But it's Saturday, you don't have to work, and I say we take advantage." He groaned as his finger entered her. "I can't wait to be inside you again, feel you quiver, make you scream. Just the thought of it—remembering how you felt—makes me harder than I thought possible."

Her body roared to life. How could he get her going with just a few words? "Who says you can make me scream?" Her voice came out all breathy. Crap! She didn't want to let on how he affected her.

"I made you call my name more than once last night." He wore a cocky smile she wanted to wipe from his face.

"Well, then maybe you won't now."

"Is that a challenge?"

She bit her cheek in an attempt not to react to what he was doing to her. He laughed all low and sexy. His lips found that sensitive place under her ear, and he tweaked a nipple. She swallowed a moan and bit his shoulder. She was going to lose and lose badly, but somehow, she didn't think she'd be upset about it.

Chapter 18

Two hours later, William pulled up to Bear Creek Coffee Co., turned off the car, and leaned over to kiss Lizzy on the lips. "Don't move."

Her eyebrows drew down a bit while she laughed. "Why? I thought we were going inside."

With a grin, he hopped out and strode around the car to open her door. "This is why. I wouldn't put it past you to get out before I could walk around." Her cheeks pinked in a way that made his heart swell a little. He'd seen her soft side with Evie and Skylla as well as when she stopped to talk to the other horses in the stable, but not so much with other people, though he was certain she had a gentler side that came out when it was just her and Chase or another member of her family.

"Such a gentleman." She took his hand as she extended a toned leg to stand.

"You don't mind then?"

"Why would I mind? Good manners just mean your Momma raised you right. Didn't you know that?"

He opened the door to the coffee shop and pressed her forward with a palm to the small of her back. Then took her hand again as they stepped into the line. "Do you want to sit down and drink your coffee here or do you want to sit by the creek?"

"The creek is nice, but the geese will make it hard to eat our pastries. They're relentless, and we don't have any food for them. We'll have more peace here."

After another round of lovemaking, they'd decided to go out for breakfast instead of cooking, which was a good thing. Yes, he'd been playing the chef for her since he moved into the house, but they'd now had sex without ever going on a date. He was a dickhead for that. If he hadn't been so caught up in his own fears, he would've known Lizzy was too good to let go.

"I hadn't considered the geese."

She pointed around the corner. "There's a nice view of the creek from the patio that's completely goose-free."

The people in front of them moved to wait for their drinks, so he and Lizzy shifted forward to order. Since they were dining in, the cashier gave them a number, and Lizzy led him around to a table on the glassed-in patio. "This is nice," he said looking at the gnarled live oaks whose branches shaded the almost greenhouse-like addition.

"It can get warm in here in the afternoon, but first thing in the morning it's perfect."

He took a chair and pulled it out for her, making a laugh bubble up from her throat. The sound made him smile.

"This is all sweet, but you don't have to do *every* gentlemanly thing possible."

With a one-shouldered shrug, he lifted their joined hands and kissed hers. "I'm happy. If it becomes too much or gets annoying, let me know, and I'll stop."

"I never said it's annoying. I just don't want you to break your neck jumping in front of me to open the door or pull out my chair."

He drew her against him and kissed her forehead, then her cheek, but a loud "I knew it!" made them hop apart before he could reach her lips. His eyes squeezed closed. He knew that voice. "I said it was only a matter of time before the two of you would get together." When he turned, Ana wore a huge grin that almost matched Chase's, who stood right behind his sister. Chase's presence shouldn't have been a surprise. Lizzy had mentioned when they passed the clinic that it was her father's day to cover.

"Good morning, Ana," William said dryly.

She gave a little squeal and danced forward to hug Lizzy. "I'm so happy!"

William shook Chase's hand while Ana continued to hug Lizzy and bounce. "I see we had the same idea this morning."

Chase shrugged. "According to Ana, my coffee is dreadful and she refuses to drink it. Most mornings, we've either had our order delivered or we've stopped in on our way out for the day."

"They deliver?"

"It's a very small radius, but yes. I live just across that bridge over there." He pointed downstream to a metal footbridge that crossed a narrower portion of the creek. Lizzy had mentioned Chase lived near the park. He'd simply forgotten. Chase put a hand to Ana's back, between her shoulder blades, and leaned closer to her ear. "Hey, let's sit in the main dining room and give these two their privacy."

Anna, who'd started talking animatedly to Lizzy, rolled her eyes. "We're in a public place, Chase. Nothing is private."

"I only meant that we sit somewhere else, so you're not staring at them while they eat with that huge grin. They may want to be *alone*."

"We need to plan a double date," said Ana. "We can go to dinner like we did before. Maybe next weekend?"

William hugged his little sister. "We'll definitely do something, but I'll call you, okay?"

Her lips were puckered to one side when she pulled back. "Okay, I get it. We'll give you some space."

Chase laughed. "*You'll* give them some space. I wasn't hovering."

Ana stuck out her tongue at him. "Fine, let's go."

As soon as Chase followed Ana back the way they'd come, Lizzy sat in her chair. "They could've joined us. I don't want her upset with Chase."

"She's not upset with him. If she was, she wouldn't have stuck her tongue out at him. That was her being her normal goofy self. When Ana's mad, the entire room frosts over."

"I suppose, now that I think about it, I've never seen Ana angry."

"All in all, she's fairly easy going. It's crazy difficult to set her off, but it can be done."

"Good to know."

"I thought I heard your voice." Lizzy sat with her back to the entrance, but she knew the oily voice since her eyes squeezed closed. Before Deputy Collins could step up to their table, she reopened them and plastered on a smile. Deputy Collins's eyes darted to William but returned quickly to Lizzy. He rested a hand on the back of Lizzy's chair. "How are you? I've been worried about you since the break-in. I've been patrolling out around the clinic and the stable whenever I have the opportunity, so don't worry your pretty little head about a thing. We'll catch him." William's spine stiffened at Collins's posture and position.

"I appreciate that, but I'm not worried." Lizzy took William's hand and gave it a squeeze. "Will's been staying at the house, and he helped my father install a security system. I don't think Wickham will be stupid enough to return."

Collins watched the movement of her hand and looked back at William for a moment before he forced a smile that resembled a grimace. William pressed his lips together. Not one hint of a grin could cross his expression—even if Lizzy's gesture satisfied him to no end.

"Well, I'm glad to know you have some protection. Just remember we don't have waiting periods here in Texas if you want to buy a gun. Even without the break-in, it's always a good thing to have around, Elizabeth." What the—? How condescending, especially with how her name rolled off his tongue. How could he have ever told Chase to persuade her toward this dickhead? The more he opened his mouth, the more William understood Lizzy's adamant refusal of Collins.

Her eyes darted to him. "I'm not interested in purchasing a gun but thank you for the reminder." Lizzy's tone was pleasant, but there was a slight shift in her manner. Perhaps it was Collins's use of her given name instead of her nickname. He'd never heard anyone call her that, even her parents. Why would Collins use it?

"Excuse me," said a young voice from behind the deputy. When Collins stepped to the side, one of the girls who worked in the coffee shop held the tray with their coffee and pastries. She set it down on the table while Lizzy smiled and thanked her.

As soon as the girl left, Lizzy looked up at Collins. "Well, I'm sure you have to go to work, and we don't want to keep you all day. Thanks for checking in."

Collins reached into a pocket and put a business card on the table. "If you have any problems, any at all, don't hesitate to call me."

"I'm sure that won't be necessary." William took the card and glanced down at it. "But we'll certainly call the sheriff's office or 911 if we need them. Thank you again, Deputy."

At the second dismissal, Collins clenched his jaw. "I'll see you around, Elizabeth."

He disappeared around the corner, and Lizzy put a finger over her lips. They sipped their coffee while Collins ordered his own drink at the counter. When the bell on the door sounded, she leaned so she could see the parking lot, exhaling in a heavy whoosh at the sight of Collins getting into his car. "Lord, he sets my teeth on edge." She grabbed the business card from William's hand and tore it into little bitty pieces before tossing it in the nearby trash can.

"Why does he call you Elizabeth?"

"I wish I knew. He's three years older than me and never spoke to me in high school. It wasn't until I graduated A&M and returned that he seemed to take an interest. He brought that service dog of his into the clinic, and the first time, it was luck of the draw that I was the vet examining him. After that, Chelsea said Collins started requesting me. The day you first brought Skylla in, he'd brought his service dog in. Chase couldn't find anything wrong with the dog and said Collins was not thrilled to have missed me. He can be so complimentary when I'm examining his dog, but always in a sort of patronizing and condescending way, even if not in the way he words things, but in his tone. 'It's a good thing to have, Elizabeth,'" she said, lowering her pitch while mocking him. "You should see him around the Lucases. He has his nose so far up their asses, I'm amazed he can manage to breathe."

He chuckled then leaned back in his seat and watched her carefully. "Do you want a gun for protection?"

"No." She shook her head while breaking off a piece of chocolate croissant. "I can't stand the things. If I wanted one, I could borrow one of my father's hunting rifles, and you notice he never offered. That's because he knew I'd turn it down." She chewed and swallowed her bite of pastry. "You know, we should go to Schertz's drug store around the corner and buy a buffet of condoms, the kinkier the better."

His head hitched back. Where did that suggestion come from? "Um, why there, and why a buffet?"

"Have you never been in Schertz's?"

"Not yet. I saw it a week or two after I moved here, and I prefer to shop local businesses, so I planned to check the place out when I had some time. It's just been one thing after another, so I've never made it in."

With a nod, Lizzy relaxed back into her chair with her coffee cup. "Mr. Schertz is the owner and a pharmacist, but he's too cheap to hire more than a couple of part-timers so his wife works the front register. The problem is that she's a terrible gossip. For fear of a HIPAA violation, her husband started ringing up prescriptions himself at the pharmacy when he realized she couldn't keep her mouth shut, or he has his tech do it. Anyway, if we go in and buy different colors and flavors and have a great time with it, I guarantee word will get back to Collins."

"Aren't you worried it'll get back to your parents?"

Lizzy almost snorted. "Well, for one, Momma hasn't gone into Schertz's since Mrs. Schertz told half the town she bought personal lubricant."

William almost spit his coffee across the table. "She what? Why would someone gossip about that?"

"That's why Mr. Schertz doesn't trust her with prescriptions. It's well known around town. Momma went into the store and called Mrs. Schertz a liar. Mrs. Schertz said she could pull up the sale in the computer system. It was an enormous mess."

He could imagine! The gossip would've died a quicker death if she'd left it alone.

"So, we go to Schertz's and buy enough condoms to last us a few months. If Momma hears anything of it, she won't believe a word. Even if she did, she'd deny it. The last thing she wants is for Mrs. Schertz to look like a reliable fount of information."

He picked at a scratch in the table. He wasn't used to having his personal information be fodder for the rumor mill, but he wasn't ashamed of Lizzy. If she really wanted to do this, he would manage, he supposed.

"Do you really think this will get Collins to back off? What if he never hears about it?"

She shrugged. "The sheriff's office is just down the street. The sheriff's secretary and Mrs. Schertz are best friends. It'll get to him. Thing is, I've told him a million times I don't want to go out with him. Maybe if he knows I'm with you and it's serious—"

"And that you're having sex every free second?"

"Exactly! Maybe if he believes that, he'll leave me alone. To tell the truth, I'd be satisfied if he just stopped requesting me at the clinic."

"A lot could go wrong with this."

"Worst case scenario: Momma freaks, and I tell her we bought them for a prank."

"Couldn't Collins think that, that we bought them for a prank?"

"I'd hope he'd take the hint of me holding your hand, but I think he needs more. Is this the most mature method? No, but I can't stand having to deal with him."

William nodded and exhaled. "Okay, I'll go along with it."

After she polished off the last two bites of her pastry and swallowed her last sip of coffee, Lizzy took his hand. "Let's go." She grinned as she led him two blocks down to the locally owned drug store. A handbasket was shoved into his grasp, and he followed her while she scanned the aisles. Why was his face already burning? No one had seen them, and they weren't even standing in front of the display yet.

When the shelves holding the condoms appeared, he struggled to keep his jaw from dropping. Holy shit! Who knew a small-town druggist would have such a selection. Lizzy meanwhile giggled like a schoolgirl, dropping package after package into the basket—flavored, ribbed, with dots, with spikes, glow in the dark. If it was different than the norm, Lizzy threw it in the pile to be purchased. Good Lord, they were going to look like sex addicts.

"Do you think it's enough?" She asked, turning to him, then frowned. "Are you okay? You're awfully quiet, and you have that grouchy expression, like when I first met you."

"I'm fine. I think." He pointed to the basket. "People are going to expect you to start walking funny with that many."

A huge grin lit her face while she nodded. "That's kind of the point." She lifted her eyebrows. "Are you embarrassed?"

"A little, I guess."

Her free hand snaked around his side. "Don't be. You'll look like a major stud," she said softly near his ear.

He pulled his head back a bit. "Does that mean I'm not?"

She kissed him then held his gaze. "Hey, I think you're amazing, and all the old busybodies will know that." She held up the basket, which was well over half full. "Come on. I can't wait to see the look on Mrs. Schertz's face."

When they reached the front, Lizzy set the basket onto the counter. "Good morning."

"Why, Miss Lizzy, I haven't seen you in an age." The grey-haired woman's eyes darted to him before she looked at their purchases. Her eyes bulged for a full ten seconds before she cleared her throat and started scanning each of the packages. "Looks like it's going to be another hot day."

"It does, doesn't it." Lizzy glanced his way and winked.

He turned back to the woman behind the counter, who was reading the front of the box of spiked condoms while she scanned it. After the last was rung up, she hit a button. "Two hundred and fifty-four dollars and fifty-two cents."

Lizzy opened her phone case to pull out her credit card, but he put his in the machine first. "I've got this."

Meanwhile, Lizzy hugged herself to his arm. "You're so good to me," she said in a gushing tone.

Mrs. Schertz just watched the interaction between the two of them. Once he'd signed the pen pad, he smiled. "Have a nice day."

"You too," the woman said weakly.

They managed to keep it together until they got into the car where as soon as they looked at one another, they burst into gales of laughter. "My mother would never believe I bought two-hundred and fifty dollars' worth of condoms."

"Did you see her face?" William held his stomach. "She was white as a sheet by the end of the transaction."

"So, you're not embarrassed anymore?"

Her beautiful smile made him warm all over. "No. I've been a private person most of my life. I think putting that out there was a shock, but once I saw her reaction and the twinkle in your eyes, I forgot all about the embarrassment."

"Good." Lizzy waggled her eyebrows. "Now, let's go home. We have some condoms to test out."

Chapter 19

When Lizzy walked into the clinic first thing on Monday morning, Chelsea grinned a mile wide. "Morning, Lizzy."

Lizzy lifted her giant travel mug. "Good morning." And what wasn't good about it? She'd woken up in William's arms. He'd even made her coffee and prepped it in her cup before she left that morning. On top of the fabulous sex, he made a terrific house husband.

She shoved open the swinging door to the back, stowed her keys in the usual drawer, and logged into the computer system as Chase strode into the room. "Morning," she said with a smile.

"You're downright chipper this morning."

"It's a lovely day."

He laughed and rolled his eyes. "It's Monday. You may love your job, but you still roll in here with a frown and a grunt most of the time. You forget that I know you're in a good mood for an entirely different reason, which I don't want to think about if I can help it."

Mary strode right in as usual. "You'd better be ready for Momma," she said, stowing her purse in its usual cabinet. "She's on a rampage this morning. Mrs. Schertz has been telling everyone that you purchased over two-hundred dollars in condoms from the drug store yesterday morning—"

Chase spit coffee across the exam table. "What?" His wide eyes turned to Lizzy. "No way."

"Yes, well, Momma is swearing up and down that Mrs. Schertz is a filthy liar and has a vendetta against the family after the entire KY incident. Daddy says it's a load of B.S., but Momma's like a dog with a bone. She's not letting it go."

"Two-hundred dollars?" Chase's voice was higher than she'd ever heard it.

Lizzy leaned against the counter. "Two-hundred and fifty-five if you round up. Did you miss Deputy Collins at Bear Creek yesterday?"

"After we ran into you and William, Ana and I ordered and took our coffees home. We didn't want to crowd you since you seemed to want to be alone, so no, we must've missed him."

After she told Mary and Chase about the run-in with Collins, she proceeded to explain her idea and what happened at the drug store. "I'd planned on paying since it was my plan, but William insisted. You should've seen Mrs. Schertz's face. I thought she would pass out right then and there."

"Oh, my God," said Chase through his laughter. "You're horrible. The only problem is Momma thinks it's a lie, and you know she's going to be furious when she realizes you did this to get Collins to back off."

"I don't know." Mary wagged her finger in front of her. "Momma's always been keen on Collins because she has favorites and has always assumed Lizzy couldn't do any better. When she discovers Lizzy is actually dating William Darcy, *the* William Darcy who bought the Saddler place, she's going to be insufferable. Think about it. First Jane marries Charlie, then she's going to start saying Lizzy's as good as married to William. With two wealthy men either married to or dating her two eldest, I don't think she'll be upset over Lizzy alienating Collins for long. I'm willing to bet a lot of money she'll start pushing me toward him." Mary shuddered. "I have other plans. I don't want Collins. He's the type to want his woman barefoot, knocked-up, and in the kitchen cooking his latest hunting kill. No way." Mary was vegan. That was definitely her idea of hell on Earth.

A moment later, Chelsea poked her head into the back. "Lizzy, Mr. Dodge is in your exam room with Fluffy."

"We'll talk more about it during surgery. I don't want to leave Fluffy waiting." When Lizzy entered her exam room, she stepped up to the table and started petting the long-haired feline. "Good morning, Mr. Dodge." She set down the file Chelsea had handed her on her way in and put the cat on the scale. "I can't believe it's already been a year since Fluffy had his last shots."

"Hasn't seemed that long, has it?" As soon as she recorded the weight, the old man smiled and scratched under the cat's chin while Lizzy stroked down his back. She was just about to turn him around to examine his eyes, teeth, and gums when a loud shriek pierced the silence.

"Where is she? Where is that ungrateful daughter of mine!"

Lizzy straightened, and her eyes bulged. "Where's Fluffy's carrier?" Mr. Dodge rushed to put the bag on the table while Lizzy lifted the cat into it and helped him zip it closed. They needed to get the cat in before her mother entered and scared the poor creature half to death. The last thing Lizzy wanted was to chase a terrified cat through the clinic. They'd just managed to get the zipper most of the way around when the door burst open and her mother stood in the open doorway.

"There you are! I cannot believe you," she said, her face red. "I was convinced Mrs. Schertz was lying. Why would my daughter need two-hundred and fifty dollars in condoms?"

"Mom—"

"But she has security camera footage with the receipt right there, superimposed over the video! What in blazes were you thinking?"

"Mom! Go in the back. Now!" Lizzy turned to Mr. Dodge. "I'm very sorry, sir. If you give me one moment, we'll continue."

"Elizabeth Bennet!"

Lizzy pointed toward the treatment room. "If you keep this up, I'll call Dad and you can deal with him. This is my job, and you're disrupting it. If you want to speak to me, you can wait until I'm done with this patient and have a free moment. The longer you argue, the more time this will take and the less likely I can fit you in."

Her mother gasped. "You wouldn't."

Lizzy clenched her hand upon the exam table to try to stop herself from shaking so hard. Her knuckles were white with the exertion. "Oh, but I would."

With a huff, her mother slammed through the hall door to the treatment room, and Chelsea appeared in the exam room door a moment later to close it.

"Again, I'm very sorry, Mr. Dodge. Let's get Fluffy back out, and I'll finish."

"Are you sure you don't want to talk to your mother?" The little old man peered over at the door then back to her.

"Not on your life. Unfortunately, I played a bit of a prank on Saturday. I thought my mother would pass it off as a lie, but I hadn't counted on there being video footage."

Mr. Dodge chuckled while he lifted the cat out of the carrier. "You really bought two-hundred and fifty dollars in condoms?"

With a grin, Lizzy started the examination. "I sure did, and in every color and texture they had. You should've seen Mrs. Schertz's face when we were done. She was as white as a sheet."

The man chuckled. "Reminds me of a joke your father would've played back in the day. He was always up to those kinds of tricks, and I bet that ole biddy Schertz was salivatin' to tell that story. I wish I could've been there." Mr. Dodge had always had a good sense of humor. What a relief that hadn't changed. "Problem is your momma's still ticked off about that KY fiasco a few years ago."

"Yeah, I know." Why was she not surprised he knew about that? The cat's temperature was normal, so she turned around to the fridge and pulled out the vaccinations. "For now, let's get Fluffy taken care of. Do you have any questions or concerns about him today?"

"Nah, he's a good boy. He likes to eat, but who doesn't?"

As soon as she was done with the shots, she helped Mr. Dodge get the cat back in his bag and carried him up to the front. "I'm sorry again for my mother."

He waved her off. "I enjoy some excitement here and there. Don't you worry about it. Besides, now that I know it was a prank, I have the inside scoop when my wife brings home the story. Since the doctor told me to cut back on my drinking, she won't buy beer, but I may just get a sixer out of this one."

Lizzy laughed and set the carrier on the floor next to Mr. Dodge's feet. "If she doesn't, let me know, and I'll bring you the six-pack of your choice. Just do me a favor and don't spread it far and wide that it's a prank. Don't want to ruin it, you know." She patted him on the shoulder. "Thanks for being understanding. I'll see you and Fluffy next year." With a wave, she backed two steps then turned. Her mother was going to get it. No matter what that woman thought, she had no right to barge into the office and demand answers when Lizzy was with a client.

She almost slammed open the swinging door as she returned to the treatment room. As she approached her mother, she put her hands on her hips. "Just what do you think you're doing?"

"I beg your pardon? I'm *your* mother. You can't talk to me that way."

"I can when you come into my place of business and start screaming. What if Mr. Dodge's cat had gotten scared and escaped? We were lucky to get him into the carrier bag before you burst into the room. Not to mention that Mrs. Schertz's gossip is not usually broadcasted through the clinic. What if I'd gone screeching into the salon, disrupting you while you were working?"

Her mother huffed. "Lizzy, I haven't cut hair in three years."

"That's not the point!" She gritted her teeth while Chase stood off to one side with his lips pressed tightly together. "What would Daddy have done if you'd barged in on him working and done that?"

"You bought two-hundred and fifty dollars in condoms with that Darcy man! What did you expect me to do?"

"Blow it off! If you wouldn't keep telling Deputy Collins that he has a chance with me, I wouldn't have been forced to do it in the first place."

Her mother's eyes bulged, and she pressed her hands against the exam table, leaning forward. "Are you kidding me? He's the best you can expect, and you insist on screwing it up. That William Darcy certainly won't look at you twice."

"And why's that, Momma?"

Chase shot Lizzy a warning gaze and shook his head, but she was shaking again. Besides, why shouldn't she know what her mother found so objectionable about her?

"Because you're as stubborn as an ox, just like your daddy, and you can't be bothered to make yourself attractive for a man. All you do is rat around this clinic and the stable. You don't wear make-up and you don't usually wear dresses. Collins is the only man who has ever been interested."

Chase's eyes squeezed closed. "Momma, no."

Lizzy pressed her palms to the exam table and leaned so she was face to face with her mother. "I'm stubborn? Maybe you should take a long look at yourself. You're always making sure Daddy has to do exactly what you want him to, and nothing can sway you from your beliefs—no matter how massively wrong you are—and you refuse to listen, which is part of why you cling to these ridiculous assumptions of yours.

"No, for the most part, I don't wear make-up. I put on a little mascara every morning, but I've never felt the need to cake a bunch of animal tested products on my face to be attractive, and cruelty-free is more money than I want to spend to wear on a daily basis.

Then there's the fact that you have a problem with me being a vet—"

"I do not!"

"You do. You praise Chase to the skies for it and you never minded Daddy doing it, but when it comes to me, no man will want me because I'm always here or at the stable. Jane is talented for the way she can train a horse and the perfect little wife, Chase is so smart and handsome, but what am I? I'm the daughter who wears gowns to the fundraisers more than once, refuses to wear make-up, and who no man will ever want besides the misogynist and patronizing William Collins. Well, Momma, I'll have you know that I *can* do better.

"I don't want to be a housewife with two point five kids and a mini-van in the driveway. There's nothing wrong with it, but it's not what I want. I love my job, and thankfully, William doesn't mind. He admires me for it. The entire thing in Schertz's was a knee-jerk reaction on my part due to running into Collins that morning at Bear Creek. He was his usual holier-than-though self, calling me Elizabeth to punctuate whatever point he wanted to make or maybe he was doing that for William's benefit since he saw us holding hands. I wouldn't put it past him to try to piss all over what he thinks is his territory, and I'd—"

"Lizzy, darlin', that's enough."

She straightened with a jolt, noticing her father standing with Chase to one side. "Fortunately, the waiting room was clear when I came in, but I'm going to take your mother home since this is not an appropriate place for this discussion." He put up a hand, palm facing her. "Before you say anything, I know this was your mother's doing. She had no right to come in here and attack you while you were with a patient." Momma gasped, and he stepped up to her and stood almost nose to nose with her. "In fact, she had no right whatsoever to scold or question you about purchasing condoms or whatever else you wanted to buy. Condoms aren't illegal last I checked, Gracie, and frankly, I'm glad she had the good sense to ignore that buffoon Collins. He takes too much pleasure in the pain his dog inflicts on those he chases down. I've told you to leave her alone and to stop encouraging Collins, but you've never listened. This morning, I told you after your sister called with that gossip from Mrs. Schertz to leave it and our daughter alone. You know darned well you shouldn't have come here." He pointed to the swinging door. "Now, let's go. Maybe if you call Lizzy once she's calmed down and apologize, she'll bring her young man to dinner on Sunday."

Momma puffed up her chest and whipped her arm away before her father could touch her. With a haughty stride, she slammed open the door and strode through.

"I'll see you this evening when you stop by the barn. Okay?"

She gave a nod and crossed her arms over her chest, fighting back the burn of her eyes. Why did she always cry after a huge argument?

"Are they gone?" Mary poked her head around the corner with a small dog in her arms.

"They're gone." Chase pulled Lizzy into a big hug. "I can't believe she decided to confront Mrs. Schertz. Shouldn't she be thrilled you're practicing safe sex?"

Lizzy covered her nose when she snorted then drew back. "Well, if anyone needs condoms, I have a lifetime supply. Don't hesitate to ask. I promise I won't ask why you need them either."

Mary set the dog down on the table while she laughed. "You should put some in Momma's stocking for Christmas. If you give them to me, I'll even do it."

"Could you imagine her face if we put a pack of flavored or glow in the dark in there?" Chase bit his bottom lip and lifted his eyebrows.

Laughing, Lizzy shook her head. "I have both. Which ones do you want?" She wiped her eyes. "Sorry, I lost my temper with her here. I hadn't planned on doing more than trying to make her go home."

"I don't blame you," said Chase. "Momma's always made little digs at you, and you've let them go for so long, you had to blow up some time."

Mary paused from clipping the dog's nails. "If only she would learn from it."

Unfortunately, Mary had a point, but Lizzy couldn't dwell on it. She needed to get back to work.

Chapter 20

William turned off the car and looked at Lizzy. She'd been quiet since they started getting dressed this morning, and the silence unnerved him. No, he wasn't particularly anticipating Sunday dinner with the Bennets, but her lack of enthusiasm was making his trepidation worse.

After all, the situation on Monday had been a shit show. He hadn't just been angry when Lizzy came home with the story of Mrs. Bennet's visit to the clinic, every muscle in his body had clenched and bristled at the woman's gall and ignorance. Thankfully, the client whose cat she'd been treating had a sense of humor and laughed the intrusion off, but that still didn't excuse the woman's idiotic notions and behavior. Why couldn't the woman recognize how amazing her daughter was?

"Why don't we go home and I'll cook? We don't have to do this today."

She sighed. "I know, but Daddy wants Momma to see how wrong she's always been." She turned her head, leaning it back against the head rest a slight curve to her lips. "You won't ditch me when she starts fawning over you, will you?"

"God, no! Don't even say that. She won't really fawn over me, will she?" God, he hated when people treated him that way.

"I was kidding about the ditching."

He shook his head. "Not a joke, in my opinion."

"As for the fawning, it's possible. I don't know how she's going to behave." She blew out a noisy exhale. "Let's get this over with." When she reached for the door handle, he stopped her.

"Don't be in such a hurry." He jumped out of the car and rushed around to open her door as he had that morning at Bear

Creek. "If your mother's watching, let her know that I'm serious and willing to treat you the way you deserve to be treated."

Her arms wrapped around him, and he held her close, kissing the crown of her head before letting her go and taking her hand. "Is that a gagging sound?"

"That's probably Lydia. Everything is a joke or annoying to her. There's no in between, and since we told her we didn't want her back at the clinic, she's been pretty irritated with us."

He glanced up to a cracked window on the second floor, which slammed shut, making Lizzy startle. As soon as Lizzy tugged him into the foyer, the scent of rose potpourri nearly suffocated him and made his eyes sting. Did people still use that stuff? Even when it was all the rage, no one kept so much it was as though you shoved your face into a gigantic bowl of dried rose blossoms. He rubbed his nose while he glanced around at the hot pink walls, glossy black trim, and black and white striped floor runner. "Um, is the entire house decorated this way?" he whispered near Lizzy's ear.

She covered her mouth, stifling a laugh. "I did tell you, if you remember—or maybe warn is a better word."

"There you are." Mr. Bennet was walking down the stairs with a medium-sized black and tan mixed breed dog hot on his heels. "I hope you'll forgive my wife's decorating choices, Mr. Darcy. If you're not blind by the end of dinner, we can escape to my study to give your eyes a break."

"I look forward to it, sir, but please, call me William." He held out his hand and shook Mr. Bennet's. "Thank you for inviting us." The dog, Lucy if he remembered correctly, trotted up to Lizzy with her tail wagging.

Mr. Bennet chuckled while Lizzy cooed and petted the friendly canine. "I know you'd much rather spend the day anywhere but here, especially after Monday, but I appreciate you coming anyway. Mary said she would be here, and Katy should be down soon. She's working on something. I'm not sure what it is. She's being secretive. And Lydia's in her room smoking." He wagged a finger at Lizzy. "She thinks I don't know because she opens a window, but I can still smell that crap a mile away." The last was said in a gruff voice while he waved them to follow.

When they entered the kitchen, William swallowed and stared. Were the cabinets sponge painted red? Every window had tiered ruffled curtains, the towels had ruffles, and to top it all off, Mrs. Bennet's apron had a huge ruffle and lace trim.

"Look who made it," said Mr. Bennet. "Don't you have something to say to them both?"

Mrs. Bennet turned and glanced at her husband as she wrung her hands in the apron. "Lizzy, I'm sorry for making a scene at the clinic. I shouldn't have gone there to confront you."

Mr. Bennet cleared his throat.

"Whether you buy condoms or not is none of my business. You've also mentioned before that you weren't interested in William Collins. I should've listened."

While her mother spoke, Lizzy's eyebrows rose on her forehead and her jaw dropped little by little. Lizzy swallowed at the end of the speech. "Thank you, Momma. I accept your apology, but if you mean what you say, you'll prove it by the way you behave in the future."

"I understand." This was unexpected. From what Lizzy had said, her mother never apologized.

"Shoot! I saved the document on the computer as soon as I heard the voices in the foyer. Did I miss the fireworks already?" His gaze jerked to the girl who had just entered. She held out her hand to William. "I'm Katy."

"William."

She opened the fridge and started ratting around inside. "I called Chase, but he and a girl named Ana are going to a matinee at the movies. They were leaving when I called."

"Chase has a date?" Mrs. Bennet whirled back around from the stove at the mention of Ana. Obviously, Chase had played it close to the belt, keeping most of the Bennets in the dark about him and Ana. "Well that won't do. He needs to bring this girl to dinner." She started wiping her hands on her apron as she walked toward a phone on the counter.

"You will do no such thing, Mrs. Bennet," said Mr. Bennet.

"And why not? We should get to meet who he's dating."

Her husband pinched the bridge of his nose. "Because our children are grown and have a right to their own private lives, and you need to learn to stop sticking your nose in the business of others." Mr. Bennet dipped his chin. "I believe Ana is your sister, isn't she, William?"

"She is." Mrs. Bennet perked up and watched him with wide eyes.

Mr. Bennet nodded in an off-hand manner. "I met her at Jane's a week or so ago. She's a sweet girl but seems a bit shy."

"Yes, she can be very shy." William was thankful for Mr. Bennet. His little sister would be nervous enough about meeting everyone, but with the already existing elephant in the room, her stomach would be in knots.

Mrs. Bennet huffed. "Well, I'll just call him later then. He can bring her next weekend."

"He can bring her when he's ready, Gracie. Don't push the boy. This is the first girl I've heard of him dating in some time. You don't want to run her off, do you?"

The woman huffed and turned back to the stove. "I hope you like brisket, Mr. Darcy. I've also got potatoes and salad to go with it. If you'd prefer I have ribeyes in the refrigerator. Mr. Bennet can grill you one instead."

"Brisket sounds wonderful, Mrs. Bennet."

"What's Mary eating?" asked Katy.

"Oh, I went by that health food store on the edge of town and bought one of those vegan meat things she likes. It's in the oven." Mrs. Bennet spun back around and waved a spatula in the air. "Why is everyone just standing there? Make yourself at home. Grab whatever you want to drink from the fridge. We've got iced tea, sodas, and beer. Help yourself. We don't stand on ceremony here." She wielded that spatula toward him. "If you can't find something, send Katy out for whatever you want."

Katy frowned. "Why me? I don't want to go out."

Her mother rolled her eyes and turned back to the stove. Once they sat down at the table, the food was excellent, but by the end of the meal, every muscle in his back was twisted into knots. Elizabeth kept one hand on his thigh, squeezing when her mother's comments or questions became too much: when was he moving back to the Saddler place? Why would he want to live in her old house when his house was so much larger? She couldn't imagine how Lizzy snagged such a handsome and rich man. The tacky questions and comments went on and on.

Meanwhile, Mr. Bennet had spent the entire meal watching his plate, seeming to tune out his wife's constant dinner conversation. Mary had a running commentary on what was said, though not verbal, but with the constant changing of her facial expressions and the rolling of her eyes. Katy ate and asked to be excused in record time, returning upstairs to work on whatever she'd left earlier while Lydia egged her mother on with her own comments. Had that been her toes grazing his ankle under the hem of his jeans?

As soon as Mrs. Bennet paused to draw breath, William stood. "Let me help you with the plates, Mrs. Bennet." He took his and Lizzy's dishes and rushed into the kitchen. Break! Dear Lord in Heaven, he needed a break! As soon as the table was cleared, Mr. Bennet waved for him and Lizzy to follow.

"You did well navigating a meal in this house," said Mr. Bennet when the door was closed behind them. "When I met Gracie, she wasn't a gossip but sweet and a kind of witty girl. Sometime after she started cutting hair, she started coming home with every rumor and story about the people in town. It wasn't so bad at first, but as the children grew up and needed her less, it became worse. For what it's worth, your rebuke Monday did have an impact but don't expect her to transform overnight. Thirty or so years of behavior won't be changed in the drop of a hat."

"I suppose that's something. It's still amazing to me that she had such a fit about it. I thought she'd blow the gossip off. She hasn't spoken to Mrs. Schertz in a couple of years."

While they sat on the sofa, Mr. Bennet laughed, sitting in a leather chair near the unlit fireplace. "I would've thought that too. Two-hundred and fifty-five dollars in condoms seems like an enormous exaggeration. She could've chuckled and gone on about her business and no one would've thought anything about it. The only benefit I see is that by your mother's confirmation, Collins may be more apt to take it as truth and move on." William wasn't going to hold his breath!

William glanced around at the floor to ceiling built-in bookshelves, lined with everything from veterinary textbooks to poetry and literature. The dark tones and dark-stained wood made for a stark contrast to the rest of the house, but at least, it didn't make him want to stab his eyes out.

"When I stopped by and apologized to Mr. Schertz for the scene your mother caused in his drug store, he apologized to me for his wife spreading the gossip. Apparently, he'd told her it was probably a practical joke of some kind, especially since you seemed to buy all of the novelty type of condoms, but she refused to listen. He and I had a good chuckle over the whole thing. He did tell me that he's going to hire a cashier, and his wife will be in the back with the accounting from now on. Goodness knows he can afford an extra hand in the front, and he won't have to worry about his wife's gossip anymore."

"That's probably for the best," said Lizzy.

"You're very quiet, William."

His gaze shifted to Mr. Bennet. "Sorry, I was looking at the room. This is nice."

The older man smiled with one eyebrow lifted, similar to Lizzy's. "I'm sure it's much better on the eyes after Mrs. Bennet's decorating. I was thankful Lizzy wanted the house up by the stable so I didn't have to redecorate that monstrosity before I put it on the market—even if I had to help her with it anyway. Lizzy took before and after photos. You should ask to see them sometime." He glanced at their joined hands. "So, when we installed Lizzy's security system, we chatted about horses. Today, I'd like to learn about you. Charlie mentioned you were his roommate during law school at Harvard, but where are you from?"

"I'm from Maine, a small town along the coast called Pemberley."

Mr. Bennet's head hitched back a bit. "I went to Maine once when I was a young man. The coastline is gorgeous. What made you want to move to Texas of all places?"

William did his best not to wince. That was a loaded question!

Chapter 21

Lizzy took a deep breath and shook her head. She'd dealt with a few hundred abscesses, but why was this one making her queasy? After a hard swallow, she lifted the scalpel, then rested it back on the table again.

"Are you alright?" Mary watched her as if she had a third eye.

"Yeah, I'm fine. Why?"

"Because you're an interesting shade of green, and I don't want to be puked on."

Lizzy lifted the scalpel one more time. She was going to do it. She would! The incision would go right down the middle just as she was taught. As the blade drew closer, she took a breath. She could do this! Right before the blade nicked the skin, she dropped it and ran for the bathroom, barely making it inside before she lost her breakfast into the porcelain bowl.

"Lizzy?" Chase knocked on the door.

Crap! "Yes," she managed between heaves.

"Let me in. I think we need to talk."

She wiped her chin with a piece of toilet paper and leaned back enough to turn the knob. "I think I have some sort of bug. I'll be fine. I promise."

Chase rolled in a stool from the hall. "I could be wrong." He made a point to close the door and lock it. "But this bug has lasted a week or so now and seems to be getting worse."

"Has it been a whole week?" She laughed, but the attempt was a miserable failure. She sagged back against the tiled wall behind her. "Have I been that obvious?"

"Well, let's see. You aren't drinking coffee." He dipped his chin and lifted his eyebrows. "You ran out of an appointment last

Tuesday 'because you really had to pee,' I think I actually smelled ginger in your usual coffee mug two days ago, and when Mary took out her barbecued jackfruit yesterday, I thought you'd vomit right there in front of her. You should've seen your expression."

She groaned and covered her face for a moment, but had to lunge back to the toilet. The water ran while she gagged and a cold paper towel hit the back of her neck. "Have you told William?"

"No," she said, taking a fresh paper towel from Chase to wipe her mouth. She couldn't tell William anything when she'd been too chicken to take a home pregnancy test. "We've only been together a month, and we used protection every time. I kept hoping the nausea would pass."

"And you were just late?" Chase snickered. "I doubt this is a bug—at least not the type you were hoping for."

She dropped her head back against the wall. "I've spent the last two weeks in denial, hoping my period would come. Everyone in this town knows we had plenty of condoms. We did use them. They weren't completely for show." There would be no way to count the number of jokes made at her expense.

Chase narrowed his eyes. "But you bought those on Saturday, the morning we saw you and William at Bear Creek. What had you used before?"

"Um, the one William had in his wallet, and the 'just in case' box I kept in the bedside table."

Her brother covered his eyes for a moment then let the hand slide down his face. "First off, you're not supposed to keep a condom in a wallet. I don't know when that became a thing, but the temperature and friction are bad for the latex."

Her eyes bugged. "What? Since when?"

He shrugged. "I don't know. I remember reading an article about it."

"And you never mentioned it to me?" She didn't read articles on condoms!

"I didn't know I was supposed to. It's not as though you were having so much sex that I thought I needed to warn you," he said, laughing. "Do you know how old the condoms in your bedside table were? You do know they expire?"

She groaned and rested her head against her knees. "I don't know. Things were kind of hot and heavy. I didn't think about whether the condoms had expired or not."

Chase grinned so she levelled the fiercest glare she could at him. This was not funny! "Sorry, but Ana and I bet on how long it would take the two of you to hook up after he moved into the house. I don't care if Dad brought a bedroom set over so William could have a room of his own. The two of you were a ticking time bomb primed to go off. I can't believe he thought the guy would actually use the spare room. The two of you giving in was a matter of time."

"For the record, he slept on top of the covers the first night and used the bedroom set Daddy brought for the rest of the first week." While she'd lost a significant amount of sleep from him just being in the house.

"And I bet he hasn't so much as touched a butt cheek to that mattress since, has he?"

Lizzy's cheeks burned, and Chase laughed even harder. "That's okay. You've been happy, and he smiles more. I think the two of you are good for each other—not that I thought you'd make me an uncle so soon."

"Don't tell anyone yet," she said in a rush. "I haven't taken a home pregnancy test, and even when I do, Daddy can't find out. I'm not ready to deal with that yet. What if he breaks out the shotgun?"

"I don't blame you." Chase leaned forward and rested his elbows on his knees. "Let's get through today first. I'll take care of the Miller cat, we can send Mary out for a home pregnancy test, and we'll make you some of that disgusting ginger tea you seem to enjoy these days. Although how you can drink hot tea in August is beyond me."

"What are we going to tell Mary?"

"Does it matter? She knows about condom-gate. Do you think she'll be surprised? Besides, you know she won't say a word to anyone, and unlike the rest of this family, she respects privacy, so she won't ask the result." He had a point.

"Now." He held his hand out to help her up. "Let's get out of the bathroom. Your stomach seems to have settled a little, and if you don't feel any better, you'll let me know. I can cover for you. We don't have a lot of surgeries, and I can manage with Mary's help for the rest of the day. That girl should go to vet school already. I bet if we knocked out the animal, she could spay or neuter it for us."

"I know what you mean. That day you called in a few weeks ago, she and I tag-teamed. She would go in and get weights, take temperatures, prep shots, and I would come in and finish while she started the next. We were busy, but it wasn't unbearable."

As soon as they entered the treatment room, Chase grabbed a pair of gloves. "Mary, would you mind running to the store for us?"

"Of course, not. What am I picking up?" She bent over and pulled her purse out of the cabinet.

"A home pregnancy test," said Lizzy in a hushed voice. Why? Chase and Mary were the only ones back here.

Mary didn't even flinch. "Got it. Do you want me to run to Fredericksburg to pick that up? I think you'd want me to avoid Schertz's, and I'm bound to run into someone we know at Walmart."

Lizzy grabbed her phone and pulled a twenty-dollar bill from the case pocket. "Yes, go to Fredericksburg and let me know if this isn't enough. Keep some for gas too."

After Mary left, Lizzy took one look at what Chase was doing and ran straight back to the bathroom.

She'd spent a good deal of time in there after Mary returned too. That know-it-all little plus sign on the pregnancy test had triggered another wave of nausea until Mary shoved a pack of saltines and a ginger ale into her hands. How had Mary known what would help? Never mind! It worked and that was what mattered.

When she reached the door of her house, it was locked, so she pulled out her keys and let herself inside. She turned off the alarm and armed it for stay, took a shower, and crawled into bed. She fell asleep in seconds.

"Lizzy?"

She blinked and put her hand on her forehead. "What time is it?" Her eyelids were heavy, as though she'd been sleeping for days.

"It's five o'clock, honey. I got home an hour ago, but I let you sleep. You're never here at that time, so I knew you had some reason for leaving work early and going straight to bed."

"I couldn't hold anything down. The Miller's cat came in with an abscess, but I couldn't drain it. Just the thought of the smell made my stomach turn." The procedure wasn't difficult, but that darned nausea made it impossible.

He sighed and laid down next to her. "I haven't said anything since I didn't know when your period was due, but are you?"

"Yes, Mary went to Fredericksburg for the test while Chase took care of the cat for me." Her eyes blurred and burned with tears. "I'm sorry. I didn't plan this."

"Hey," he said, cradling her cheek. "I was there too. I'm sure we both would've preferred to wait until we were more settled as a couple, but I do want children—you know, before my knees are so eaten up with arthritis that I can't play soccer or football with them."

"I'm a few years away from being considered a 'geriatric' pregnancy. Even then, I won't be ready for someone to use that word for me yet." She did her best to smile but quickly rolled over to grab the saltines. After she shoved one in her mouth, she sat up to chew and swallow. Evie sat near her knees. "I wonder when she cuddled up to me."

"She was there when I came home." He picked up the bottle of ginger ale and handed it to her. "Do you think you'll feel well enough to eat dinner? Ana and Chase are coming over. They're bringing pizza." He chuckled and shook his head. "You know, I should've known something was up. While Ana and I were out at the stable, Ana received a phone call from Chase and squealed."

"I'm not surprised Chase would tell her. He promised not to say a word to my parents yet. I'm not ready to deal with that shitstorm." Could they wait until they had no other choice? Maybe after the baby was born?

"It wouldn't be fair to ask him to keep it secret from Ana anyway."

"True," she said with a sigh. "Why was Ana at the stable with you?"

"I had an appointment with a man from the Austin area, and she wanted to be there. He wanted samples from Bram and Eddie."

"You didn't mention you needed me for that."

"Because I didn't. He brought his own vet down with him. They collected the samples and left."

She rested her head on his shoulder. "Oh, well, that's okay then. I have to admit that while I can collect semen samples, I'd rather not."

"Kind of like anything that involves a long glove."

She laughed. "Exactly."

His phone beeped, and he checked at the screen. "It's Ana. They're turning onto the stable road."

"Do you think I need to put on something besides pajamas?" she asked while he took her hand and helped her stand. She didn't want to change. What she was wearing was nice and comfy.

"No, I don't think so. I doubt either of them would expect it when you haven't felt well."

She pulled the front of her hair back into a clip, grabbed her saltines and ginger ale, then let William lead her down the stairs with Evie hot on their heels. As soon as he let Ana into the house, she squealed and ran over to Lizzy, making Evie flee right back to the master bedroom. "I'm so excited!" She threw her arms around Lizzy's neck and squeezed. God, she loved this girl. She was this bundle of energy once she was comfortable with you. One day, Ana would be as close to her as Jane or Chase. She was sure of it.

"We're not telling anyone yet, Ana," said William.

Chase held up three large boxes from Antonio's. "Pizza sound okay? We got three cheese with spinach and pesto, prosciutto and artichokes, and steak and Portobello mushrooms."

Ana pulled a shopping bag off her shoulder. "We also found ginger beer at the store. When I traveled to England, I ate something once that didn't sit well, and it was great for nausea. Saved my trip actually. Oh, and we also got cupcakes from that bakery on the corner of Main and Rosewood."

Lizzy's stomach growled. "It sounds incredible."

After Chase set the pizzas on the table, William handed everyone a plate, and they each took pieces and sat down. Lizzy selected one of each, then stacked two of the pieces and took a bite, moaning when the rich cheese melted on her tongue. So good!

"Lizzy, you know that's artichoke," said Chase with a slice paused mid-air.

"It's amazing."

Chase's grin was huge. "You hate artichokes. I got that one for Ana."

"Oh, I'm sorry," said Lizzy. "I won't take another slice."

Ana giggled and shook her head. "No, if you and the baby are craving my artichoke pizza, then go for it."

"Next time we can get you a pizza with everything if you want." Chase opened a Guinness and set it in front of William. "Since you're eating artichokes, I'm curious to see if you'll eat anchovies."

Her stomach clenched, and she put up a hand. "Please, don't even mention those."

Chase grinned. "Don't worry. I'll stop. I've seen enough of what happens when the hormones turn your stomach. By the way, we're going tubing on the Guadalupe next weekend. Do y'all want to go?"

"What do you think?" William looked at her and smiled. "Could be fun. I've never been tubing before." What? How?

"Ana said she hadn't either," said Chase. "That's why we're going. I also invited Mary and Katy. Lydia whined and threw a tantrum. She finally found a job, but she has to work weekends, which she hates."

Lizzy jerked back from her pizza before she could take another bite. "Well, she can't return to the clinic. She can whine and beg all she wants. It's so much nicer not having to listen to the complaints about her attitude and thumbing through her social media accounts instead of helping clients."

"Don't worry. I already said the same thing when Momma insisted we take her back. She believes we're unfair not to consider it, but you know how our mother is: something else will catch her attention in the next few days, and she'll be ranting and raving about that."

"Your father seemed to do okay with her when we went over there for Sunday dinner."

"That was for one afternoon. Dad's tried to instill some responsibility in her, but over time, she wears him down in the same way she does everyone else."

William grabbed a chilled pint glass from the freezer and sat down beside her. When she glanced around the table, Chase and Ana laughed and glanced at each other in that cute way typical of new couples while they told William about what happened at the Bennets' before they picked up dinner. Lizzy smiled. She hadn't been unhappy before William, but having him and Ana added to their circle was so much better. This was perfect: good food, good company, and William. Yeah, she loved this.

Chapter 22

Lizzy relaxed back into the inner tube, her head resting on the side and her fingers trailing along the surface of the chilly water. Her vintage-looking, red and white floral bikini top may have had wider straps than others, but that knot of fabric between her breasts made him crazy. William wanted more than anything to tug one of those ends and let the sides fall open, revealing the treasures underneath. He shifted in his own tube and adjusted the legs of his swim trunks. His mind needed to stop fixating on what was under Lizzy's clothing or everyone around them would know exactly where his mind had wandered!

He had to admit that when she'd first come out of her closet in that top and the short denim cut-offs, he'd stripped her out of them before they'd departed. How could he have resisted? They'd been late meeting Chase, Ana, and the younger Bennet sisters at the tube rental shack, but boy, the sex had been worth Ana's chastising expression when they'd pulled up. Hopefully, his grin hadn't been too telling, but he wasn't going to stress over it if it was.

"What do you think?" asked Chase. He must have noticed William's current preoccupation since he was laughing. Could Chase tell he was staring at Lizzy's breasts? "We've been pretty lucky. Since school started last week, the river is pretty empty today. Some weekends are so busy, you couldn't pay me to come out. If you catch the right day and time, it's relaxing to float along with some friends."

"I've enjoyed it, though I think my sister may have an objection after that cow peed in the water."

"That was gross." One side of Ana's nose lifted.

Chase's shoulders shook. "And it was diluted to nothing within seconds. In the meantime, you squealed like a piglet."

"I did not." Ana crossed her arms over her chest and lifted her eyebrows.

He rolled his eyes and laughed. "You did, but I'll stop saying it. I don't want you to get mad at me."

Ana gave a light snort. She reached down and tugged the rope that attached the tube carrying the cooler. "Anyone want something to drink?"

"Ooh! I'll have a ginger beer," said Lizzy.

Ana's suggestion of ginger beer last week had been liquid gold. Between the saltines and the strong ginger soda, Lizzy had been worshiping the porcelain gods much less than before—at least that was what she'd told him. She'd been at work most of the time she'd had morning sickness, so William hadn't been able to keep tabs. Her stomach wasn't perfect, but she seemed to feel better.

"I'll take a beer." William pulled himself closer and took both bottles, handing Lizzy hers before he released the line attached to him. Mary and Katy both requested sodas, which Ana passed across. She handed Chase a beer and removed a small bottle of Sangria and unscrewed the top.

"How much longer are we on the river?" asked Ana as she settled back into the tube.

Chase looked ahead, leaning back to see some around the bend. "We're not far from the end, actually. I thought we'd go to El Rio when we're done. It'll be right there, and they have lots of outdoor seating."

Lizzy lifted her head. "That's a great idea. I'd love some of their carnitas tacos right now."

With a glance at her belly, he smiled. This morning, she'd complained her shorts were snug. She'd admitted it was too soon for her to be showing, but he'd had to press a big kiss near her belly button. A peace had settled inside his chest. Why was that? He'd been so resistant to starting a relationship with her. He was happier than he'd ever been in the past, which had to be a factor. With Anne, he would've panicked at her being pregnant so soon, but with Lizzy, he hadn't blinked an eye. The situation seemed right and how it should be, despite how little time they'd been a couple. The only reasonable explanation was that she was the one—she had to be the one. He still didn't want to rush things, but he wasn't going anywhere either.

With a crooked grin, she stuck out her foot and pulled herself closer until their innertubes touched. He grabbed her foot and dug his fingers into the arch, making her head drop back. "That feels amazing."

He peered over to where Chase and Ana had their floats close together while they talked. Katy and Mary had tied on to the group, giving themselves plenty of slack so the couples could have some alone time while they floated lazily down the river. It had been a perfect way to spend the day.

"Your sister Mary is very serious," he said softly.

"She has her moments." Lizzy shrugged and glanced at the girls. "She would make an excellent vet, but I'm not sure what's in her head. My father was surprised when she opted to get an associate's degree and work for the clinic as a tech, but she's a godsend. We rely on her a lot. One of our clients has a teenager interested in veterinary medicine. She'll be volunteering some around the clinic to decide if it's what she really wants to do. Mary's not going to know what to do with the help."

"Is she the only tech?"

"We have a couple of guys who work in the kennels and one other girl who comes in on a part-time basis. Those who work in the back take care of the animals who board with us and groom some. They also give medicated baths when necessary. On occasion, one will hold an animal for us or assist her, but they don't work in the treatment room often unless Mary is ill. Mary is happy staying busy, and she's so efficient, we'd rather pay her more than hire more people."

"Lizzy!" They turned to Chase, who pointed behind them. "There's the bridge."

"We need to get to the side," she said, steering herself toward the shore with her free hand.

Lizzy sighed when they pulled up to the house. "Today was fun. I can't remember the last time a group of us went out to the river. Did you like it?" Her head was turned to the side while she watched him, her eyes blinking slowly.

"I did. I also enjoyed getting to know your sisters some too."

She laughed all low and seductive, making his heart stutter. "You say that, but Katy noticed when Chase almost spilled about the baby. Now that Condom-gate has blown over, if Momma doesn't call tonight, ecstatic and praising me for my 'catch,' I'll eat my hat."

He squeezed her hand. "We'll need to tell them soon. It'd be messed up for them to find out through the rumor mill. I don't think we want to do that again." Longbourn was too much of a small town to keep anything a secret for long.

A lazy grin crossed her face. "Yeah, I'm just not looking forward to it. Momma wanted Jane to get pregnant to force Charlie to propose. She'll think I took her advice with you, and I'm worried my father will start cleaning his shotguns when I bring you to the house."

"Will he shoot me?" Why had his voice come out high-pitched? He wasn't scared of Dr. Bennet, was he?

"Dad? I doubt it. He's a big softie." Why wouldn't she meet his eye when she said that?

She unbuckled and opened the door. "I don't know about you, but I'm glad to be home." After they emptied their towels and the cooler from the back of the SUV, she took his hand and led him through the house to the patio and down the steps to the creek. She removed her denim shorts and backed into the water, lowering into the steady current then rising onto her knees.

He swallowed—hard. She'd put on a thin white button-up shirt in the car and removed her bikini top, saying it was digging into her ribs. His concentration on the road became near impossible when she dropped the top on the floorboard in front of her and groaned. Now, that thin white top was almost transparent, her rosy nipples playing peek-a-boo through the wet folds of the material. "What are you doing?"

"I thought about this a lot while we were tubing." She released one button, then in a slow movement a second. "Are you not interested?"

"Um, no, I never said that. What if someone sees us?"

She released her hair and shook it out. "The trails go in the other direction. It's pretty rare someone comes this way."

He whipped his shirt over his head. That was good enough for him! Lizzy reached for another button, and he grabbed her hand. "Don't you dare." He traced his fingers down her slick skin to her breast, tracing around the center and making the nipple pebble under the sheer cotton.

Her chest rose and fell in an increasingly faster rhythm as he slipped his hand under the fabric. "You're so gorgeous. I kept watching you drop your head back against that tube. I so wanted to nibble on that spot under your ear—the one that makes you gasp—untie that knot holding your breasts and free them."

He turned her around and suckled that place that had been calling to him since they left the house that morning. Most of her perfume had faded while they'd been in the water, but a hint of its delicate floral scent still lingered and did as much to turn him on as the whimpers coming from the back of her throat. His palm flattened against her stomach and pressed her back against him. She had to feel what she was doing to him.

She gasped when his fingers slid home, a high-pitched noise that ratcheted his need for her to unbearable heights. Her response to his touch and his kiss never disappointed. She released every inhibition, abandoning every ounce of reserve and making him even more desperate for her.

He brought her with him as he sunk to his knees, leaning her slightly forward while he bit her shoulder. She gazed back at him, her damp hair plastered in places to her cheeks and her mouth open. He'd never seen anything sexier in his life.

She was so perfect and warm. He buried his face into her shoulder while he loved her, doing whatever he could to make her come undone. There was nothing like it—nothing like being with Lizzy. The way her eyes rolled back, how her back arched to take him in as far as she could, the incoherent cries that burst from her lips—she gave him everything. He would never tire of that. Her supple curves consumed him, preoccupied him from the moment she left for work every morning until the moment she was in his arms again. Was this normal? If asked, he would say he was a man obsessed, and he would've worried if his heart hadn't been as taken by her as his mind.

"Oh, God, William. I can't."

She wasn't far along, but she'd confessed to being more sensitive since realizing she was pregnant. He couldn't complain. Every gasp and moan was like the crescendo of a symphony, and when her orgasm hit, he lost control, following her over the edge. As much as he'd tried to hold off, he just couldn't help himself. Without the condom dulling the sensation, her cries and the pulsing of her climaxing around him was too much, and he was pulled under by the wave that overtook him.

Once he returned to himself, he took her with him as he relaxed back into the water, his hand drawing lazy circles over her breasts and stomach while he caught his breath. "Feel free to share any fantasy you have. That was amazing."

An uncharacteristic giggle bubbled from her lips. "If they all turn out like today, then you don't have to worry."

"Yeah?" He couldn't help a grin from overtaking his face.

"Don't gloat," she said in a rough voice, elbowing him lightly in the ribs. "I need to take a shower. Want to conserve water and join me?"

He closed his eyes for a moment and nuzzled her hair. "Sounds good to me. After that meal, I don't think we need a big dinner. Are you craving anything special?"

"No," she said, sitting up. "I'm not hungry. El Rio always serves so much food. I'm glad we shared a plate."

"I am too. If I'd eaten that entire meal on my own, I'd be miserable."

She picked up his clothes and threw them at him with a silly grin before she retrieved her shorts and jogged ahead of him up the steps. Once they were inside, she fed Evie, then dropped their clothes into the washing machine before prancing upstairs as naked as the day she was born. He smiled as he followed her lead. Moving to Texas had been an inspired idea. He'd considered staying up north, which would've been a much easier move, but if he hadn't taken such a huge leap, he wouldn't have met Lizzy, she wouldn't be expecting his child, and he wouldn't have been this content. He opened the glass door of the shower and admired the view before joining her inside.

Lizzy peered over her shoulder. "Are you just going to stand there and watch, or are you coming in?"

He closed the door behind him and took her in his arms. What had he ever done to be this lucky?

Chapter 23

"What a day!" Lizzy let the kitchen door swing closed behind her and set her travel mug on the counter. "I swear we were up to our ears in spays and neuters. It seemed as if every spring kitten and puppy had to be fixed today. From what Chelsea told me, we have a full surgery schedule tomorrow as well."

He set down the spoon to whatever he was cooking and tucked her hair behind her ear. She loved it when he did that. "Are you hungry?"

"A little," she said, "but I need to drink some ginger beer and eat some saltines to settle my stomach. You know how it gets when I haven't eaten recently. I tried, but the pace at the clinic never slowed down enough for a real lunch. One more month and the doctor promised me it would get better. I just need to wait it out." She was so looking forward to that. After all, who loved being nauseated at the drop of a hat? Women were supposed to glow during pregnancy, and she was more than ready for that part. She'd spent enough time swallowing or heaving into a toilet, her complexion had probably maintained a green tinge since that little plus sign had changed her life a month ago.

He pressed a sweet kiss to her lips then opened the fridge, pulling out a bottle of her now favorite drink, opening it, and holding it out. "Why don't you take a shower? I'll finish dinner and have the food on the table for when you return."

"What are we having?" Lizzy had never eaten so well in her life. She could cook, but most evenings, by the time she got home from the clinic, she couldn't muster the energy to fix more than the boxes of macaroni and cheese he'd once teased her about. Hey, at least she'd made veggies to go with it.

"Honey ginger salmon with rice and broccoli."

"Oh, that sounds amazing. I'll be—" The front door sensor beeped. Lizzy frowned and glanced toward the foyer. "Are you expecting someone?"

He shook his head. "No, Ana said she and Chase were going to a movie. Your dad dropped in earlier without calling or texting, but I imagine he left for home already."

The knock on the door finally came, so Lizzy made her way through the house to the foyer and glanced through the peephole. She frowned. "It's Lamonte."

When she opened the door, the man held his worn cowboy hat in his weathered hands. "Forgive me for bothering you folks, but I think something might be wrong with Skylla."

William was at Lizzy's shoulder in seconds. "What do you mean?"

"I'd locked up the office and was heading for my truck when I saw that Wickham fella ducking out of your horse's stall. I yelled at him, but he took off before I could stop him. I don't know what he did, but I imagine he was up to no good. I called the sheriff and Doc Bennet. Doc said he'd be up as soon as he could, but I didn't want to leave it for too long—you know, just in case."

Lizzy's stomach clenched, and she shook her head. "No, you were right to get us." She grabbed the backpack she kept by the front door, while William turned off the stove and oven and joined her to follow the older man to the stable.

At first glance, nothing appeared off in Skylla's stall. She placed a hand on the gelding's shoulder. He wasn't too warm. "How are you boy? Did that nasty man think he could scare you?"

William strode immediately to the hay. "It's not moldy. The shavings are clean and dry. I don't see any broken glass or metal."

He shifted his foot back and forth, no doubt checking under the shavings in case whatever Wickham did wasn't so noticeable at a glance.

Meanwhile, Lizzy took out her stethoscope and listened to Skylla's heart and lungs. When she turned, Lamonte's eyebrows were drawn toward the center while he stared into the feed bucket. "Lizzy, you better take a look at this."

When she stepped beside him, her heart stopped at the neon green sheen on what was left of his feed. "Oh, God."

William straightened. "What is it?"

Lamonte took a quick whiff. "Smells sweet. I'd bet everything I own it's antifreeze."

William's eyes shot to her. Right before her, the color drained from his face until he was so deathly pale, she rushed forward and pressed her hands to his cheeks. He couldn't faint. She would need whatever help he could give her if Skylla was to make it. "What does that mean?"

"It's not good," she said. She didn't want to freak him out, but she refused to lie. "We're on the clock here. We need to get some activated charcoal in him and quick." Lamonte took the bucket of feed and rushed out of the stall while she leaned forward to catch William's eye. Please don't pass out! "Look at me. Are you okay? I need your help if you can manage so breathe."

"Why would he eat contaminated feed?"

"Because ethylene glycol is sweet, and he doesn't know better. The problem is we need to absorb as much of the poison as possible before it can be metabolized. If we don't act soon, he can go into kidney failure."

William's eyes widened, and he ran a hand through his hair before letting it slap against his leg. Had she been too honest?

When Lamonte returned, he had the steel bucket and everything she'd need to put a tube into Skylla's stomach. William went to his horse's side and started rubbing in long strokes down his neck while Lizzy worked, getting the tube in place and injecting the charcoal followed by some water to flush the treatment through.

She hooked up an I.V. and started a bag of fluids. "It's not enough," she said shaking her head. "We need some ethyl alcohol, and we don't have a big enough dosage for a horse, but we do have a vial of antidote at the clinic. We keep it just in case, but this isn't common in horses. Skylla's much bigger and would take a substantially higher dose than our biggest dog. I need to call Garrett over at Hillside on my way and see if they have more."

Lamonte pulled out his phone. "I'll call your father. He can stop at the liquor store on the way over."

She hurried out of the stall and toward the doors. "I'll be right back." Let's see, she needed the antidote, some diazepam in case he began behaving as if in pain, more fluids, charcoal to replace what she'd used.

"Lizzy!" When she turned, William came running up behind her. "You can't go."

"I have to go. Your horse needs the supplies."

"Not by yourself, you won't. What about Wickham? Don't you think we should wait for the sheriff? What if this was his plan?"

"I don't know," she said shrugging and letting her hands drop to her sides. "I could sit here and question every move I make all night long, but we don't have time to wait for the sheriff. What if he doesn't show up for a half-hour or more? In the meantime, your horse needs help, and I'm not willing to sacrifice him because this might be what Wickham has planned. I *have* to go to the clinic. "

"Then I'm going with you." He fell into step beside her, his hand grasping hers.

"What about Skylla?"

"Lamonte is with him. I trust him as much as I do you when it comes to my horses. I know Lamonte will do whatever he can to help him. He's proven that already, and I don't want you down there by yourself. Wickham hates me, and that's more than enough reason for him to poison Skylla since he's done something similar before. I just don't think that's all there is to it this time."

Lizzy didn't bother putting up a fight. Instead, she rushed to the house to grab her keys. As they hurried to the clinic, she pulled out her phone and pressed a number she had on speed dial. Garrett picked up after two rings. "Hello?"

"Hey, Garrett, it's Lizzy Bennet."

"You don't call me after hours very often. What's going on?"

"I've got a horse someone tried to poison with antifreeze. I've given him activated charcoal, but I was wondering if you had any antidote. I have one vial, which I doubt will be enough."

"Shit," muttered Garrett. "I ordered a bottle last week, but I haven't seen it come to the back. Let me run up to the clinic and check my office manager's desk. She references what we get in with the orders to make sure everything is correct. I'm hoping it's still sitting in her inbox. Where are you?"

"I'm at the Longbourn stable, but I can send someone out for it."

"No, don't do that. I'll text you when I know more, but if I have it, I'll drive it out."

Lizzy rubbed her forehead and blinked to keep from crying. "Thank you. You don't know how much I appreciate that."

"Don't mention it," he said. "Your father's done something similar for us on more than one occasion. I'm glad to finally be able to repay the favor. I'll text you one way or the other in the next ten minutes."

"I'll be waiting for it." She hung up right as they approached the clinic, which was dark and quiet, the only lights on inside were the usual ones behind the front desk and down the hallway.

"What did he say?"

She glanced over to William. "He has to go to the office and check. They ordered some but he's unsure if it's come in. He's going to let me know. We should have it soon, especially since he offered to drive it over himself."

William exhaled in a ragged, weary way. What was he going to do if she couldn't save his horse? Even if they did everything right, they had no way of knowing how much he ingested.

She cleared her throat and tried to shake off how on edge she was, her hand trembling as she put the key in the lock and turned it. With a deep inhale, she pushed the door open, disarmed the alarm system, and headed back to the treatment room with William right behind her.

She grabbed a crate and threw in several bags of fluids, new tubing, and I.V. catheters, followed by some syringes and vials so she could do blood work as the night progressed. They would need to keep a close eye on Skylla. Several other medications were tossed into the crate, and a box of activated charcoal was set next to it. With that on the table, she skimmed the bottles of medicine on the counter to be sure she hadn't missed anything, her hand halting at the anesthetic they used to put an animal to sleep. Her eyes burned as she picked it up and tucked it into the corner of the crate.

"What's that?"

"It's for just in case. I don't want to have to return if he's suffering."

He picked it up and shook his head. "No, we won't need that."

"William, I'm going to do all I can, but if we can't keep the chemical from getting into his bloodstream, and he's in pain, we may have to make that decision. Please understand this is something I pray I will not need. I don't want to have to use it. You know how much it hurts me when I have to put down an animal. You saw last week how hard I take it with that seventeen-year-old Corgi, but it doesn't mean I can't be practical when necessary. You have to let me plan for every contingency without challenging me, or we'll take longer than we should when time is of the essence."

He closed his eyes and winced as he returned it to the box. "I'm sorry. I should know better than to argue with you. You want him to come through as much as I do."

"He's your best friend. I get it." She pulled her key ring out of her pocket, flipped to the smallest key, and opened the cabinet with the controlled substances. She'd just pulled out the diazepam when the whoosh of the swinging door made her spin around.

Wickham stood just inside the treatment room with a gun aimed straight at her chest. He wore a smirk that made her skin crawl and bile rise into her throat. "I'd hoped you'd need something out of that cabinet, and lookie here. I was right."

Chapter 24

William's heart pounded like a jackhammer against his ribs. He'd known coming to the clinic without the sheriff was a horrible idea. He should've insisted Lizzy wait, but he hadn't wanted to argue with her—he'd also trusted her when she'd said they couldn't delay treating Skylla so he'd ignored his reservations. The problem now was how to get out of this.

Wickham was never the type to be satisfied with what he had. Of course, his supply of drugs was probably dwindling fast, and he always needed money. He couldn't stick around Longbourn after this. Breaking into the stable and stealing some medication was one thing; holding up two people at gunpoint was another entirely. "Are you stupid, Wickham? You do know we called the sheriff after you were spotted in the stable? They'll be here any minute."

The asshole turned and sneered. "I also called in a home invasion on the other side of the county." His eyes shifted. "I saw you there, Darcy, but since you don't have what I want, you can shut your fucking mouth. I also much prefer looking at Liz than your ugly face." The smirk he wore made William's stomach turn.

"What do you want?" Lizzy's voice was strong considering the weapon he pointed at her.

"You know what I want, and if you don't, you aren't as smart as I thought you were."

"Drugs."

"Very good." He laughed, then tossed a large duffle bag in Lizzy's direction. He flicked the pistol toward the cabinet. "I'll take whatever you've got, and make sure you throw some syringes in there. I ran out two days ago. I don't like using dirty needles if I can help it." He aimed the gun at William for a moment before training it back on Lizzy.

She held up a large bottle of injections. "You know these are veterinary formularies. They aren't made for humans."

He rolled his eyes with a derisive chuckle. "Oh, please. They won't kill me."

"Animals metabolize drugs differently, so there are certain drugs that could kill a human just as there are human drugs that can kill animals."

"Spare me the dramatics. I don't care," he said through his teeth. "Now quit with the science lesson and put the drugs in the bag!" Wickham resituated his stance and stood a little taller, straightening his arm as though about to shoot.

Every muscle in William's body tensed further. "Lizzy, do as he says, so he'll leave."

William, who stood off to the side, started breathing again when she turned and began stuffing bottles into the bag. While she worked, he watched Wickham. He'd lost some weight since the last time William had seen him, and he was sweating. If one looked close enough, a slight tremor was noticeable in the barrel of the gun. Was he nervous or going through withdrawals? Perhaps a bit of both?

"What are you staring at, Darcy?" He didn't remove his eyes from Lizzy as he spoke.

"Just seeing how different you are from a few years ago."

His laugh was high-pitched and manic. "I don't think I've changed that much, but I've changed more than you. I don't have to ask to know that you're still the same dickhead you were back home. How's Ana by the way? Does she miss me?"

William's hand clenched so tight his fingernails dug into his palm and his knuckles ached. He'd love to punch that smug grin from Wickham's face, but he had to hold himself back while that Glock was trained on Lizzy. He couldn't risk her getting hurt, even for revenge.

"I've missed her, your sister. She always loved me—until you convinced her otherwise."

"You're delusional," said William. "And you *will* stay away from her."

"What are you going to do?" Wickham cackled in a way that sent a chill down William's spine. He was insane. "I'm the one holding the gun. You're as helpless as your girlfriend over there." He tried not to react, but Wickham only laughed harder. "Do you think I didn't watch the two of you while I made this plan? I admit I'd hoped Liz would come by herself—I couldn't imagine you leaving that stupid horse of yours to follow a woman. I thought she and I could have a little fun after she got me my drugs and the money from the safe in the office."

"How'd you know about the safe?" asked Lizzy. She stood with her hand poised over a glass vial.

"Your precious sister, that's how. She's a real piece of work. She hates you, by the way." His grin was one William had seen before. He didn't even have to ask to know Wickham used Lydia. The asshole grinned and smacked. "Not that it mattered. I was happy to listen to her bitch all about this place and you. She was useful to me in more ways than one too. Let me tell you, she gives one hell of a blow job."

Lizzy covered her mouth with the back of her free hand and gagged, but thankfully, hadn't needed to dive for the nearby trash can. William started toward her.

Wickham's aim changed direction. "Don't move, Darcy, or I kill her. She can puke on the floor if she can't stomach my talking about her whore of a little sister." He flicked the gun's barrel toward Lizzy. "And why've you stopped? I don't have all night. Hurry!"

After she tossed the last two bottles into the bag, she held it out to Wickham. "The syringes are in those boxes on the shelves down there." She leaned and pointed under the countertop in the treatment room.

Wickham shifted back and gestured with the Glock towards the surgical room. "Get in there with her, Darcy, so I have both of you in my line of sight." William reached to grab Lizzy, to tuck her behind him. He needed her to be safe. "I never said touch her! Don't touch her. Keep more than an arms-length between you so you can't pass her anything either. Do you understand? And make sure you keep your hands where I can see them." Wickham tossed the bag onto the counter and started shoving the boxes into the duffel.

"Are you okay?" William said as softly as he could.

"I'm surprised I managed not to get sick, but I don't know how much longer I can last without having to go for the sink. I haven't eaten, and it's making things worse."

"You're doing great."

"I should've listened to you."

"You just want to save Skylla. I can't blame you for that so don't go blaming yourself." He meant it. He understood and appreciated her impatience when it came to treating his horse. Who wouldn't? He wanted Skylla healthy, but what he wanted more than anything was Lizzy and their unborn child away from Wickham and back at their house where she belonged. Their house? When had he started thinking of the Bennet homestead as his home? Would he have considered the Saddler place their home if Lizzy had moved in with him there? Something in him whispered it wouldn't be the same. He liked the ranch he'd purchased, or he would've never made an offer, but he hadn't come to feel comfortable there in the months since he'd moved in. Once he let his fears and reservations go, Lizzy's house had become his home from nearly that first night. As long as she wanted him there, he never wanted to leave.

Her hand pressed to her stomach, and she breathed deep and slow. No more than a minute passed before she lunged at the sink, the sound of her retching filling the small room.

"What the fuck is this?" Wickham moved into the doorway, his nose crinkling. "You're so nervous you puked? Your girlfriend is a coward, Darcy." William started toward Lizzy, but Wickham raised the gun at him once again. "Not one more step. She's a big girl. She can manage without your help."

She gagged a couple more times before the water turned on, and she reached for a paper towel.

"You don't have to clean up right this second," said Wickham in a hard voice. "Get your ass out to the front office." William turned to Lizzy, watching her instead of Wickham. "Why are you watching her? She's not the one with the gun, I am, so I call the shots. Move. Now!"

When they started forward, Wickham grabbed Lizzy around the waist and yanked her against him. "Not so quick. I didn't say for you to go just yet. I need to keep you close in case your boyfriend decides to try something stupid. He's not the smartest, you know."

"I beg to differ. He went to Harvard. Where'd you go?"

He scoffed and pressed the muzzle of the gun to her cheek. "Harvard is overrated. I didn't need to go to some expensive school to prove that I'm smarter." She cried out as he whipped her back around and jabbed the gun into her side.

"You better not hurt her." William tried to keep his tone as hard as he could. If he could keep the fear out of his voice, all the better. That gun was a huge problem. But how was he supposed to get it away from Wickham without putting Lizzy in further danger?

"What are you going to do? Cry?" Wickham sniffled. "Boo-hoo." He cackled and let go of Lizzy just long enough to throw the duffel bag over his shoulder, then pull her to him again. "Why are you standing there like an idiot? Get your ass through that door."

William turned and stepped through. He needed to do something, but with no weapon and no way to fight off someone with a gun, he was useless. The knock of something hitting the door, and the footsteps that followed let him know that at least Wickham was behind him with Lizzy. William walked behind the front counter and looked behind him. If only he could get Lizzy away from him.

"Into the office," said Wickham, pointing with the Glock. "Get behind the desk."

He shoved Lizzy into the corner on the opposite side of the room. "Open the cabinet and unlock the safe."

"The deposit was made on Friday," she said. "We have no more than what's necessary to make change."

"I don't care! Open the safe!" Spittle flew from his mouth, and sweat poured from his forehead. The hand holding the gun could barely hold it still. The tremors had to be withdrawals, and they seemed to be worsening.

She flinched and pulled the cabinet door, reaching in, and turning the dial. When the last number rotated to the top, she tried to turn the lever, but it wouldn't budge.

"Stop screwing around!" The weapon shook harder when he yelled, making Lizzy squeeze her eyes closed.

She clenched and released her hands. "I'm not screwing around. I'm shaking because I got sick. The gun you have pointed at me isn't helping either."

"Well, it's not going anywhere, so get over it and do what I told you."

"Take a deep breath, Lizzy. You can do it."

Wickham rolled his eyes. "Oh, aren't you two just adorable." He spoke in a heavy, mocking drawl. "Shut up! I've heard enough of your sanctimonious voice to last me a lifetime. Before I leave, I should shoot you in the mouth. That'd be one way to guarantee I never have to hear you speak again." His eyes lit when the safe door clicked, and Lizzy opened it. She withdrew a bank bag and held it out in his direction. "Aren't you accommodating." He set down his bag on the desk, then shoved the money into the side pocket with one hand and zipped it, keeping the gun trained on them during the process.

"Well, this has been loads of fun," he said as if they'd been having drinks at the local cantina. He put the bag back on his shoulder and stared at them. "Now, what do I do with the two of you? I can't have you following me."

"We have no intention of following you," said William. Anything to persuade him to go, and soon! "You have what you came for. Leave."

A faint siren pierced the silence. Please let Wickham decide he was going before the sheriff arrived! The last thing William wanted was for Lizzy to be in the middle of a standoff between Wickham and the deputies, and with the desk between them, he couldn't get to her to protect her.

Lizzy gasped when Wickham moved the gun to aim at William's chest. He opened his mouth to speak, but Wickham grinned and shifted the gun back to Lizzy. "Eeny, meeny, miney, moe." With each word, he swapped between them as the target.

When William glanced to the side, tears poured down Lizzy's cheeks. He inhaled and turned back to Wickham. "Stop this shit and leave. You have what you came for."

"You're right. I do." The gun was again pointed at William. "But since I don't want you coming after me, I need to make sure you're preoccupied with something."

"What's that supposed to mean?"

"This." Without warning, Wickham's arm glided left, and he pulled the trigger.

Chapter 25

"No!" The shot rang out, and as William lunged, everything around him moved in slow motion.

Wickham spun on his heel and tore through the door, but William didn't follow. He hurled himself forward, catching Lizzy before she hit the floor. "Lizzy!" He pulled her into his arms as a dark stain spread across the front of her navy work Polo, and he touched his hand to it. When his fingers came up stained dark red, a whoosh of air left him. "Lizzy!"

"Stop yelling." She grimaced and clutched the stomach wound. "Is he gone?"

He glanced over his shoulder. "Yes, I think so."

"Good. Lock the door. Hurry, before he comes back." Her words came out in an uneven cadence, and she breathed heavily.

William took out his phone and dialed 911. "He's more interested in getting away. He won't be back."

She rolled her eyes. "He will if he has no choice. The sirens—they're louder."

He kissed her forehead and carefully laid her down on the floor. The phone rang while he rushed to the door and turned the lock. "911. What's your emergency?"

"Yes, my name is William Darcy. My girlfriend has been shot. I need an ambulance at Longbourn Veterinary Hospital, 8215 Bennet Oaks Drive."

"Is the shooter still on the premises?"

"He's not in the building. As soon as he ran, I locked the door. He has a gun, but I don't know if he's managed to drive off. I can hear sirens." He slammed the swinging door to the treatment room open and began opening and closing cabinets until he found a stack of surgical towels. He grabbed them and rushed back out to the front while he answered a myriad of questions asked by the operator: the phone number he was calling from, whether Lizzy was awake, whether she could talk. "The stable manager up the road already called the sheriff because my horse was poisoned."

"By the shooter?"

"Yes." When he entered the office, Lizzy's eyes were fluttering. "The baby," she said softly. Her lip quivered as a tear tracked down her cheek.

After he nodded, he pressed several towels to the wound as she cried out in pain. He had to get the bleeding under control. While he used both hands to try to staunch the flow of blood, he used his shoulder and cheek to hold the phone.

"Is everything okay?" asked the operator.

"I'm applying pressure to the wound."

"That's good. I have an ambulance on the way to your location. Sir, do you know the name of the shooter?"

"Yes, Greg Wickham."

"Can you give me a physical description?"

As he rattled off Wickham's description, Lizzy's hand wrapped around his wrist. "I love you."

"No, you don't." He pressed harder. "You're not leaving me."

Her eyes fluttered. "I don't want to, but I'm so tired."

"Just stay awake, sweetheart. Please! I love you too. Please!"

"Sir, the ambulance is a couple of minutes away. I have word that the sheriff's deputies are outside the building. Can you let them inside?"

He jumped up and ran for the door, turning the lock before rushing back to Lizzy. He swapped the soaked towels for fresh ones and continued to press.

"Sir, I'm going to leave you now that you have help. May God bless you and your girlfriend."

"Thank you." As soon as her end of the line clicked, he let the phone drop to the hard, ceramic floor. At this point, he didn't care if it broke. He'd buy another. The only thing that mattered was Lizzy. "Where's that ambulance?"

"Pulling up now, sir," said a deputy as he entered. He gave Darcy an odd glance. Did the deputy think he was the shooter? "Can you tell us what happened before the paramedics come in?"

"Greg Wickham poisoned my horse. Lizzy and I came down for medication to help him—she's a veterinarian. Wickham planned the whole thing and followed, holding us at gunpoint for drugs and the petty cash. Before he fled, he shot her to keep me from chasing him." When he looked down, her eyes were closed. He let out a sob and pressed harder. "Come on, Lizzy. Fight, damn it!"

A paramedic dropped to his knees across from William. "Sir, I need to see the wound." When had the paramedic entered? The room was now teeming with first responders and he had no idea where they all came from.

"Sir?"

William lightened his pressure on the wound, so the man could lift the cloths. "Keep putting pressing on that for me. Can you do that?"

He nodded while the man yelled some orders over his head. The paramedic checked her pulse, her blood pressure, then pried open her eyelids one at a time. As soon as he put in the I.V., he nodded to the man who had rushed in with a board. "Let's get her out of here." They moved efficiently, loading her up, then carrying her out to the ambulance while William did his best to continue the pressure.

"Lizzy?" Chase barreled up to the stretcher with Ana close behind him, her hands covering her mouth.

"Oh, God!"

Chase cradled Lizzy's cheek in his hands. "You're not going anywhere. Do you hear me?"

The paramedics lifted the stretcher. "I'm sorry, but we've got to go."

"I'll meet you at the hospital," said Chase to him. "Take care of her."

"I will." William clapped Chase on the shoulder as he climbed into the rig. No one asked if he was a relation, and at this point, he sure as hell wasn't offering the information. He would be riding with her whether it was their policy or not.

As soon as they were rolling, the paramedic moved around Lizzy with a cell phone to his ear, rattling off numbers and vitals while he continued to assess her. He reached over his shoulder and held out more toweling for William, who swapped it with what he'd been using. "Do you know if she has any allergies to medication?"

"No," he said, shaking his head. "But she's pregnant."

The man's eyes flared for a second. "How far along?"

"Nine weeks. Her OB is Dr. King." A beep came from Lizzy's pocket, and he removed one hand from the towels to pull her phone from her jeans pocket.

"I found the antidote. I'm on my way." was lit up on the screen. A part of him breathed a tiny bit easier. Dr. Bennet would have another vet to help him when the vet from Hillside arrived.

The paramedic tapped his tablet and put the phone back to his ear. What came after was a blur. William kept pressure on the wound while the EMT communicated with the hospital and kept them apprised of her vitals.

The moment they emerged from the ambulance, a nurse grabbed him by the sleeve. "This way, sir."

"Can't I just—" His eyes followed Lizzy as they whisked her down a bright white hallway.

"I understand, but you'll only be in the doctors' way. Let them do what they can to save her. Meanwhile, I need you to tell me all you can about her history, and we'll get you a pair of scrubs. The rest of your family will freak out if they see you all covered in her blood."

For the first time since the gunshot rang out, William glanced down at his own clothes. His hands were sticky and red, his favorite athletic t-shirt was smeared with blood as was his khaki shorts. She was right. Mrs. Bennet would undoubtedly be here soon, and that woman would be in hysterics if she saw him like this. "Thank you."

A million questions and one clothing change later, William sat in a chair in the surgical waiting room, his elbows propped on his knees and his hands steepled in front of him. As soon as he'd come out of the bathroom where the nurse had taken him to change clothes, she'd ushered him up the elevator and parked him in that chair. They'd taken Lizzy directly into emergency surgery, and now he waited for someone to bring him word—any word—while he prayed with every last cell of his body for her to live. What would he do without her? No! He couldn't even consider that possibility.

"There he is!"

He jumped to his feet when Ana entered, Mrs. Bennet and her younger daughters trailing behind her. "She's in surgery. That's all I know."

Mrs. Bennet nodded and sank into a nearby chair, tears running down her cheeks. He'd never seen the woman so composed. Between the gala, the two Sunday dinners they'd attended, and the one time she'd dropped by the house, she seemed to whirl in and out of a room like the Tasmanian Devil in the Bugs Bunny cartoons. He'd expected her to moan and wail instead of this terrifyingly quiet resignation. Under normal circumstances, he'd welcome her calm. Why did her sudden sedate behavior make things worse? She was so quiet it was eerie.

Ana sat beside him. "Chase wanted to come, but he stayed behind with Dr. Bennet to work on Skylla."

"Shit, Skylla! I hadn't had a chance to text Dr. Bennet yet. How is he?"

"They made a call to a vet over at Hillside, but apparently, he was already heading to the stables because of a call from Lizzy. Anyway, they told him about Wickham stealing their supplies, and thankfully, he'd decided to bring the clinic van, just in case they needed anything else. The three of them are collaborating to get him well. From the way they talk, I don't think this happens very often in horses, and the scene at the Longbourn clinic is a mess. Chase couldn't go inside, so one of the sheriff's deputies removed the crate of supplies Lizzy had prepped and the machine they needed to do the bloodwork. I suppose since Wickham wasn't interested in it, they could make an exception and remove it. They've set the lab work machine up in the stable office for now."

She touched her shoulder to his and took his hand. "Have they said anything at all? What about the baby?" She whispered the last after a glance at Mrs. Bennet.

"I don't know. I told the paramedic on the way here and the nurse when we arrived, so I'm sure the doctors know."

She nodded and clasped her hands in front of her. "Who wants coffee?" His little sister looked around at everyone. "I have a funny feeling we're going to be here for a while. We may as well have some fortification."

"Is there any news about Wickham?" When he asked, everyone in the room stopped to stare at him.

"State trooper pulled him over on I-10, heading toward San Antonio," said Ana. "He had a fake passport on the seat. They think he was heading for Mexico."

"He didn't shoot the trooper, did he?"

"No, he cooperated. I made sure sheriff's deputies knew he's wanted in Maine, though they said you'd informed them before. From what they said, he'll have to serve out his sentence here first. The deputy I spoke to expects him to go to jail for a long time. Attempted murder alone can be twenty years."

"Twenty years is nowhere near enough, but he'd also face charges for the robbery, trespassing at the stable, and possibly an animal cruelty—"

"Oh yeah! Chase mentioned that as long as we can prove Wickham poisoned Skylla on purpose, he should be charged for that. Animal cruelty in Texas is a felony and can carry ten years for each count."

He wiped his face with his hands. With any luck—and a sympathetic judge and jury—they may never have to deal with Wickham again.

"Okay, I'm going to that fancy coffee shop I saw downstairs. Do you want to go?"

He shook his head. "No, I need to be here in case—"

"I understand. Don't worry. She'll be fine."

She spoke to Lizzy's mother and sisters before she left, and he sagged back into the chair in the same position as before. Had it even been five minutes later when Chase arrived? He hugged each of his sisters and held his mother for a moment before he sat down beside William.

"Ana went down for coffee."

"I saw her when I arrived. Dad made me leave the stable and come here. He insisted three vets was overkill and that there was such a thing as 'overtreating' an animal. Skylla's bloodwork so far is coming back okay. We're hopeful he'll be fine. I just want to make sure you know he's still good so you can concentrate on Lizzy."

"Thanks," said William. "I do appreciate it, but your dad should be here. I'll pay the vet from Hillside for his time and effort. I don't mind. You need to call your father and persuade him to come."

Chase squeezed his shoulder. "Dad would go stir-crazy sitting here waiting for hours on end, and he knows it. Heck, Lizzy would tell you that herself if she could. The only thing keeping Dad from falling apart is your horse. Let him do what's necessary. I don't want him to seem callous or uncaring—"

"No, I think I get it. Sitting here helpless is impossible."

"Skylla has Garrett there too, so my father's not alone. Both are excellent vets."

William rubbed his eyes. Lydia sat in the far corner with a pout on her face. He clenched his teeth and gripped his hands. The last thing they needed was a scene.

Ana came in with two coffee caddies, set them down on the table, then handed the youngest Bennet sister her drink. She worked her way around the room before finally giving a cup to both Chase and William before taking a sip of her own. "Any news?"

William shook his head and turned to Chase. "Look, while it's just the three of us, I need to tell you something about Lydia." He sighed and told Chase exactly what Wickham had said, even including the comment of her certain talents. Ana sat beside her boyfriend and took his hand, and Chase groaned at the worst of it.

"How am I supposed to tell that to Dad? Then there's the question of whether she knew what she was doing."

"I didn't get that impression," said William, "or I couldn't sit in the same room with her, especially right now. I think Wickham somehow found out she used to work at the clinic and turned on the charm to get the information he wanted. After he learned about the drugs at the stable, he wanted access to the full stock. Lydia was a means to an end. She'll need to see a doctor though. He even said in front of us that he's had to reuse syringes."

Chase squeezed his eyes closed. "Stupid, stupid girl. We keep waiting for her to use that brain of hers, but I'm beginning to worry she never will."

"Since Wickham lied to get the job at the stable," said Ana. "He may have told her a fake name."

"I'm going to get Mary to take her home."

William lifted his eyebrows. "Won't Mary want to be here?"

"I'm sure she does, but she can always take Lydia home and come back. I'm not going to make her babysit." Chase strode across the room and pulled Mary to the side. He spoke near her ear so no one else could hear, but to William, it was obvious when he told her what had happened. Her jaw dropped, and her eyes were huge. She strode over to Lydia and punched her in the arm.

"Ow! What was that for?"

"We're leaving. I'm taking you home."

"What are you talking about, Mary?" said Mrs. Bennet. "Lydia should be here for Lizzy."

Chase shook his head. "Momma, she needs to leave."

"I don't understand." His mother glanced between Chase, Mary, and Lydia.

Lydia crossed her arms over her chest. "I don't care about being here. I don't even know why I'm here. Mary can take me home. At least I can call my friends or watch TV."

"Come on," said Mary. "Let's go."

When they were gone, Mrs. Bennet stomped over to her son. "When is someone going to tell me why Lydia had to leave?" At least Lydia left without everything being revealed, Chase just needed to make Mrs. Bennet stand down.

"Dad will tell you later," said Chase. "As soon as I talk to him." Mrs. Bennet threw up her hands, let them fall to her sides, and sat down with a huff.

William caught Chase's gaze. "I didn't expect you to do that."

"I know you didn't, but after hearing what you said, I couldn't sit here and look at her for another minute. That was as much for me as it was for you."

All William could do was nod.

Chapter 26

William dragged his head up from the edge of the mattress and groaned. Dear Lord, had he been hit by a bus? He rubbed the sleep from his eyes and blinked, clearing the fog from his brain while his fingernails managed to penetrate the stubble he hadn't bothered to shave since the shooting. As much as he wanted her eyes to open, Lizzy was still unconscious, a monitor beeping the steady rhythm of her heart while she slept. She'd been out for three days since the surgery. Three days too long if you asked him.

He closed his eyes and rested his forehead against her hand. They'd waited several hours for some word before the surgeon had come to the waiting room and explained the damage done to Lizzy's abdomen. They'd patched everything up, but she'd required several units of blood. The only thing left to do was wait until she woke. The prognosis was good, but the doctor had left out one important thing.

As soon as the surgeon left, he and Chase followed.

"Excuse me," said William a few steps outside the waiting room. "May I ask you a question?"

The surgeon turned and gave a single nod. "Yes, of course."

"You didn't mention the baby."

The surgeon's eyes flitted down to the scrubs and back to his face. "You were with her when she came in."

"He's the father," said Chase. "Lizzy is my sister."

William closed the distance between them some. "We hadn't told everyone yet. It's why I waited until you left to ask."

The surgeon nodded and shoved his hands into his coat pockets. "I'm afraid we couldn't do anything to save the baby. Too much was stacked against such a new pregnancy: the stress of being held at gunpoint, the trauma of being shot not to mention the surgery. I wish we could've done more. I'm very sorry."

William's eyes closed, and he shuddered in an inhale. He couldn't imagine how the baby would've survived, but he'd allowed himself to hope. "When can I see her?"

"She'll be moved to a room soon. I'll ask a nurse to notify you when she is."

"Thank you. I appreciate everything you've done for her."

When the surgeon walked away, William swung his arm as if he was going to punch the wall but slowed before his fist made contact. "Damn, Wickham." He pressed his palms against the smooth pastel surface and leaned against it.

Chase put his hand on William's shoulder. "I'm so sorry. I know it wasn't planned, but I do know how excited Lizzy had become in the last few weeks. She's mentioned you were just as happy." He was. The baby wasn't the sole thing making him so content, but as a result of the pregnancy, he'd realized how much he wanted a family, a family with Lizzy. What would he do if something happened to her as well?

Ana hugged him, and when she pulled back, tears glistened in her eyes. "Oh, William. I'm sorry, but at least you have good news about Lizzy."

His eyes burned, and he blinked, swiping at a bit of damp near the edge. Lizzy needed him to be strong. He would not cry, at least not yet. Chase had been correct. Their timing had been off, but they'd stayed up late arguing over baby names and whether it was a boy or a girl. How was he going to tell her? Nothing he could say or do would soften the blow.

"Anything?" Dr. Bennet suddenly stood beside him with an extra-large cup of coffee held out. When had he arrived?

"Nothing. I just keep thinking that she has to wake soon." He took a sip of the hot brew, letting its warmth seep through him. He was cold and had been since he entered this room.

Her father squeezed his shoulder. "She's a strong one, always was. I'm sure she'll wake up soon." He cleared his throat. "She did a good job getting that charcoal into your horse so fast. With everything, I hadn't gotten to mention that. Lamonte's still keeping an eye on him, but he hasn't shown any signs of kidney damage, which is a miracle if you ask me."

"I'll need the contact information for the vet at Hillside. I want to pay him for his time."

Dr. Bennet shook his head. "When Garrett showed up and learned what'd happened, he refused to take my money in payment for the medication we needed. I doubt he'll take yours either."

"I'd still like to try."

"I understand, son." Dr. Bennet leaned against the hospital bed and crossed his arms over his chest. "When was the last time you left this room?"

He looked back at Lizzy. "I don't know."

"Why don't you go get some food? You won't do her any good if you pass out."

William shook his head. "No, I can't. I won't leave her. I have to be here when she wakes up."

The older man sighed. "I figured you'd say that, but I hoped I could persuade you otherwise."

As he took another sip of his coffee, Lizzy's hand turned under his. She'd moved her fingers before but rotating her arm was new. He set his cup on the table and stood. "Lizzy? Lizzy, baby, open your eyes for me, please."

Her father took her opposite hand as her eyes fluttered, and she groaned. "Hurts," she mumbled.

William glanced at his watch. "You're due pain medication soon. I'm sure that'll make you feel better."

"Hey, Lizzy," said her father. "Can you open your eyes all the way?"

She managed but frowned. "I'm so tired."

"You lost a good bit of blood." William cradled her cheek. "I should call for the nurse, but your dad and I have been waiting for three days for you to wake up." He pressed the button but returned to cradle her cheek again. "Baby, can you stay awake a bit longer?"

The nurse bustled in, and Dr. Bennet moved to the side for her to evaluate her patient. "You're finally awake, Miss Bennet."

"Dr. Bennet," said William. "She's a veterinarian."

"Sorry." One side of the nurse's lips quirked upward. She checked the monitors then stopped at the foot of the bed. "She improves a little more every day."

"She says she's in pain and that she's tired."

The nurse smiled. "Her fatigue is normal and probably exacerbated by the pain medication, which I'll give her in a moment. It's good to see you awake, Dr. Bennet."

Lizzy faded back to sleep almost as soon as the nurse left the room. Her father dropped his head, then clasped his hands together as he lifted it again. "Well, at least I can go into the clinic and tell everyone she was awake. Speaking of the clinic, I should go. I don't want to leave Chase to do all the heavy lifting alone."

"I know she'll appreciate you covering for her."

Dr. Bennet smiled. "I enjoy it—not that I want to have to work for this reason, but that I can practice without so much of the obligation these days. Semi-retirement suits me, I suppose." He clapped William on the back. "I'm sure my wife and daughters will be in later." He started to leave, but right before his hand hit the door, he turned. "I thought you should know I spoke to Lydia. She never watches the news, so she had no idea of what she'd done. When I showed her Wickham's mug shot online and explained what'd happened, I expected hysterics or anger, but instead, her reaction was the oddest thing I've ever seen."

"What's that?"

"She stopped talking. In fact, we can hardly get a word out of her. Mary says she heard Lydia crying in her room last night. I just hope this opens her eyes. She's been self-centered for far too long in my opinion. You see, when she was born, I told my wife Lydia'd be our last. She kept wanting to try for a boy, but I thought five girls was going to mean I worked until I dropped dead in the clinic one day. Since Lydia was the last, she spoiled her, and I let her. I shouldn't have. If I hadn't, maybe all of this wouldn't have happened."

"You can't blame yourself," said William. "I knew Wickham before I moved to Texas, remember? If we want to consider the situation in those terms, we can both claim fault. In the end, it's Wickham's—all Wickham's doing. If he hadn't been involved in drugs and continuing whatever sick vendetta he had against me, this wouldn't have happened." Dr. Bennet didn't respond. He just nodded and left.

People came and went during the day. Ana brought breakfast—not that William ate much these days. Mary brought him lunch, and later that afternoon, Mrs. Bennet spent her time at Lizzy's bedside crying until Katy forced her from the room and took her home.

"Why'd you let Momma in here?"

He spun around from digging in the bag Ana had brought him that first night. "Don't you want your mother to visit you?"

Lizzy exhaled and shook her head. "She makes me crazy when I'm sick."

"You can keep pretending to sleep through it."

She managed a smile before her expression fell, her eyelids already drooping. "Did they catch him?"

He stepped over to the bed and sat on the edge. "They did. He's been indicted on a boatload of charges: trespassing, armed robbery, animal cruelty, attempted murder."

"Good," she said weakly, then drifted back to sleep. He slumped and rubbed his face. He knew she'd ask about the baby eventually, but he hoped with all that was in him that she'd do it when she was stronger. How was he supposed to break her heart?

His had cracked and bled when the surgeon had told him. He couldn't even imagine how hers would shatter at the news. Even Ana hugged him tighter whenever she came to visit.

While he traced Lizzy's features, she frowned, her eyes began to move under the lids, and she whimpered. "No."

"Lizzy?" He laced their fingers.

Her head whipped back and forth and her legs shifted. "No," she said louder.

"Baby, wake up." He placed a palm to her cheek. "You're dreaming." Goodness knows he'd had enough nightmares in the past few days. He'd wake up in the middle of the night, sweating and disoriented. After remembering where he was, he'd peeked into the hall to see if he'd made any noise that would've disturbed the floor. Thankfully, the nurses all moved from room to room and milled around the nurse's station as though nothing had occurred.

"No!" With a flinch, her eyes shot open. She blinked several times and relaxed when their gazes met. Tears flooded her eyes, and she choked back a sob. "He'd shot you."

"I wish he had." How often had he thought that in the past two days? Anything to keep from watching her suffer.

She shook her head while her lip trembled. "No, I couldn't have taken it if he'd killed you. I meant what I said."

"That you love me?" He guessed, but it was the best one he had.

"Yes, and I heard you say it back. I don't know how because most of what happened after is muddled, but I do remember that."

"Then you've chosen to keep the best part." He kissed her forehead, fighting against the burn in his own eyes.

"William?"

He squeezed his eyes closed and waited. As much as he wanted her awake and better, she wasn't ready for this yet. "Yes?"

Her hand came to the back of his head, and she pulled his face towards hers so they were almost nose to nose, a lone tear tracked down her cheek. "The baby's gone, isn't she?" In the last week, she'd started referring to the baby as a girl. She couldn't explain why but staunchly refused to say "it."

He pressed his forehead to hers, then kissed her cheek and held her as carefully as he could while she broke down into wracking sobs.

"Is everything okay?"

With a start, he drew back and wiped his eyes. A familiar face from the evening shift stood near the foot of the bed. "We're fine. She had a nightmare. We're sorry if it disturbed anyone."

"I can't say I'm surprised after what the two of you went through." The heavy-set Black lady tsked in a way that reminded him of his grandmother. "Thank the Lord that man is in jail where he belongs." She wrote down the numbers from the machines, then propped a hand on her hip. "Now, I'm here all night long, and I won't tell a soul if the two of you cuddle. I say that's the best thing when something horrible happens. So, missy, you're on a liquid diet for now thanks to that rat bastard. I'll bring you some water, tea, or Jell-O. Just name it, and it's yours."

"Maybe some water?"

"You got it." She moved closer and held out a hand, which Lizzy took. "Since you were brought up to this ward, you've been in my prayers. I know not everyone is a praying sort, but—"

"Thank you," said Lizzy before the woman could explain herself. "We appreciate the time and thought. We'll never turn down someone's prayers."

The nurse smiled and patted the hand she held. "I feel the same way. Now, I'll be back with that water in a moment. If you need anything at all, my name's Pam. Just holler, okay?"

"Are you hurting?" he asked as soon as the nurse left.

"I ache, but I think it's from being in bed. How long has it been?"

"Three days."

"Tell me about what happened and what the doctor said."

One look at the resolute expression on her face, and his shoulders slumped. He shifted to lay beside her and wrapped an arm around her, high enough so he wouldn't press on her wound. "Where do you want me to start?"

"From the moment Wickham shot the gun. Just don't be surprised if I fall asleep. I'm fighting some to stay awake."

"I think you will be for a while."

She sniffed near his arm. "William?"

"Yeah."

"Don't take this the wrong way, but you smell." Tears still poured down her face but a slight smile peeked through. He held her a bit tighter. Things would be hard for a while, and they'd have to mourn the baby, but they'd be okay. He was sure of it. They had to be.

Chapter 27

Lizzy opened the shower door and grabbed the fresh towel William set out before leaving for the ranch. She patted most of the water from her skin, then wrapped the soft towel around her while she made her way to the mirror. When she leaned forward, she touched her face, grazing her fingers down her nose and along her cheekbones. The dark circles and most of the paleness had disappeared in the almost month since the shooting. She almost resembled her usual self, which was something, but when would she once again feel like her usual self? She was tired of the fatigue and everything else that went hand-in-hand with her recovery.

The trees outside her window swayed with the early October breeze, so she threw on a comfy pair of black joggers and her heather grey and maroon rhinestone Aggie t-shirt. After a quick kiss to Evie's head and avoiding the paw that tried to slap her in return, Lizzy went downstairs, put on her sneakers, and stepped outside.

Before she left the porch, she took a deep breath, inhaling the scent of falling leaves combined with a hint of smoke. Someone was burning on a nearby property—never a good idea in a place as prone to drought as the Hill Country. It was either that, or they'd taken advantage of the cool October day to use their fireplace.

With a steady pace, she headed toward the stables. Other than sitting on the patio by the firepit or walking to the car for a doctor's appointment, she hadn't been outside, and moving around was definitely a lot better than lounging on the sofa for days on end. William wouldn't even let her clean. At this point, she was just plain desperate if she was hoping to do housework to alleviate boredom!

Her first stop was at Luna's stall. She stroked down the grey mare's face. "Hey, sweetie. Have you missed me?" Luna nickered softly while she chewed on some hay.

"I hadn't expected to see you out here yet." When she turned, Lamonte stood a few feet away, leaning against a stall door. "Will I find Darcy out here hunting you down after you go?"

"He went to the grocery store, and I wanted to get out for a bit. I promise not to wear myself out, and I give you permission to lie and say you never saw me."

He laughed and waved his hands in front of him. "No way. I'm not getting between whatever the two of you have going on."

She gave Luna a kiss on the nose then continued on, stopping in front of Skylla's stall. "Is he really okay? I know what Daddy said, but I wouldn't put it past him to sugarcoat the situation after everything."

Lamonte stepped beside her and draped his arm over her shoulders. "I was here for most of the night with your father and Doc Garrett—heard every word they said and helped them too. Between your quick start of the treatment and them taking up where you left off, all of you made sure none of that poison hurt him. He's been a spry thing too. You should've seen him kicking up a storm out in the paddock this morning. You'd think he was a two-year-old. That boy of yours better get out here and ride him soon, else he's going to become spoilt."

She smiled, and when the horse stuck his nose out of the window, she leaned her forehead to his cheek. "Hey, boy." Her vision blurred, and she blinked madly. Skylla was here, and he was fine. Even with all that happened that night, everything had worked out. Dr. Annesley, the therapist she and William had been seeing for the past two weeks, was right. This did help.

After she turned, she hugged Lamonte. "Thank you."

His wiry arms held her as though he would crush her if he wasn't careful. "I'm glad you're all right. I'm sorry I ever hired that good for nothing. If I'd known—"

"It wasn't your fault. William blames himself; he thinks Wickham followed him here. In the end, Wickham did what he did. No one forced or coerced him. Don't blame yourself, because I can tell you no one else does. Do you hear me?"

"Yes, ma'am." he said with a partial smile and mock salute.

She rolled her eyes and grinned. "If William comes searching for me. I'm just walking around. Between you and me, I'm sick to death of reality television. Whoever decided that was entertainment needs more therapy than either William or I do."

"Don't go telling Doc that. You know how much he loves The Bachelor."

"He loves laughing at that show."

Lamonte chuckled. "True."

After a quick wave, she walked from the stables and stopped in front of her house, staring down the lane toward the clinic. Could she? Should she? She shook her hand as though that helped her nerves, and took a tentative step down the hill. One step turned into two as her pace increased. When she reached the bottom, she stared at the front windows and sucked in a breath. She could do this. She would do this.

She trembled when she opened the door. Chelsea looked over from the monitor and gasped. "Lizzy!"

Mrs. Goulding stood and rushed over to hug her, her obnoxious little rat terrier yapping at Lizzy's ankles. When Lizzy turned, a huge grin overtook her face. "Henry!" Her eyes burned as she knelt down and held out a hand. "Hey, boy." The chunky

Bassett Hound wagged nearly his entire body when he approached, bumping her and sending her butt to the floor.

"Oh! I'm so sorry!" Mrs. Schwarz jumped forward and gasped. "He didn't hurt you, did he?"

Lizzy burst into laughter. "I'm okay." Henry climbed into her lap and rolled onto his back, begging for tummy scratches. "Okay, but just for a bit." She started at his chest and worked her way down to his belly while Henry's tongue lolled out of his mouth in pure unadulterated ecstasy.

"Lizzy?" When she lifted her gaze, Chase stood by the front counter, his eyes wide. "What are you doing here?"

She shrugged. "I thought I'd check in and make sure y'all were holding down the fort. Henry insisted I give him a belly rub first, though."

Her father entered the waiting room with a chart in his hand. He laughed when he caught a glimpse of her position on the floor and Henry's blissful expression. "I should've known you'd visit with one of your patients before us."

Mrs. Schwarz lured Henry off her lap with a treat, and Chase helped her stand. She caught a glimpse of the business office while she brushed the pet hair off her butt, and her smile met a quick end.

"You don't have to do this yet," said Chase in a soft voice.

"I know, but if I don't face my fears, I'll never be able to come back to work." She pointed toward the treatment room. "I want to start back there first. You both have patients, so do what you need to do. I'll be fine."

Her father lifted his bushy eyebrows. "Are you sure?"

She nodded. "I promise. Besides, Mary's probably back there doing a dental or something useful so I won't be alone." At their raised eyebrows, she sighed. "I promise I'll scream if I get scared. Okay?" As soon as she kissed both Chase and her dad on the cheek, she walked to the swinging door, pressing her palm to it for a full minute before taking a deep inhale and pushing it open.

Mary glanced up from the dental on the table. "Lizzy?"

Lizzy stopped, wringing her hands in front of her. She nodded toward the dog on the table. "Who's that?"

"New patient. Four-year-old pit bull. He's from one of the rescues. They wanted him neutered, vaccinated, and ready for adoption. Dad said to clean his teeth before I disconnected him from the anesthesia. They're pretty bad."

She peered over Mary's shoulder. "That one needs to be pulled. Do you want me to do it so you don't have to wait?"

"That'd be awesome." Mary tossed her a pair of gloves and pulled out a sterile pack of tools. The tooth gave easily, and Lizzy stripped off the gloves, tossing them in the trash.

"His teeth look good. I'd call it a day and unhook him."

While Mary worked, Lizzy stepped inside the surgical room, staring at the new locked metal cabinet that replaced the old wooden one. She shuddered. A hand to her shoulder nearly made her jump out of her skin.

"I'm sorry," said Mary. "I wasn't sure if you could help me get him off the table."

She shook her head. "I can't yet. Do you want me to get someone?"

"Please. I don't want to leave him up there unsupervised."

She exited into the hallway and caught Chase taking Mrs. Goulding into his exam room. "Sorry to interrupt, but Mary needs you for a minute. I can't help her lift that dog off the table."

237

Mrs. Goulding patted Chase on the shoulder. "Go on ahead. We can wait."

"Thank you," said Lizzy while Chase disappeared into the treatment room. After a smile to Mrs. Goulding, Lizzy walked to the front desk, shifting behind the counter and ducking into the business office before she could second-guess herself. Her heart raced, and she shook as if she stood in a raging ice storm, not inside the warmth of the clinic as she was. She shoved her hands into the pockets of her joggers while her eyes darted around the room. The cabinet that contained the safe, the spot on the floor where she must've fallen when Wickham shot her. She stared at her feet where a cracked tile stood out among the rest of the ceramic. Wickham had stood exactly where she was standing right now. A tear landed on her cheek, and she swiped it away.

"Hey," said Chelsea softly at her shoulder. "Screw that asshole."

A laugh spluttered from her. "What?"

"You heard me. I can't imagine how it must feel to stand there, but screw him. I think it's a good thing to confront what happened or you'd never be able to set foot in here again, but I also think whenever it all starts to get to you, you repeat a mantra to yourself."

She smiled. "Screw that asshole?"

"Precisely." Chelsea gave a nod and a wink. "You're alive, you're getting better every day, and he's going to rot in prison—hopefully, for the rest of his life—so screw 'em."

"I agree." When Lizzy looked over, Mrs. Schwarz stood at the counter. "Don't let that man take even the tiniest fraction of your peace of mind. Do you hear me? Give him no further power over you. He's not worth it."

One side of Lizzy's lips remained curved. "Thank you." She wrapped an arm around Chelsea's shoulders. "Thanks especially for creating a memory in this room I won't forget anytime soon."

"I hope it works," she said.

"I'm not going to say I can stand here and not remember, but I can't think of it without your words in my head." Her eye was captured by a flash of the same midnight blue William was wearing when he left, outside, at the base of the hill. "I think William has tracked me down. It was great to see everyone."

"When will you be back to work?" asked Mrs. Schwarz.

"I have another two weeks before I'm cleared. My father and Chase want me to go slow, so start part-time and work myself back up." She gave Henry one last scratch behind the ear before she exited the clinic. William waited, leaning against a live oak just outside the parking lot. "You could've told me you wanted to come down here. I would've driven you."

She smiled but rolled her eyes. "That would've defeated the point."

"What's that?"

"I really wanted to walk around. I'm so tired of sitting on my butt. You've done so much for me since—" She waved her hands about. "—but I needed to confront some of my fears, and do so on my own."

He sighed and held out a hand. "Dr. Annesley and I have talked about this. I know I have to let you stretch your wings again, but it's hard. I don't want you to get hurt. Can't I wrap you in bubble wrap and not let you out of my sight?"

She took his hand and pulled herself into his arms. "It's going to take time for both of us to be secure again. Thank you for not becoming angry."

His head popped back a bit. "Were you worried I would?"

"A little."

After pressing a kiss to her temple, he tugged her toward home. "I admit to being frantic when I couldn't find you. When I ran into Lamonte, he told me what you were doing, and the last he saw you, you were heading down the hill. It didn't take a genius to know where you were going. But, if Lamonte hadn't told me, I probably would've been upset when I found you. All I ask is that next time you leave me a note. Please."

She leaned her head on his shoulder. "I think I can manage that." She inhaled deeply. "William?"

"Yeah."

"As soon as I'm cleared by the doctor, I want to get pregnant again. I don't want to wait."

His hand gripped hers a little tighter before he entwined their fingers. "I think I'd love that."

"You would?"

He lifted their joined hands to his lips, closed his eyes, and kissed her knuckles. "I know we haven't been together a long time, but whether there's a ring on your finger or not, I know you are my forever, so yes, I would. I really would."

"The doorbell is a visitor for you."

Lizzy pulled on a comfy pair of leggings with a frown. She'd just finished her first day back at work and had immediately showered and changed. "For me? Who?"

"I think you should see for yourself."

She strode around him and started down the stairs but stopped at the sight of Lydia in the living room. Her youngest sister bit her bottom lip and wrung her hands while she paced in a small circle.

"Lydia? What are you doing here?"

Lydia tucked her hair behind her ear. "I hope it's okay that I came. You probably don't want to see me, but I needed to tell you something and came anyway."

As soon as Lizzy stood at the base of the staircase, she clenched her hands, resisting the urge to cross her arms over her chest and throw out a leg. Her insides writhed, and she didn't want Lydia to know she was shaking. "What do you want?"

"I came to apologize. Daddy took me to San Antonio a little over a week after you were shot, and I stayed with Aunt Maddie until this weekend. We've been talking a lot about what happened—you know working for the clinic, leaving, Greg. She's helped me see how immature I've been for, well, I don't know, forever. I was mad at you and let Greg use me. I know he's to blame for a lot, but I understand that I'm responsible for the information I gave him. I messed up." Tears welled in her eyes. "I'm sorry, Lizzy. I know I'm a brat and a bitch, but I never wanted this to happen. I didn't know who Greg was or what he was planning. He told me his name was Gregory Taylor. He told me a lot of things, all lies from what Daddy and Mary have said." She choked back a sob. "I know you have to learn to trust me again, but I hope that you won't shut me out. Mary told me about the baby, so I wouldn't blame you if you hated me. I cost you a lot, and Aunt Maddie made sure I understood that you would be recovering from this for a long, long time."

"Lydia—"

"I swear I won't tell Momma or anyone else about the baby. Mary wanted me to know what you'd lost, and she was right to do it."

Lizzy held both hands up. "Lydia, stop."

Her sister swiped at the tears on her cheeks and stood stock-still.

"I'll admit that I was shocked when I learned what you'd told Wickham. He bragged about it while holding a gun on us—how you'd willingly given him what he needed. When I woke up, I knew the baby couldn't have survived. She was just too young and between the stress and the blood loss..." Lizzy shuddered in a breath. "I was angry with you—furious actually—and I admit I still am sometimes. I know you weren't nearly as responsible as Wickham, but what you did was vengeful. You're my sister, and I don't want to hate you. I won't shut you out, but you're right that it'll take time, maybe a long time, to trust you again."

Lizzy took in a deep breath. Thank goodness, her stomach had relaxed some, and she'd stopped shaking like a leaf. "That said, if you want to prove yourself, I do have an idea."

Her sister lifted her eyebrows. "What's that?"

"Mary is finally putting in her application for vet school, and Katy wants to take her place as a tech. She's been coming in on her days off and learning the ropes, but it would be better if she could train full time. If you'd like to come back and take Katy's place, up front with Chelsea, we'll try it on a trial. You'll have to prove yourself: no social media, no attitude, and no swearing in front of the clients." Was she doing the right thing? Lizzy had no idea. One thing for certain: Chase was going to have a fit!

Lydia nodded vehemently. "Yes, I'd love to. I promise to do a good job this time."

Lizzy did her best to smile, but Lydia had to know it wasn't genuine. "I'll tell Chase and Chelsea tomorrow." William came downstairs and squeezed her hand on his way to the kitchen.

"Are you going to marry him?"

"I hope so, but probably not anytime soon."

"Well, I think you should because he's smokin' hot." She whispered the last in a way that resembled the old Lydia more than the girl who'd so far stood in front of her today. "Anyway, I'll leave you two alone." She bobbed in place for a second or two before throwing herself into Lizzy's arms. "Thank you."

What the heck? The old Lydia never hugged anyone except for her cheerleader friends from school, and even that was a loose snobby sort of action that involved a peck to the cheek. Before she could hug her in return, she was gone.

"You told her she could have her old job back?" When she turned, William leaned against the door frame with his arms crossed over his chest. "Chase will have something to say about that."

"I can't abandon her. She seems to be trying—wanting to be better than who she was. What kind of sister would I be if I ignored that?"

He straightened and took her in his arms. "I get it. I've tried to imagine how I would feel if it were Ana."

"Ana has never struck me as ever resembling Lydia."

"I think that's why it's so hard for me to understand, but I admire your willingness to forgive her. You have a good heart, and I love that about you."

"I love you too."

Chapter 28

<u>A year later — November</u>

William's gut clenched as Lizzy grabbed the bench in front of her and used it to stand so she could waddle to the podium. No matter how much she'd argued, he should've made her stay at home and take it easy. Sitting day after day during the trial and now appearing for the sentencing had put too much stress on her, not to mention the baby. He hadn't missed that she'd been rubbing her bulging belly since they'd arrived this morning. Why did she have to be here? She didn't have to give her statement in person. Wickham had been found guilty on all counts. This was the sentencing. Not the trial itself.

"Your Honor, I am Elizabeth Bennet, one of the victims of Greg Wickham. On the evening of September 2nd 20__, Mr. Wickham poisoned William Darcy's horse, then held William and me at gunpoint while he stole drugs and money from my family's veterinary practice. To prevent William from pursuing him, Wickham shot me in the stomach." Her eyes darted to the back of Wickham's head. He sat with his attorney, with his back to them and not acknowledging Lizzy's presence at all, which wasn't a shock. Wickham, who had remained cocky all the way until that fateful guilty verdict had been read, had offered no reaction to William's statement either.

"That evening, I lost a great deal to Mr. Wickham's single bullet. I lost so much blood, I required transfusions while the surgeons worked to save my life; I lost almost two months of my life recovering from the physical toll of that one bullet—my full recovery took much longer; and I lost my unborn child."

Mrs. Bennet sniffed and dabbed at her eyes. They hadn't originally intended to inform the entire Bennet family, but when the prosecutor told them the state could charge Wickham for the death of the baby thanks to the Unborn Victims of Violence Act, they both agreed to pursue that possibility. Who wouldn't embrace any avenue to keep Wickham behind bars for as long as possible? They'd told Mr. and Mrs. Bennet of their decision that Sunday after a large family dinner. Mrs. Bennet had burst into tears and reacted just as Lizzy had predicted, making Lizzy plead fatigue so they could leave as soon as possible.

"The trauma of the entire evening, and not just the shooting, required months of therapy so I could once again sleep through the night. I still catch myself staring at the controlled substances cabinet at work, remembering the terror we faced staring down the barrel of Mr. Wickham's handgun. I also avoid the business office where Mr. Wickham pulled the trigger and forever changed our lives. Despite the year of therapy since that night, I still experience anxiety when I try to enter that room. Mr. Wickham has stood trial for those actions as well as the loss of our child and has been found guilty by a jury of his peers. While I am pleased the jury agrees Mr. Wickham is guilty of his crimes, I am disturbed by Mr. Wickham's insistence of his innocence, not to mention his decided lack of remorse for his actions and their repercussions, particularly the loss of my baby whom I can never replace. He has hurt members of the Darcy family in the past and is wanted in Maine to stand trial for his actions there. What I ask of this court is to sentence Mr. Wickham to the maximum penalty under the law—to ensure he is locked up and unable to harm another animal or human being. Give not only myself, but also Mr. Darcy and his sister, who has also suffered by Mr. Wickham's hands, the peace of mind to know he can never harm any of us again." By all outward appearances, Lizzy appeared strong, but he knew her better than the judge. The slight waver of her voice and the occasional sniff hinted that she struggled to hold back her tears. Yet, there was something else. He was certain of it. She nodded, her lips pressed in a thin line. "Thank you, Your Honor." Her hand continued to massage the upper left side of her belly when she sat beside him.

"Are you all right?" he whispered.

"Don't be mad."

"What?" His voice dropped. He couldn't help it. Whenever Lizzy started with "Don't be mad," whatever she had to say wasn't good.

"I've had a headache all morning, and I'm having a pain in the top of my stomach." They jumped when the judge struck the gavel. People stood and began to mill about them. The prosecutor weaved through the gallery, headed in their direction.

"We're going to the hospital."

"I'm sure I'll be fine once I'm home in bed."

He stood and helped her up. "What if something's wrong, Lizzy? Do you really want to take a chance after...?" He couldn't say it. As much as he thought it, he couldn't hurt her that way.

Her eyes flooded with tears. "No, you're right. I'm sorry."

When the prosecutor stepped beside him, William shook her hand. "I apologize, but Lizzy isn't feeling well. I'm taking her to the hospital to get checked out."

"It would be better if you came to the final sentencing, but I understand if that's not possible."

"Thank you," said William. "You have my number. Text me when you know anything, and I'll let you know if I can make it."

"Will do." With an arm around Lizzy, he urged her into the aisle, pointing and mouthing "hospital" to Chase and Ana, whose eyes bugged.

Ana mouthed, "Time?" pointing at her watch, but William shrugged.

Once they were buckled in and William had started the car, Lizzy sighed. "You're angry."

"No, I'm worried. I understand why you wanted to deliver your impact statement in person, but the doctor warned you of the stress. Your blood pressure has been borderline since the trial started. I only wanted you to rest."

"I know, but I wouldn't be any less stressed at home. I'd just be freaking out while I wondered what was happening." She pulled out her phone and touched the screen.

"What are you doing?"

"Calling Dr. King's office."

He continued to drive toward the hospital while Lizzy spoke, keeping one ear trained on their conversation. As soon as she put the phone down, she winced and rubbed her stomach. "Park in the garage as we would for appointments. She wants to evaluate me in the office. If she has any concerns, she'll admit me directly to the OB ward."

"What's wrong with the ER?"

"She doesn't want me sitting around waiting to be seen."

When they arrived, a young woman in scrubs stood waiting with a wheelchair. "Good morning, Miss Bennet."

"Hi, Rachel. Is that for me?"

"Yes, ma'am. Dr. King insisted."

Lizzy plonked down into the offending chair and rolled her eyes. "I really hate these things."

He squeezed her shoulder, keeping his hand there while they headed for the doors. "You needed it when you were shot. Besides, I'm glad the doctor thought of this today."

She grumbled but continued to rub on that same spot while the nurse took them into the back entrance and into the closest exam room. She slapped a blood pressure cuff on Lizzy's arm, pumping the bulb until Lizzy winced. A moment later, she ripped the band from her arm. "160 over 109." His heart dropped. "We'll need a urine sample." Rachel pointed at the bathroom to the side. "You know where everything is by now. I'll let Dr. King know the results and see what she wants to do."

As soon as the girl left, Lizzy looked at him with wide, glistening eyes. "I'm sorry. I really am. I didn't think it would get that high."

"Lizzy, I'm not mad at you, but we'll talk after you go pee in that cup."

When she came out, she was wiping tears from her cheeks and his heart clenched. He took her in his arms and rubbed her back. "Shh, everything's going to be okay. You're thirty-seven weeks. If things aren't good, the baby can be delivered. Is he moving?"

"Yes, *she's* been using my belly button for a punching bag all morning." Something in him settled at that. The baby was okay—or seemed to be anyway.

The door opened as Dr. King strode in without pause. "Alrighty, let's take a look at that baby. Lizzy, on the table, if you please, and as soon as we're done, you are to lie on your left side. I want to see if that changes anything."

The doctor squirted the cold goop on Lizzy's lower belly, then moved the wand around. She took a few photos. "The baby is active, which is good. I don't see anything concerning." The young nurse came in and handed the doctor a piece of paper. After a glance, Dr. King exhaled. "You have protein in your urine." She patted the table. "Roll over while we talk."

William sat on a stool so he was face to face when Lizzy shifted to her side. "Hey," she said softly.

Dr. King stood beside him and leaned against the wall. "It's no secret you've been under a lot of stress. This could be related to that or something else entirely. Some women just have pregnancy-induced hypertension for some unknown reason. Your weight gain is a bit high—we've discussed that—but not as high as some. With your blood pressure reading when you came in and the results of the urinalysis, I'm going to admit you. You're a little over thirty-seven weeks, so we don't need any more time for the baby's lungs to develop, so you're going straight to OB with orders to induce. Let's get that baby out where he or she is safe and healthy, and get your blood pressure down."

When Lizzy's eyes met his, William exhaled. "I'd rather not take any chances."

Lizzy closed her eyes and nodded.

"Good, I'll call over to OB, and Rachel will wheel you over." She patted Lizzy's leg. "I hope you're ready, Mom and Dad."

His heart began beating a mile a minute. They needed their bags, and then there was Evie. He pulled out his phone and touched his messages app. "*Lizzy's BP too high. She's being induced. We need our bags, and Evie will need to be fed.*"

"*Chase and I are on it! Send a room number when you know.*"

The next hour was a giant blur. Rachel wheeled them across the elevated walkway from the office buildings to the hospital, Lizzy had an I.V. and fetal monitor slapped on almost immediately. Lizzy's contractions began a few hours later. Chase and Ana dropped by long enough to bring the bags and kiss Lizzy before they headed home to wait with the rest of the Bennets.

Nurses came in and out, checking vitals and Lizzy's progress. The contractions increased and became stronger. William mainlined coffee through the night, courtesy of deliveries from Ana, and refused to sleep when Lizzy encouraged him to.

"Son of a bitch." Lizzy groaned and stiffened. She'd been at it for twenty-eight hours. The doctor had even broken her water four hours ago. He would need to up his game to espresso if something didn't happen soon. This couldn't go on for another night, could it?

"Breathe." William rubbed her back. "You can do this."

"Screw you."

He flinched but kept massaging as a smiling nurse entered. "As soon as you're done with this contraction, let's see where that baby is."

Lizzy flopped to her back, panting. She grimaced and gripped the sheet until her knuckles turned white. "Remind me why I wanted to do this again?" The words were gritted out between clenched teeth.

"Because you and I both wanted a baby?" His voice was weak, and he tried to brush a curl from her face, but she swatted his hand away.

The nurse patted her knee. "Ten centimeters. Are you ready to have this baby?"

A jolt went through his heart. "Do you hear that, Lizzy?"

She whimpered while she shifted. "I'm in labor. I'm not deaf." Another nurse joined the first while they prepped the room for the birth. Meanwhile, he couldn't even hold Lizzy's hand. She shook him off.

When the next contraction hit, she grabbed the railing and moaned. "I need to push."

One of the nurses rushed over and hurriedly threw on some gloves. The first nurse situated Lizzy and showed him what to do. Thankfully, Lizzy let him touch her this time. "I love you," he said near her ear. She groaned and bore down.

The nurse across from him smiled. "You're doing great, Daddy. She's in her own space right now while she tries to deal with the pain, so she may not respond to you. It's also why she probably didn't want you to touch her earlier. It's not uncommon at all."

He nodded. The problem was if she was going to ignore him, what else could he do to help her?"

"Don't stop talking to her. Just don't be hurt if she doesn't seem to notice."

Dr. King strode in and stood beside the nurse while she got ready. "This little one snuck up on us. When I checked you earlier, I thought you'd be laboring until tonight, at least." She glanced up and grinned at him. "Take a deep breath, William. If you feel like you're going to faint, sit down. We don't want you passing out."

"I'm good."

"You sure," she said laughing. "You're as white as a sheet." She patted Lizzy's knee. "Okay, Lizzy, you're doing great. On the next contraction, keep pushing just like you were, and we'll have this baby out in no time."

Lizzy's head flopped back to the pillow. "I'm so tired."

"You've got this, honey." Her foot flexed when the next contraction hit. "We're almost there. I know you want to hold her."

Air hissed from her, and her face was red with the strain. When the pain let up, she rolled her head to him. "You're conceding she's a girl?" Really? Of all things, that got her attention?

"I'm conceding nothing. I simply didn't want to upset you."

"Dickhead," she said when she bore down for the next contraction.

He pretended she hadn't said anything but continued to talk her through each pain. How much longer could she do this? She hadn't slept last night, and she had to be exhausted. Still, she kept on until she finally dropped back one last time and shook her head. "I can't. It's too much." She sniffled and put her hand over her eyes while a nurse put a receiving blanket on her chest.

"Lizzy." He took her hand and gripped it. "You're almost there. You can do it."

"The head is almost out, Lizzy," said Dr. King. "Two, maybe three more pushes, and you're done."

"Two more?" She grabbed her thighs and bore down again, this time crying out as the baby's head freed itself. With wide eyes, he watched as the doctor helped the shoulder, taking the wet, wrinkled, and screaming baby and placing it on Lizzy's chest. She gasped and lifted the tiny hand with her finger while the nurse scrubbed it clean. When the baby rolled to its side, Lizzy laughed. "I was right. I win."

He grinned and kissed Lizzy's forehead. "She may not be a boy, but I still win, you know."

"How's that?"

"Because I have the two of you, and you're both healthy and happy. I just enjoyed watching you purse your lips and pretend you were insulted when I teased you." He brushed her hair behind her cheek. "I went through a time where I thought I'd never find that perfect someone much less be a father. Now, at this moment, I have no complaints—none whatsoever."

Chapter 29

Lizzy sighed and stroked Ella's downy soft head while her daughter nursed intently at her breast. The last six weeks had been a crash course in living in a near sleepless state. She was tired, but she was a happy tired. Her mother had tried to help out after the birth, but after several intense disagreements, Mrs. Bennet had huffed and gone home, which was exactly what Lizzy had hoped for by that point. No, Lizzy was not interested in supplementing with a bottle, particularly one with Karo syrup laced formula. Who did that anyway? At least who did that in the last thirty or so years?

"Here's your coffee." William set her cup on the end table and sat beside her, wrapping his arm around her shoulders. "When's your family coming?"

She rested her head against his shoulder. "I expect them any minute now. Momma said something about making cinnamon rolls for breakfast. I'm sure she's been up since five a.m."

"Well, the turkey is stuffed, and in the oven, and I'll get working on everything else after we open gifts."

"Are you sure I can't help? I feel rather lazy sitting here by myself, holding the baby. I *can* cook you know." Not that he ever let her.

He chuckled and shook his head. "I've got it covered. You sit here and relax. Besides, I don't plan on having box mac and cheese for Christmas dinner."

She laughed and shook her head. "You're such a dick."

"Hey! Don't swear in front of my daughter." The moment Ella released her nipple, William scooped her up to his shoulder and began patting her back. "Go ahead, Ella. Tell Mommy you're too young to hear those words."

"You're one to talk."

"Hey, I don't say them in front of her." He stood and grabbed a small wrapped box from her stocking. "I'd hoped we could open a gift or two before our families arrive, and I wanted to start with this one."

The tiny box set off a roller coaster of flutters inside her, starting in her chest and doing a loop-de-loop inside her stomach. Her hand curled around the package when it hit her palm. With the size, it could only be one thing—jewelry. She swallowed down as much of her nerves as she could. Was it what she hoped? After his previous engagement, she'd never wanted to pressure him, so she never mentioned it. He'd ask when he was ready. The problem was what if it was earrings or a necklace. How could she open it without showing her disappointment? Disappointment was a bad word. She'd love the gift, of course, but she'd been ready for him to ask for months, especially since Ella was born. Waiting only became harder and harder.

"Well? Are you going to open it?"

At his raised eyebrows and small smile, she inhaled gradually through her nose and steadied herself while she removed the paper. Sure enough, when the paper was pulled away, a deep blue velvet box sat in her hand. "What is it?"

His low chuckle washed over her and tugged at some invisible string attached to her heart. "Maybe you should open it and find out."

She gripped it so her fingers wouldn't shake and pried the lid open, gasping at the sparkle of the emerald cut diamond ring nestled inside. Oh my God. It was huge! How was she supposed to wear it to the clinic? Okay, maybe it wasn't big when compared to Beyoncé or any of J-Lo's, but it was what? Two carats?

When she looked up, William was on his knee before her, Ella perched on his shoulder. "Elizabeth Bennet, you know by now that I'm a stubborn ass. My heart knew you were for me from the first moment I saw you, but I was so thrown by my reaction to you, I behaved like an idiot. If I hadn't already been attracted, that snarky response you gave me when you propped your hand on your hip and recited every school you'd ever attended would've made me want to kiss you senseless. I consider myself the luckiest man in the world that you didn't slap me at the fundraiser, and that you gave me a chance when I finally stopped being a coward. We've done everything in the wrong order to what I would've planned, but I don't regret any of it. I have Ella, and I have you, and now, I want to have you for the rest of our lives. Elizabeth Bennet, I love you so much. Will you marry me?"

A warm tear hit her cheek when she nodded. "Yes, you sentimental and perfectly lovely man. I will marry you." Since he held the baby, she scooted forward and wrapped her arms around them both. "I love you." After a sweet kiss, she drew back and wiped her eyes.

"I'd put the ring on your finger, but I don't want to drop Ella."

"Here," she said, taking the baby. When Ella was cradled in her right arm, William took her left hand and slipped the ring onto her finger. "How'd you get the size so perfect?"

He grinned as he rose to sit beside her. "You, my dear, have slept like the dead since the baby was born."

"I don't see how when I wake every time she cries."

"But in between, you're out, and I mean out. I checked your finger size a couple of weeks ago while you were napping. You never even twitched." He was so smug. She should just kiss that cocky grin from his face.

She adjusted the white gold band and examined the way the ring split into two smaller diamond-studded bands that cradled the bigger diamond. "How am I supposed to wear this to work?"

"It was my mother's, but not the same one I gave Anne, in case you were wondering. I could never bring myself to give her this one. Anyway, I had it cleaned and the prongs checked when it was appraised for insurance. If something happens, we can have it replaced, though I do understand if you want a silicone ring for work, particularly when treating horses. I don't want you to lose it or worse, have some issue and lose a finger."

"We'll see how it goes. I've got another six weeks before I go back to the clinic." She took her left hand and pulled his head down for another kiss. "When do you want to get married?"

He bobbed his head back and forth. "I was thinking this spring when the bluebonnets are blooming. We can get married in the back with the view of the creek behind us and the bluebonnets and Indian paintbrush on the opposite bank, then have tables set up under the oaks on the side of the house."

"I like that. Ella can nap in her own crib when she needs it, and she'll hopefully be sleeping through the night at that point."

At a knock on the door, William jumped up and answered it, letting in Chase and Ana. "Let me have my niece." Ana stretched out her arms. "I haven't gotten to hold her in two whole days."

Chase laughed and slapped William on the back before he sat across from Lizzy. "Be warned. The family is about five minutes behind us."

As soon as Ella was settled in Ana's arm, Lizzy started to draw back, but Ana grabbed her hand. "Is that Mom's ring?" She gasped. "William! When?"

"This morning." He wore the biggest smile she'd ever seen on his face.

"Oh! I'm so excited," said Ana, giving Lizzy a one-armed hug. "Do I get to be a bridesmaid?"

With a chuckle, William shook his head. "How about my best woman?"

Her eyes widened, and she laughed. "Fun! I'd love that. Do I get to plan your bachelor party?"

"No strippers!"

Lizzy smiled while Chase hugged her. "I'm so happy for you, Sis. Do you know what you want to do for your side of the wedding party?"

"Well, I've always figured you'd be my 'Man of Honor,' then our sisters can be the bridesmaids." Who would've thought she'd ever want Lydia in her bridal party? Since her little sister apologized for what'd happened with Wickham, she'd been a different woman. She'd even been going into San Antonio two days a week for college classes and had been making A's. It wasn't A&M, but Lydia was already talking about going to College Station for her Master's degree.

"I love the gender-swap going on here," said Ana with a giggle before she gasped. "I saw the most adorable black strapless jumpsuit online. I think there's a physical store in Austin. Chase and I can go shopping some weekend after the holiday madness is over. What do you think?"

William shrugged. "I think you can wear whatever you want."

"What am I going to wear?" Chase gave her a side-eye. "Don't say a dress."

Lizzy started laughing. "How about the girls wear cornflower blue, and you can wear charcoal grey pants and a vest with a matching blue shirt? Will that work?"

With a gasp, Ana grinned. "Oh, that sounds hot! I'll have to find the jumpsuit in gray so I match. "

Chase nodded. "Yes, it'll work."

"Does anyone want coffee?" Before anyone could answer, a light knock came from the door right before it opened to the remaining Bennets. Momma tiptoed over beside Ana while giving a soft squeal. She'd wanted a grandchild for a long time, only she'd expected it to come from Jane before Lizzy. After all, Jane was married. She'd be obnoxious once she noticed the engagement ring. Couldn't they wait and tell her after the wedding?

"She looks just like William," said Momma while taking the baby from Ana. "But why you named her Ella? Your grandmother always said she hated her name. She's probably rolling in her grave."

How many times had her mother repeated that same story since Ella was born? "Yes, Momma, I know, but I happen to like the name and so does William."

"Well, maybe we'll give her a more fashionable nickname. You know, like Elle or Ellie."

Chase frowned. "Ellie is fashionable? It makes me think of those Beverley Hillbillies reruns Dad likes to watch."

Her mother waved him off, then returned to cooing at the baby. Chase rolled his eyes and followed William into the kitchen with her father, who'd carried in what must've been the cinnamon rolls.

When she joined them, her father's eyes widened as he pointed to her ring. "Tell me before you let your Momma see that.

I'll go to the stables and call Lamonte to give me a ride home later tonight. On second thought, I may sleep on his sofa." Chase's shoulders shook from laughing. Her father looked between them, and his eyebrows shot up. "I'm serious. After Jane told her she was going to marry Charlie, that woman had me fit to be tied. I won't do that again. You can't make me." He jumped as if remembering something vitally important. "Then there was the planning. I won't be offended if you elope. I'll even pay."

Lizzy slapped her father's arm. He could be ridiculous! "Daddy, stop it. William and I don't want anything fancy. We're going to get married back on the patio with just family and set up some tables under the oaks for a barbecue after. All we need is to find a minister, order flowers, and set up a caterer."

"And a bar service," said Chase. "If we load Momma up with champagne, then she'll pass out early."

She slapped her brother's arm too. "You're horrible."

"Hey, I'd go with the elopement if it were me."

William shook his head with a chuckle. "Good luck with that. Ana's been dreaming of the perfect wedding and dress since she was little. I busted her playing bride more than once."

Lizzy's eyes darted back and forth. "Am I missing something?"

Her brother groaned. "I asked William's permission to marry Ana." She gasped. "But, I haven't proposed to her yet. I'm thinking about being super cliché and doing it on Valentine's day."

Lizzy grabbed him and wrapped him up in a huge hug. "She'll love that!" Ana adored anything sappy and sentimental. When Lizzy had been in the hospital, William's sister had sat with her twice, and both times, tortured Lizzy with Hallmark movies. "I'm so happy the two of you found each other."

"Well, if I don't bring her a cinnamon roll soon, she may just say 'no' when the time comes."

"Then what are you doing, Chase? Get your ass over there."

While Chase and her father brought coffee and cinnamon rolls to the living room so everyone could eat, William pulled her back into his embrace, his arms wrapped around her stomach. "This is amazing. Ana and your family, all here and happy. There's only one thing that could make it perfect."

She frowned and looked back over her shoulder. As far as she was concerned, they had everything they could ever want or need: a roof over their heads, work they found fulfilling, a healthy baby, Evie cuddled between them every night, and a full life ahead of them. What could he possibly believe was missing? "What's that?"

"A dog."

The End

Acknowledgements

Oh my! Where do I start? I've wanted to write a story with Lizzy as a veterinarian for so long. I love most animals (not a huge snake fan!) and this was just a fun thing for me to do. I was a bit surprised at how everything played out in the end, but you know, the characters do have minds of their own!

I wouldn't have been able to write this book without the years of animal experience I've gained. From my first forays into riding when I was little to the horses I had growing up, and finally, showing horses for two people who became a second set of parents to me while I was in college.

My grandfather was a rancher and butcher in the Texas Hill Country, and my mother had an entire childhood of stories of his life as well as of her and her horse. I tried to be faithful to the area and used many of the towns I knew as surrounding my fictional Longbourn. The Hill Country was once a very German area, so many of the old families have those old German last names. Of course, many other people have moved into the area, but it wouldn't be the Hill Country without some of those influences.

My mother spoke often of my grandfather who had his own ranch and was the local butcher/shop owner. I learned a ton about horses from my mother then furthered that knowledge on my father's farm, and later when I showed horses for some friends of the family, the Murphys, who taught me a lot.

Growing up, I wanted to be a veterinarian, so I worked for a veterinary hospital in Baton Rouge where I had a crash course in what happens behind the scenes, from drawing blood and starting IVs, to assisting the vets with surgeries when needed. Of course, life got in the way of that dream, but as life happens, dreams and goals change. I don't regret my road less traveled one bit and what I learned way back when has come in handy, even if I did have to still research how up to date my information was!

I also need to thank my friends and family. Thanks to Carol for her editing prowess, Debbie for her betaing, and Marie for her proofreading. The gang at Austen Variations for their support, and my fans who flatter me so often with their re-reads and recommendations of my books.

Thank you!!!

About the Author

L.L. Diamond is more commonly known as Leslie to her friends and Mom to her three kids. A native of Louisiana, she spent the majority of her life living within an hour of New Orleans before following her husband all over as a military wife. Louisiana, Mississippi, California, Texas, New Mexico, Nebraska, England, Missouri, and now Maryland have all been called home along the way.

Aside from mother and writer, Leslie considers herself a perpetual student. She has degrees in biology and studio art but will devour any subject of interest simply for the knowledge. Her most recent endeavors have included certifications to coach swimming and a number of fitness certifications. As an artist, her concentration is in graphic design, but watercolor is her medium of choice with one of her watercolors featured on the cover of her second book, *A Matter of Chance*. She is also a member of the Jane Austen Society of North America. Leslie also plays flute and piano, but much like *Pride and Prejudice's* Elizabeth Bennet, she is always in need of practice! She also adores travel.

Leslie's books include: *Rain and Retribution, A Matter of Chance, An Unwavering Trust, The Earl's Conquest, Particular Intentions, Particular Attachments, Unwrapping Mr. Darcy, It's Always Been You, It's Always Been Us, It's Always Been You and Me, Undoing, Confined with Mr. Darcy, He's Always Been the One, Agony and Hope, His Perfect Gift,* and *That Perfect Someone.*